The Night Before Christmas

The Night Before Christmas

Lori Foster

Erin McCarthy

Jill Shalvis

Kathy Love

Katherine Garbera

Kylie Adams

BRAVA

KENSINGTON PUBLISHING CORP.

http://www.kensingtonbooks.com

CONTENTS

WHITE KNIGHT CHRISTMAS

Lori Foster

Chapter One

With the sluggish winter sun hanging low in the gray sky, Detective Parker Ross dragged himself out of his salt-and-slush-covered car. Howling wind shoved against him, jerking the car door from his hand to slam it shut. His dress shoes slipped on the icy blacktop and he almost lost his footing. The frozen parking lot echoed his muttered curse.

Cautiously, he started forward, taking in the depressing sight of his apartment building. The landlord's attempts at decorating had left bedraggled strands of colored lights haphazardly tossed over the barren, neglected bushes that served as landscaping. Some of the bulbs had blown, while others blinked in a drunken hiccup.

On the ground near the walkway, a dented plastic snowman lay on its side, half-covered in brownish slush, cigarette butts, and scraps of garbage.

Damn, but he'd be glad when the holidays passed and life returned to normal.

Slinging his soiled suit coat over his shoulder, his head down in exhaustion, Parker trudged along the treacherous, icy walkway. He didn't have an overcoat with him because the last perp he'd tangled with had destroyed it. Weariness and disgust kept him from noting the frozen snowflakes that gathered on the back of his neck; after such a bitch of a day, even the frigid December weather couldn't revive him.

A hot shower, some nuked food, and sleep—that's all he needed, in that exact order. Once he hit the sheets, he intended to stay there for a good ten hours. He had the next week off, and he didn't want to do anything more involved than camping on his couch and watching football.

God knew he deserved a rest. The past month of holiday-evoked lunacy and criminal desperation had left him little time for relaxation.

Parker saw Christmas as lavish, loud, and downright depressing. With his planned time off, he intended to hide out and avoid the nonsense.

Now, if he could just slip into his apartment without Lily Donaldson catching him . . .

Thinking of Lily sent a flood of warmth through his system, rejuvenating him in a way the frozen weather couldn't. He was old enough to know better, but no matter how he tried, Lily tempted him. She also infuriated him.

She aroused his curiosity, and his tenderness.

She made him think, and she made him hot.

She had trouble written all over her. *He* wanted to be all over her.

In the ten months he'd known her, Lily had influenced his life far too often. Smart, kind, gentle. She carried food to Mrs. Harbinger when the old lady fell ill. She argued sound politics with fanatical Mr. Pitnosky. Both intelligent and astute, Lily smiled at everyone, never gossiped, and had a generous heart.

She *loved* Christmas, which rubbed him raw.

And she had a terrible case of hero worship. That was the hardest thing to deal with. Parker knew he didn't possess a single ounce of heroism. If he did, then resisting her wouldn't be so damn difficult.

In a hundred different ways, Lily made it clear she wanted to be more than friends. But her age made him wary, her enthusiasm scared him to death, and her love of a holiday he scorned showed they had little in common.

On top of all that, he had serious doubts about her occupation.

Yep, a conundrum for sure. Parker hated to think about it, yet he thought about it far too often. Not once had he ever noticed any work routine for Lily. Sure, she left her apartment, but not dressed for anything other than a real good time. Always made up. Always decked out, dressed for seduction.

Sometimes she left early, sometimes late.

Sometimes she stayed gone for days, and some days she never left the apartment at all. But that didn't stop a steady stream of admirers from calling on her. The only reason Parker could tolerate that situation was because the guys seldom lasted more than a few hours, never more than a day.

Whatever Lily did to support herself, she sure as hell didn't punch a time clock.

He'd tried asking her about her job a couple of times, but she always turned evasive and changed the subject, leaving Parker with few conclusions to draw.

He was a selfish bastard who refused to share, so even if the other roadblocks didn't exist, no way could he let their friendship grow into intimacy.

That didn't mean he could keep his mind off her. Throughout the awful day—hell, the awful *month*—thoughts of Lily made the hours more bearable. He imagined her sweet smile, the special one she saved for him. He imagined that deep admiration in her eyes whenever she looked at him.

He imagined her lush bod, minus the sexy clothes she wore.

Seeing her now would shove him right over the edge. Avoiding her was the smart thing to do.

He planned to duck inside as fast as his drained body would allow. If she knocked, and he knew she would, he'd pretend he wasn't home.

After rubbing his bloodshot eyes, he opened the entrance

door to the apartment building and stepped inside. Whistling wind followed in his wake—and still he heard her husky voice, raised in ire.

Shit. With no way to reach his front door, Parker paused by the mailboxes and listened. Lily's usually sweet voice held a sharp edge of annoyance. She probably had another smitten swain who didn't want to take no for an answer.

Peering out the glass entrance doors, Parker considered a strategic retreat. Maybe he could drop by a bar and get a beer. Or visit his mother—*no, scratch that.* His mom would start trying to rope him in for a big family get-together, caroling, or God-knew-what-other holiday function.

Maybe he could . . .

Lily's voice grew more insistent, and Parker's protective instincts kicked in. Damn it, even if it fed her goofy misconceptions about him being heroic, he couldn't let some bozo hassle her. Giving up on the idea of escape, Parker trod the steps to the second floor. Halfway up he saw her, and he forgot to breathe.

A soft white sweater hugged her breasts. Dangling, beaded earrings in a snowflake design brushed her shoulders. Soft jeans accentuated a deliciously rounded ass.

Previously spent body parts perked up in attention. Nothing new there. No matter what Parker's brain tried to insist, his dick refused to pay attention.

Lily's pale blonde hair, pinned up but with long tendrils teasing her nape and cheeks, gave the illusion that a lover had just finished with her. Heavily lashed brown eyes defied any innocence.

And her bare feet somehow made her look half-naked.

His heart picked up speed, sending needed blood flow into his lethargic muscles. Predictably enough, he went from exhausted to horny in a nanosecond.

Vibrating with annoyance, Lily stood just outside her apartment. A fresh, decorated wreath hung from her door, serving as a festive backdrop.

Lily loved the holiday. And he loathed it.

But for now, he couldn't let that matter. Lily had a problem. She had a dispute.

She had . . . *a guy on his knees?*

Parker blinked in surprise at that. Lily's confrontations always involved men. More specifically, they involved Lily rejecting men. But a begging guy?

That was a first.

Glued to his spot on the stairs, Parker stared, and listened.

"It was *not* a date, Clive. Not ever. No way. I made that clear."

"But we had lunch," Clive insisted, reaching out to grasp her knee. "Just the two of us."

While stepping back, out of reach, Lily exclaimed, "I picked up the bill!"

Clive crawled after her. "But I would have."

She slapped his hands away. "I didn't let you—*because it was not a date.*"

"Lily," he moaned. "I thought we had something special."

"Tuna fish on rye is not special, Clive. Now *get up.*"

At her surly reply, Parker bit back a smile. Lily excelled in brokenhearted boyfriends, and this guy looked very brokenhearted. Poor schmuck.

As Clive obediently climbed to his feet, Parker looked at Lily—and met her gaze. The surprise in her brown eyes softened to pleasure; she gave him a silly, relieved smile—expecting him to heroically save the day.

And Parker supposed he would.

He'd taken one step toward her when good old Clive threw his arms around her. "I love you!"

"Oh, *puh-lease.*" Lily shoved against him, but Clive wouldn't let go.

"I do," he insisted. "Let me show you how much."

Glancing toward Parker, Lily said, "Don't be stupid, Clive. I know why you're here."

Parker knew why, too. Lily was sexy and sweet, and Clive wanted in her pants.

"You're after my money," Lily stated, causing Parker to do a double take.

"Lily, no!" Clive cried.

"You're broke, Clive. I know all about your business going under, the losses you've sustained."

"Temporary setbacks, I swear."

"Right. Temporary, because you figured I could shore you back up." She leaned away from Clive's hold.

"*Noooo.*" Clive tugged her close again.

Straightening her arms to hold Clive off, Lily looked at Parker. "Well, don't just stand there."

Smirking, Parker took the remaining steps to the landing and caught Clive by the back of his coat. Because he was tired and annoyed—and damn it, he didn't like seeing other men slobbering on Lily—Parker rattled him.

"The lady said to leave." For good measure, he shook Clive again before setting him several feet away from Lily. "Now beat it."

Flustered, Clive straightened his coat with righteous anger. "Who the hell are you?"

"Just a neighbor."

"Then this doesn't concern you."

Given his height of six feet four, Parker had the advantage of looking down on most people, especially shorter people like Clive. "I'm a cop. I've had a shitty day." He leaned toward Clive, forcing him to back up. "I've dealt with a three-car pileup. Got knocked into a damn curb full of blackened slush by a mob of *happy* shoppers. Got jumped by a crazy woman stealing a bike for her kid. Had to break up a riot during a VCR sale. *And* wrestled with a goon robbing Santa of donations for the homeless. I am *not* in the mood to tell you twice."

Clive gulped. "I just need to explain to her . . ."

"She's not interested in your explanations."

Lily moved to stand beside Parker. "No, I'm not." She curled her arms around one of his for no reason that Parker could find. She did that a lot. If she spoke to him, she touched him—almost as if she couldn't help herself.

And it drove him nuts.

"All right." Dejected, Clive fashioned a puppy-dog face. "But you're making a mistake, Lily. I do love you. With all my heart." He turned and slunk down the stairs like a man on the way to the gallows.

When the door closed behind Clive, Parker mustered up his good sense and peeled Lily's hands off his arm. "Good night, Lily." He headed for his door.

"Good night?" She hustled after him. "But . . . what do you mean, 'good night'?"

"I'm beat. It's been a hell of a day." Parker refused to look at her. Just being near her made him twitchy in the pants. If he looked at her, he'd be a goner.

"Sounds like." She scuttled in front of him, blocking his way. "I never realized that detectives got into so many physical confrontations."

That damned admiring tone weakened his resolve. "It's the holidays." He couldn't help but look at her, and once he did, he couldn't look away. "It brings out the worst in everyone."

Gently, Lily said, "That's not true."

His day had been just bad enough to shatter his resolve. He wanted to vent. To Lily. Somehow, he knew she'd understand.

To disguise his level of emotion, Parker snorted. "The wreck I mentioned? It sent two innocent people to the hospital."

Concern clouded her beautiful eyes. "I'm so sorry to hear that."

"I got called in because the arresting officer found psilocybin mushrooms in the car of the idiot who caused the wreck. Enough to know he's a dealer."

"Hallucinogenic drugs," Lily breathed, surprising Parker. "How terrible. Will the victims be all right?"

Parker eyed her. What the hell did Lily know about mushrooms? "I don't know," he grouched. "Last I heard, the woman was in surgery." She had two kids who'd be counting on her to be there Christmas morning. Parker hoped like hell she made it.

"The dealer?"

"Escaped without a scratch."

"But you'll see to him, I'm sure."

Parker ground his teeth together, pissed off all over again. Lily sounded so confident in his ability. "I'd already arrested him once on a charge of manufacturing methamphetamine, but he failed to appear in court. At least this should cinch a conviction."

Lily inched closer, her expression sympathetic, her mood nurturing. "Your job isn't often an easy one, is it?"

Damn, she looked sweet and soft, and far too appealing. Parker cleared his throat. "Look, Lily, I'm beat. I don't want to talk about work." He didn't want to tempt himself with her. "I need to get some shut-eye."

Her hand settled over his, her fingers warm and gentle. "At least let me explain about Clive."

Cocking a brow, Parker said, "It was pretty self-explanatory."

Leaning on the wall beside his door, her gaze somber, she studied him. "I had no idea Clive harbored an infatuation. He said he wanted to talk about business, my schedule was clear . . ." She shut down on that real fast. "It was not an intimate lunch."

The nature of their business made Parker's stomach roil. "So you said."

"I guess you got an earful, huh?" She didn't sound all that embarrassed. "He lied to me, Parker, saying he wanted to help with a project of mine, telling me he wanted to be friends. Can you believe his nerve?"

"The world is full of creeps, Lily." What project? No, he didn't care. "Good night."

Lily's voice dropped. "It's barely six o'clock."

Sticking his key in the lock, Parker tried to ignore her nearness. An impossible task. "I've been up over twenty-four hours. I can't see straight anymore. Fast as I can get a shower and find some food, I'll be turning in." His door opened. He stepped inside . . .

Lily followed. "Poor baby." She touched him again, this time on his right biceps.

Even through his shirt, Parker felt the tingling jolt that shot through his system and fired up his gonads. She might as well have grabbed his crotch for the way it affected him.

Unaware of his rioting libido, Lily said, "I feel terrible that you got pulled into the middle of my mess after all you've been through today."

Before he could censor himself, Parker said, "It's getting to be a habit."

Lily tilted her head and smiled. "I can think of worse habits than drawing your attention."

Please don't go there. "Sorry." Parker ran a hand over the knotted muscles in his neck. "I didn't mean that the way it sounded."

"I understand. I . . . I do seem to have a bad track record with guys."

"Lily . . ."

"I don't blame myself, though." Rather than explain, she brightened her smile and changed the subject. "Now that Clive's gone, why don't you let me thank you with dinner?"

Parker took a step back, then stopped to curse himself. Damn it, since when did women have him retreating like a green kid in middle school?

Since Lily had moved in—smelling, looking, probably tasting like sex.

His body flinched in excitement, and he quickly steered his thoughts in a new direction. "That's all right. I'll just grab a sandwich or something."

"I have plenty of fresh leftovers. Fixing you a plate of ham and potato salad won't take any longer than making a sandwich." Coy, Lily ducked her head, and one long blonde curl fell over her breast. "Besides, today is my birthday."

Ah, shit. "Yeah?" And he heard himself say, "So are you legal yet?" The second the words left his mouth, Parker clamped his lips shut. Too late.

"Actually," Lily said, gazing up at him in adoration, "I've been legal for a while. I'm twenty-four now."

So it wasn't as bad as he'd told himself. He still felt ancient. At thirty-eight, he was old enough to be her . . . older brother.

"My folks are on vacation," Lily continued, and she took a tiny step forward, full of entreaty. "They won't get home till Christmas morning. My friends are all with their families. I don't have anyone to celebrate with—but now you're home."

Just the thought of spending the night with Lily had Parker's heart dropping to his stomach.

With anticipation.

"Really, Lily, I'm shot. I'd be lousy company."

"You don't have to entertain me."

Peculiar desperation clawed at him. If he ever had her, he wouldn't want to let her go. But the roadblocks all remained. "I need a hot shower."

Her gaze dipped over him with approval, lingering on his belt buckle, then the open collar of his shirt. Parker felt his nostrils flare at her interest, and knew he fought a losing battle.

"I think you look . . . fine."

Coming from her mouth, *fine* sounded like the greatest flattery.

"But if you want, go ahead and clean up and change out of those wet clothes. I'll get the food ready."

Seeing no help for it, Parker caved. "All right. Thanks." He made a move toward the door, hoping she'd take the hint and skedaddle so he could regroup. "Throw a plate together and I'll come over and grab it as soon as I'm done."

"Don't be silly." Lily patted his chest, then let her fingers linger. Her attention on his sternum, her voice low, she said, "Leave your door unlocked." Her gaze lifted, warm and intimate. "I'll get everything heated up and bring it to you."

He'd just bet Lily could heat things up . . . No. Hell no. "I don't want to put you to any trouble."

"I insist." She traipsed out, giving one flirtatious smile over her shoulder as if she hadn't just manipulated him. "It's the least I can do since you played White Knight for me again."

Damn. Parker shut the door behind her. Now what? Hands on his hips, he looked around at his apartment, seeing the newspapers everywhere, the layers of dust, the dishes in the sink. His neck stiffened.

So what? He worked so damn many hours this time of year, he didn't have time for fussing around the apartment.

Stalking into his bedroom, mumbling under his breath, Parker rummaged around in his dresser until he found clean clothes. In the bathroom, he stripped down to his skin and stepped under the steamy, relaxing spray. Tension eased, and his thoughts drifted—to Lily being only twenty-four, young and ripe, and so sexy.

To Lily smiling at him, touching him. Understanding him, admiring him.

To Lily naked, stretched out over his kitchen table while he—

With a groan, Parker stuck his head under the water and tried to clear his brain, but the past ten months flashed by with highlights of Lily. He saw her in her shorts, her shapely legs lightly tanned. He saw her speckled in yellow paint when she'd redecorated her kitchen. He saw her fussing over him when he got stitches in his head from a car chase that went bad, and laughing at him when he came home covered in mud for the same reason.

When with her, he felt younger and happier—and that made him vulnerable.

Dealing with the dregs of society had taught him that good didn't always prevail over evil. Right didn't overcome might. Crimes went unpunished, while good people sometimes paid with their lives.

But Lily gave balance to the futility of his job. Her enthusiasm for life made him less pessimistic. Time and time again, she told him what a difference he made—and when she said it, he almost believed it.

Almost.

His trained ears detected the sound of his door opening. He straightened abruptly, straining to hear Lily, his heart suddenly galloping a wild beat. If he didn't greet her, would she join him in the shower?

Liking that thought far too much, Parker washed with a vengeance, rinsed, and turned off the water.

He could hear Lily singing . . . to Christmas music.

Damn. Dredging up his bad attitude, his disgust with the holiday, he scowled toward his closed bathroom door.

He didn't have any Christmas music. None. Was it on the radio? Probably. Lately, that's all they played.

She had a nice voice.

He groaned.

Parker quickly dried and dressed in loose sweatpants and a T-shirt. He finger-combed his wet hair, peered in the mirror, saw the dark whiskers on his face, the circles of exhaustion under his red-rimmed eyes, and disgusted, left the bathroom.

Before he saw Lily, he noticed the portable CD player, blaring Elvis's holiday tunes. Then he noticed the red, cinnamon-scented candle, its smell potent enough to assault his nose. He saw that the dishes, placed just so on his beat-up table, were all red and green.

And he saw Lily, standing at his counter, pouring a big glass of milk. She sang along with Elvis while rocking her hips to the beat of the music. An air of happiness surrounded her, and Parker simply stood there, watching her, his heart thumping and his mind in turmoil.

She must have felt the intensity of his gaze, because she glanced over her shoulder and gave him a quick once over, her expression warming. "I figured you must like milk, since you have a gallon of it. I couldn't see beer with dinner, and there's nothing else." She turned to face him. "Unless you want me to run back to my place and grab some eggnog?"

The thought of eggnog nearly made him gag. "Milk is fine." He gestured at the table presentation. "What the hell is all this?"

She laughed. Of course. Lily was forever laughing, because Lily was always happy.

"You sound like the Grinch, Parker."

"Who?"

"You remember. That green nasty guy who wanted to do away with Christmas in Whoville."

He grunted, thinking the similarity apt. All but the green part.

"Don't be like that. It's the holiday season. A time for good cheer." She pulled out a chair and waited for him to sit.

Determined to get the festive meal over with, Parker strode forward and took the chair. "Ladies don't hold chairs for men."

"Now you sound like a sexist grinch."

To his surprise, she pulled out a chair for herself and joined him at the table. When Parker just looked at her, she grinned. "Go on. Dig in. I want to see if you like it."

"I haven't eaten since . . . well, I forget what time it was, but somewhere around six in the A.M." And then he'd only had a hardened biscuit with a congealed hunk of sausage and cold egg. "Believe me, I'll like it."

He forked up a big bite of ham . . . and wanted to moan in sublime pleasure. Honey and brown sugar and some vague spices exploded on his tongue in a taste mamba. His eyes closed. He swallowed. *Heavenly.*

"Good, huh?" Delight sounded in her voice. "I love these caterers. They always do a fabulous job."

Parker gathered himself and opened his eyes back up. "Caterers?" That made sense. He glanced at Lily's heavy breasts beneath the soft sweater and called himself a fool. A woman like her had no use for cooking skills. Still, he asked, "Why does a single woman need a caterer?"

Her head tilted in that familiar but curious way. "To help feed the homeless. Why else?"

Chapter Two

Parker choked on his food. "Homeless?" he rasped, and started wheezing.

Leaving her seat, Lily approached him and pounded on his back until he caught his breath. "You okay now?"

Jesus, he was in bad shape if getting a fist between his shoulder blades turned him on. But it was Lily's fist, and she stood close, and he could smell her. More than enough reasons for arousal.

He nodded, took a large drink of milk, and managed an almost normal breath. "Thanks."

Smiling, trailing one finger across the table, Lily headed back to her seat. Parker stared at her ass in the snug jeans, knew he stared, but couldn't seem to pull his gaze away.

After reseating herself, Lily put her right elbow on the table and propped her head on a palm. The position left her breasts resting on the edge of the table. His table. Right in front of him.

"Parker . . ." She fidgeted with her hair. "May I ask you something?"

Mesmerized, he watched her delicate fingers as she teased that long, loose curl hanging over her shoulder, twining it around and around. He asked, "What?" and was appalled at how hoarse he sounded.

"It's kind of personal."

His gaze shot back to her face. She looked far too serious, and alarm bells went off in his beleaguered brain. "This might not be the best time . . ."

"Why don't you like me?"

Damn it. Her blurted words hung in the air. She looked anxious and young, and Parker wanted to reassure her—then ravage her for about a day and a half.

"Don't be ridiculous." Unable to meet her gaze, he stared down at his plate of food. "Of course I like you."

"But you've never asked me out."

Trying to appear blasé instead of edgy, Parker forked up another big bite of ham. "We're neighbors, Lily. Friends."

She folded both arms on the table and leaned toward him, giving him a clear shot of her cleavage. His tongue stuck to the roof of his mouth. Lust churned in his belly. Heat rose.

"I'd like us to be more."

A man didn't get to be his age without meeting plenty of women. He'd liked some, he'd lusted after others. A few he'd really cared about.

But none of them had ever looked at him the way Lily did. None of them had ever sent a jolt to his system that obliterated all thought. More times than he cared to admit, he'd gone to sleep thinking of her and had awakened in the middle of an explicit dream.

"I've tried," she pointed out, as if he might not have noticed all the ways she deliberately provoked him. "But you don't even see me as a woman."

Parker did a double take, and sputtered. "That's just plain stupid."

"Is it?"

Gaze dipping to her breasts, then darting away, Parker snorted. "Trust me, Lily. Your . . . *femaleness* is not something I'd miss."

"Then you must find me unattractive."

He rolled his eyes. She deliberately put him on the spot, but Parker couldn't stop himself from reassuring her. "You have mirrors. You know what you look like." When she remained quiet, just waiting, he huffed out a long breath. "You're beautiful. Okay?"

Pleasure brought color to her cheeks. "Thank you."

"You're welcome."

"So if you like me and find me attractive, why haven't you asked me out?"

A full frontal attack. And at a time when his defenses were down. Stalling for time, he took another bite of ham. Hell, he was too hungry *not* to eat. He swallowed, then eyed her with cynicism. "What's this all about?"

Lily pushed out of her seat and began to pace.

Parker again noted her bare feet. She really did have cute, sexy toes.

Turning to face him, she folded her arms under her breasts and drew a deep breath. "I want you."

His heart did a somersault. Every muscle in his body clenched. His neck already had more kinks than a porn star, and now he winced.

Easing back in his seat, his watchful gaze locked on her, Parker rubbed at his neck. He decided being straight with her would be his best strategy. "Look, Lily, you're a little sexpot, okay? Very sweet on the eyes. No one can deny that."

Her arms dropped and she gaped at him. "A . . . a sexpot?"

Did she have to sound so startled? Parker rolled one shoulder, trying to ease the rising tension. "That's right. But the thing is—"

An odd, unidentifiable look came over her face, alarming Parker for a heartbeat. Jesus, he hated it when women turned to tears. He opened his mouth, more than ready to apologize, to do whatever necessary to fend off the excess of emotional upset—and she threw back her head, roaring with hilarity.

He went rigid. "What's so damn funny?"

"Oh God, Parker." For several moments, she laughed too hard to answer. Her blonde curls bounced—and so did her boobs. Tears of mirth filled her eyes. She pressed a hand to her belly.

Finally, wiping her eyes and still grinning big enough to blind him with her pearly whites, Lily said, "I know you're older than me. But using a word like that makes you sound like a grandpa."

Grandpa his ass! Never mind that he'd always considered her too damn young. Now he felt challenged. "I'm thirty-eight."

Lily bit her lip, trying to stifle her laughter. "Ah. I see."

Parker's teeth ground together. He'd sounded frigging defensive even to his own ears.

"Come on, Parker. It's not like forty is old."

"I am *not* forty." Shit. More defensiveness. Just shut the hell up, Parker.

"Right. My apologies," she teased. "Thirty-eight. A gorgeous, sexy, mature, kind, and protective thirty-eight."

Was she poking fun at him? Or indulging more of that asinine hero worship?

Or was she just plain admiring?

Her lips curled. "So, by sexpot, did you mean I'm sexy, or was that an aspersion on my character?"

Another kink formed in his neck. Christ, he hated these types of confrontations. "Both." There. Let her deal with that.

But her gaze focused on his hands and on how he rubbed at his neck, and before he knew it, Lily stood behind him, pushing his hands away and touching the naked skin of his neck and shoulders, soothing, caressing.

Parker stiffened. So did the old John Henry.

"All right, Parker. Time for us to clear the air." She leaned down to the side of his face, saw his stock-still shock, and frowned. "I mean it, Parker. Pay attention."

"Trust me." He swallowed hard. Gentle breath brushed his

jaw. Slender fingers dug into tense muscles, forcing them to relax. Feminine heat, scented by Lily's curvy body, drifted around him. "You have my undivided attention."

He drank in her light womanly perfume and turned his head just enough so that his jaw brushed one plump breast.

Lily straightened. A sigh shuddered out and, voice shaking, she said, "You've got it all wrong, you know."

Did he? Her fingers slid into his hair, rubbing at his scalp, his temples, then smoothing down his neck and into his shoulders. Oh God, it felt good. Better than good. Close to orgasmic.

Real men didn't melt from a woman's touch—but he wanted to. He wanted to strip those skinny jeans right off her and pull her onto his lap.

He wanted to come and then to sleep for about a week.

"I'm independently wealthy."

Jerking hard, Parker rekinked everything she'd just relaxed. "Ow, shit." Twisting to face her, Parker demanded, "What did you say?"

"Hold still." She pressed at his shoulders until he gave up and sank back into his seat.

It was as much mind-numbing shock as anything else that had Parker staring straight ahead at nothing in particular. His brain struggled to make sense of her ridiculous statement. "You say you're independently . . ."

"Wealthy."

"I see." He didn't see a damn thing, except maybe that expanding divide between his world and hers. He'd always known she was naïve about life, blind to the ugliness in it. How else could she stay so damn happy all the time? "That explains everything."

"You don't have to be sarcastic."

He was horny, not sarcastic. Okay, maybe a little sarcastic. And *real* disbelieving.

"My grandmother doted on me. I was her only grandchild." Her warm fingertips moved to his temples. "When she passed away, I became financially set. I was nineteen when that happened. I tried to find a job, but you know, I'm just too spoiled to want to work for anyone else."

He'd never considered her spoiled. Pampered, maybe. Innocent. But also generous and kind.

Definitely not spoiled.

"I donate."

Head swimming, Parker looked at her over his shoulder. "Donate what?"

Her hands rested on his shoulders. They stared at each other. Neither of them moved.

"My time. My money." Her lashes lowered. "My optimism and good nature and happiness."

How the hell did you donate happiness?

"You know, that's why you've seen so many guys hanging around my place. Like Clive, they're looking to get rich the easy way."

Aha. Finally something he could sink his teeth into. "Reality check, Lily. If you're really rich—" Which he doubted. "—then money might be a perk, but it wouldn't be the first thing on a guy's mind."

He could tell she didn't believe him, and for some reason, that annoyed him. "When men come sniffing around you, they're looking to get laid, not rich."

His crude words brought a curl to her mouth and put a twinkle in her eyes. "How come you aren't sniffing a little?"

Sniff? He all but hyperventilated around her. "A lot of reasons—but it sure as hell isn't because of the way you look."

"Enlighten me."

"All right, fine." Parker turned to face her. "You're young, and you have a very skewed outlook on life."

Her brows lifted in surprise. "What's wrong with my outlook?"

"You run around in rose-colored glasses, seeing what you

want to see." Especially where he was concerned. "And this crazy fascination you have with Christmas . . ." He shook his head. "There's nothing like the festive season to force you to face facts."

"What facts?"

"That life isn't always as joyful and triumphant as we're led to believe."

While appearing to digest his comments, Lily went back to caressing his shoulders. "I can't do anything about my age, Parker. Not that twenty-four is too young, anyway."

"It's a fourteen-year difference."

She shrugged. "So?"

What could he say to that? At the moment, her age didn't bother him a bit. "I can't say as I approve of your career choices, either."

"Why? What do you have against philanthropists?"

Being a detective came to Parker's aid. He caught Lily's wrists and lifted those small, teasing hands away from his flesh. Holding her captive, he eased her around to the side of him, turning at the same time so that they faced each other.

"I'm not buying it, Lily."

She didn't try to pull away. A little breathless, she whispered, "Why not?"

"For starters, look at where you live."

"You live here, too."

"Because I make a cop's salary. If you're as loaded as you say . . ."

Lily inched closer, edging her knees between his open legs, and Parker went mute. He still clasped both her wrists in his much bigger hands, and now he caged her in, damn near embracing her.

She didn't seem to mind at all.

Focus, Parker, focus. He cleared his throat and tried to ignore the stab of sexual awareness. "Why the hell would you live here if you could afford something better?"

Her gaze softened, and she gave him a very sultry look. "Because you do."

Parker shoved back his chair and managed to stand without touching her. "What the hell is that supposed to mean?"

"Do you remember the first day I met you?" Her breasts lifted against the soft material of her sweater in a deep sigh. "I do."

Of course, he remembered. "Some yahoo was arguing with you at your door. You told him to get lost, but he didn't want to."

Lily nodded. "Another fortune hunter. I've dealt with them since my inheritance. You were all sweaty, and you had a black eye. You didn't explain, you just moved up behind him, gave him this certain look that sent chills all over me, and said in a deep, I'm-in-command-voice, *Is there a problem?* And just like that, conflict solved." She pressed her clasped hands to her heart. "You were so powerful and gallant."

Her admiration threatened his resolve. Day in and day out, he worked his ass off trying to help people, trying to serve the public. More often than not, he got disappointment and complaints instead of gratitude.

But with Lily, she appreciated every damn thing he did for her. In her eyes, he was a hero. He was the man he'd always wanted to be.

Parker retreated, which annoyed the hell out of him. He didn't retreat from anyone. Anyone except Lily.

She strolled after him.

He stepped back again—and butted up against a wall. Shit. Trapped. "I'm a cop," he said fast. "It's second nature to interfere."

"With you, it's more than that. I bet you were always a defender of the underdog, huh?"

"No." But he was. He could never tolerate bullies, and he detested cruelty of any kind. He'd become a cop because he wanted to help, wanted to make a difference.

"So modest." She stared at his mouth. "There's something so sexy about the strong, silent type. Know what I mean?"

"No."

"I bet you always wanted to be a cop."

"Wrong." God, he was a lousy liar.

"And now I know that you're attracted to me." She stopped right in front of him, with only a thin space of air separating them. "So why fight it?"

Any second now, Parker knew he'd crumble. "You wanna know what I thought you did for a living?" He didn't give her a chance to reply. She'd left him little space to maneuver, and she looked so appealing staring up at him like that—the situation called for desperate measures. "I figured you for a hooker."

Lily blinked at him.

Neither of them moved.

Even Elvis quit singing. That stunned him, until a new CD, this one Neil Diamond, clicked into place.

"A hooker?"

Feeling dumber by the moment, Parker nodded.

Her lips twitched a little, then firmed. "As in a woman who makes her living selling sex?"

Another nod, this one more curt. He waited for her to slap his face.

Instead, she giggled. "Oh my. You're giving me more credit for my sexual experience than I deserve."

Parker drew himself up. *Just what the hell did she mean by that?*

"What a dilemma for you, Detective Ross. Here you are, the quintessential defender of evil—"

"Knock it off, Lily."

"The epitome of all that's good—"

Growling, he said, "You're asking for it."

"A regular White Knight, and you thought the damsel in distress was a soiled dove."

How dare she poke fun at him! Parker loomed over her.

"You keep irregular hours. You have strange men at your door all the damn time. And you look . . ." His agile tongue tripped to a halt. Jesus, he'd backed himself into a verbal corner.

She batted her lashes at him. "I look . . . what?" Fighting a laugh, she said, "Like a . . ." The laughter won, and she barely managed to get the word out around her hilarity. *"Sexpot?"*

Furious, Parker slid away from the wall and stalked over to the table. He grabbed up another chunk of ham and tossed it into his mouth. "Listen, I'm too shit-faced to be heckled right now. Take your little party home and let me get some sleep, why don't you?"

Rather than leave, she occupied his spot on the wall, collapsing back in amusement, her dark eyes all lit up and pretty. Her laughter never failed to affect him. He felt his ill humor slipping away.

And the way her breasts jiggled . . .

Parker stormed up to her, caught her upper arm, and pulled her away from the wall. "Time to go, Lily." In about two more minutes, he'd be flat on his face, passed out.

If he lasted three minutes, she'd probably be under him.

Taking him by surprise, Lily drew up short, pulled him around, and threw herself into his arms. "You're precious, Parker, you really are."

Precious? Fighting the urge to snuggle her warm little body against his, Parker ground his teeth together. "You're laughing at me," he accused.

"Because it's funny." She chuckled again and shook her head. "Believe me, if I was a hooker, I'd starve to death."

Don't ask, Parker. Just don't ask.

Her hands came to rest on his chest, and she tipped her head back to see him. "You've fascinated me from the first day we met. And now that I know why you've kept your distance . . ."

Her reaction defied logic. "I can't believe you're not insulted."

"Plenty of men have been after my money. That's a whole lot more insulting."

Somehow, his hands ended up on her waist. He could feel the heat of her, the supple softness. "Idiots."

Her gaze warmed. "But you had no idea I was rich. You thought I was a hooker." Her fingers curled, subtly caressing him. "And still, you've always been kind and considerate. And you're attracted to me."

"I'm a man. How could I not be attracted?" The words no sooner left his mouth than Parker wanted to cut out his own tongue. He needed to dampen her pursuit, not encourage it.

Didn't he?

He started to step away, and Lily launched into explanations. "I chose this apartment because it's close to one of my favorite shelters. I spend a lot of time there helping the homeless, abused women, and kids of addicts."

So that's how she knew about mushrooms. His next thought made his guts cramp: *Maybe she wasn't so innocent and naïve after all.* As much as her rosy demeanor had always annoyed him, he detested the thought of her facing the ugliness in life.

"While my house was being built, I needed a place to stay. But then I met you, and I didn't want to move until I got things straightened out between us. Only you refused to make a move beyond being friendly. I knew I had to do something to get your attention."

She waved at the table where the candle still burned and Neil Diamond growled out an old familiar holiday tune. "So I forced dinner, and a little holiday cheer, onto you."

"The dinner was great."

Cuddling closer, she asked, "But the holiday cheer?"

"It's a myth. The holidays depress the hell out of most people."

Her brows came down in a frown. "That's nonsense. The holidays give people hope. They give them something to focus on other than their troubles."

"Like lack of funds, lack of family and friends, lack of . . . faith." Damn it, he sounded maudlin. "Do you have any idea how many suicide attempts get called in?"

She put a hand to his jaw. "There will always be lonely and unhappy people, Parker. Neither you nor I can reach everyone. But during the Thanksgiving-to-Christmas season, the suicide rate actually drops."

"You can't prove it by me."

Now she looked indignant. "Parker, this is what I do. I know what I'm talking about." And to prove it, she added, "The American Association of Suicidology has proven that December has the lowest suicide rate of any month of the year. And the National Center for Health Statistics has documented a suicide drop by at least twenty percent during the holidays."

Anger rippled through Parker. "Christ, I fucking hate hearing people classed as statistics."

Lily's smile wobbled, not because his temper scared her, but because she interpreted his words all wrong. "You're an incredible man, Parker. A hero." She hugged herself against him again. "You care, when a lot of other people don't." With a sigh, she added, "It's what I find most attractive about you."

She offered herself so openly. It'd be beyond nice to lose himself in her slanted perception, to take all her softness and block out the ugly truths. But as a realist, Parker faced his own demons. And it was past time Lily did the same.

Hands shaking, Parker clasped her upper arms and levered her away. "Red light, Lily." He gave her a slight shake, making her eyes widen. "Put your damn brakes on that fantasy, will you already? I'm sick of it."

Appearing genuinely confused, she asked, "What fantasy?"

"I'm a cop," he rasped, "nothing more and nothing less. What I do doesn't even put a dent in the shit going on in our world. So quit deluding yourself—about me and about everything else."

She sighed again, this time in exasperation. "You refuse to soften up even a little?"

And Parker, being too tired and too horny to think straight, stared at her mouth and said, "Honey, right now, I'm about as far from soft as a man can get."

Chapter Three

Lily knew when to take advantage of a propitious moment, and after Parker's bold admission, it wouldn't get much more propitious than right this very second.

Tonight, more so than at any other time, Parker needed her. Pressing into him so that she felt the hard length of his erection against her belly, she whispered, "Please kiss me."

"Lily, damn it . . ."

She smiled—and closed her fingers around him.

Parker sucked in a startled breath. His erection pulsed, grew bigger. "Stop."

Very gently, she said, "No."

"*Lily.*" He said her name like a warning.

Loving him more by the second, Lily caressed him, squeezed him . . .

And he broke. A growl rumbled from deep in his throat. His jaw locked. All his muscles went taut. And he rasped, "*I give up.*"

Crushing her mouth under his, he moved forward, driving against her until it was her back pressed to the wall—with Parker firmly against her front.

Lord, she'd unleashed a storm. And she loved it. He tasted good. And he knew how to kiss. Or devour. Whatever. Lily couldn't breathe and didn't care.

With one hand curved around her nape, he held her head

still while his tongue delved into her mouth. With the other hand, he felt her. Everywhere.

Lily moaned.

From the moment she'd met Parker, so strong, so quiet and honorable and caring, he'd touched her heart. He was every woman's dream, a hero, a real man, exactly what the world needed, exactly what she wanted.

His fingers tightened in her hair, but she didn't flinch away. He kissed her throat, nuzzled against her ear while urgently kneading her breasts.

"Is this what you want?" The low, rough words sent a shiver down her spine.

"Yes."

His groan drowned out her gasp of pleasure. He took her mouth again, stifling her excited cries as he groped over her backside, her belly, and finally between their bodies to cup her mound.

"And this?" His fingers pressed.

The sensation was so erotic, Lily tore her mouth away and gasped.

With fierce intensity, Parker watched her. His eyes were burning and bright, his expression dark and hard. He looked wild—and he looked turned-on.

He looked determined.

Wow. Barely forming the words around her escalating need, Lily whispered, "I've never had angry sex before." She swallowed, lightly touched his jaw. "I . . . I like it."

In the blink of an eye, Parker changed, pulling back to let her breathe, his scowl lifting. He looked at her eyes, her mouth. After several deep breaths, he put his forehead to hers. "Either tell me to stop, or plan on getting fucked. Your choice."

Poor Parker. She knew which choice he'd prefer her to make. She licked her lips. "Your room or mine?"

Accepting the inevitable, Parker squeezed his eyes shut, then opened them again. He hefted Lily over his shoulder, feeling like a deranged caveman, and not caring.

She reared up. *"Parker."*

"You had your chance." He cupped her rounded backside to keep her still, and he liked that enough that he fondled her as he strode into his bedroom. He'd wanted Lily too long to dredge up any nobility now.

Lily, hanging upside down, said, "Finally."

He tossed her onto his bed, bent one knee on the mattress beside her, and tackled the fastenings to her jeans. Urgency pounded in his brain. Need clawed through him.

"Lift your hips."

She did, and he stripped off her jeans. Her panties were white with little candy canes all over them. He could see the shadowing of her pubic hair beneath. He could smell her aroused scent.

Ravenous and out of control, Parker gripped the hem of her sweater and yanked it up and over her head.

She covered herself with her arms. "No fair. You have to take something off, too."

God, she had a beautiful body. Staring at her belly, he muttered, "Right. Whatever." Nearly blind with lust, Parker shoved to his feet, stripped his T-shirt off over his head and, staring at her body, shoved out of his jogging pants and boxers.

Lily started to sit up to look at him, but he said, "No way." He tumbled her backward onto the mattress and worked her panties down her legs. A little finesse wouldn't have hurt, but he couldn't dredge up even an ounce. The fact that he wasn't yet inside her showed remarkable restraint, as much as he could muster.

Her bra nearly ripped under his fumbling hands, but within seconds he had her naked. He wanted to touch and taste her all over, and to that end, he fell on her like a marauding berserker, his mouth at her throat, her shoulder, his hands sliding over warm skin and soft curves.

Lily laughed as he touched her everywhere. For only a moment, he suckled a nipple, and enjoyed her rising sounds of excitement. But at any moment, he'd lose it, so he levered up on one stiffened arm, opened her thighs and, breathing hard, stared at her pink sex while sliding one finger deep.

"Parker." She arched up. Wet, hot.

Ready.

Breathing raggedly, he found a rubber in the nightstand, rolled it on, and then he was over her, groaning, on fire at the feel of her silky flesh, her stiffened nipples, the warmth between her thighs.

He closed his mouth over hers, stroking with his tongue while pressing into her, rocking deeper and deeper until she'd accepted all of him. Her slim arms wound around his neck, her ankles locked at the small of his back, and damn it all, he started coming.

He threw his head back, managed to growl out "*Sorry,*" while thrusting deep and hard, giving over to the draining of tension and anger and regret, and accepting the pervading numbness, the awesome calm.

Vaguely, he felt Lily's hands touch his chest, cup his jaw. He heard her gentle sigh, and when he sank onto her, wrung out, shot to hell, he noted the soft kiss to his shoulder.

The events of the day got the better of him, and Parker had only enough wits left to roll off to her side, sprawling on his back, before sleep claimed him.

Smiling like a goof, Lily lay there while her heart continued a mad gallop. She could easily guess how Parker would react to his carnal faux pas when he awoke. He was such a big, macho guy, so determined to always be strong and honorable. Leaving her would probably seem the ultimate insult to him.

She turned her head to look at him, and the smile faded to tenderness. God, he was so sexy, even now while dead to the world. And she wanted him so much. Her belly tingled and her thighs trembled and her breasts ached. But she could wait until he awoke. Even heroes needed sleep.

Carefully turning toward him and lifting to one elbow, she

touched him, smoothing back his dark brown hair. To her surprise, his green eyes snapped open and stared right at her. But they looked more blank than aware, and suddenly he mumbled something unintelligible and dragged her close. Lily found herself cradled to his warm chest, one muscled arm around her back, one heavy leg over hers.

She couldn't move.

But then, she didn't want to. It was too early for her, but after a while, sleep beckoned, and she relaxed enough to drift off.

The lights were still on when Lily awakened, but she sensed a lot of time had passed. A distinct chill filled the air—and a warm, wet mouth tugged at her breast.

Her eyes widened. "Parker?"

"You betcha." A teasing tongue licked across her chest, then curled around her other nipple. "You let me fall asleep."

Her breath caught. "I don't think I could have stopped you."

"I'm a pig. Mmmm, you taste good." And he started sucking at her breast again.

Shockwaves of pleasure moved over her, reigniting her earlier arousal. She tunneled her fingers into his hair. "What time is it?"

"Who cares?" And then, "Open your legs."

Wow, he sure had awakened with a "prove-himself" attitude. "Why?"

"I want to finger you. I want to feel you and get you off, and then find another rubber and take you again. The right way. The way you deserve. The way I've been thinking about for months."

She shouldn't have asked. Heat throbbed beneath her skin—and she opened her legs.

"Nice." His hands were big and rough, and he knew what to do and how to do it. "Poor baby," he crooned, while touching her intimately. "You fell asleep all hot and wet, didn't you?"

Lily couldn't talk, not with his fingers moving over her like that, pressing into her and retreating and teasing . . .

"I should be shot. How does this feel?" Parker pushed two fingers deep, stretching her, carefully thrusting, and then his thumb rolled over her clitoris.

Her muscles jolted in reaction, stealing her breath so that she couldn't answer.

Voice low and thick with satisfaction, he whispered, "You like that, Lily."

She arched her neck and managed a small sound of agreement.

Parker smiled against her breast. "I'll make this good for you."

And true to his word, he kept up the wonderful foreplay until her entire body burned.

"Come for me, Lily. Let me redeem myself."

Such idiocy! How could he blather on while she—*oh God.* Tension suddenly gripped her and her fingers bit into his hard, sleek shoulders while her hips lifted in rhythm. Pleasure rolled through her, and then, by small degrees, ebbed away, leaving her limp.

Before she could open her heavy eyes, Parker rose over her, kneeing her legs apart to press into her, deep and deeper still. With his warm breath coming fast, he cupped her face and kissed her gently. "Just relax," he instructed, "and I'll take care of you."

"Protection?"

"Already in place." He leisurely kissed her, long and slow and consuming, then kept on kissing her. He filled her. His heat and scent surrounded her. Yet other than his tongue, he didn't move an inch.

Lily shifted her hips, felt the sweet friction of his erection inside her, and decided moving was a good thing. But when she tried it, Parker pressed down, holding her still.

She pried her mouth away from his. "Parker . . ."

"Shhh." He kissed her throat, took a soft love bite of her shoulder. "I want you to be with me this time."

"I am."

"Not yet."

Ready to press the issue, Lily trailed her fingers over his chest—and got her hands pinned above her head.

"Behave," he admonished, then his attention caught on her breasts, and he lowered his head to tongue a stiffened nipple.

She couldn't move at all, not with his hips between her thighs, his weight holding her down, her hands restrained by his. It was frustrating. And a turn-on. And she didn't want to wait anymore.

"I'm ready, Parker." And to taunt him into action, she said, "Remember, I'm younger than you. I recover quicker."

His head shot up. "I'm the one who woke you."

"I know." She stared at his mouth, a little breathless, a lot in love. "Now show me what you can do."

He seemed to harden even more, his expression, his muscles, the erection deep inside her. One side of his mouth curled in a predatory smile. "You want to come, is that it?"

"I want you to love me."

Her deliberate wording took him off guard. But Lily held his gaze, letting him form his own conclusions. No matter how he took it, he'd be right.

Releasing her wrists, his eyes locked on hers, Parker trailed his hands down to her thighs. He hooked his elbows beneath her knees, lifted her legs high, and tilted her hips up so that he sank into her even more.

Breath catching on a gasp, Lily braced her hands on his shoulders—but she didn't look away from him.

Without a word, he began a steady rhythm that gained in strength with each thrust. Harder, deeper. Gaze burning, Parker watched her. His hair hung over his brow, his shoulders strained, every muscle delineated.

Lily came first, the release taking her by storm, forcing a high cry from her throat.

Parker muffled his answering groan against her shoulder. They went limp, arms and legs tangled, hearts beating together.

Lily had to bite her lip to keep from telling Parker about her feelings. She'd been half in love with him a week after making his acquaintance. Since then, she'd fallen a little more in love every day.

Now that they'd been intimate . . . well, she just couldn't imagine any other man in her life.

When her breathing calmed enough so that she could speak, she turned her head and saw the clock. Two A.M. She smiled and whispered, "It's Christmas Eve, Parker."

He grunted, struggled up to his elbows, and stared down at her. He wanted to say something, Lily could tell, and she held her breath, waiting.

But then he shook his head, kissed the end of her nose, and rolled out of her arms and out of the bed.

"Be right back," he said, and she watched the muscles flex in his shoulders, butt, and thighs as he left for the bathroom.

Should she get up, dress, and leave? Should she ask to stay? Would he *tell* her to leave?

She heard running water and splashing, the flush of the toilet, and she got up to take her own turn in the bathroom. Parker paused to absorb the sight of her nude body as she passed him in the hall. He didn't touch her, and he didn't say anything.

When she returned to the bedroom, the lights were out, but she could see the distinct shape of his long body beneath the covers.

She'd almost figured out what to say when he lifted the blankets aside to invite her in.

"Come here," he said. "It's cold. I don't want you to get ill."

Relieved, Lily slid in beside him, felt his arms close around her, and wanted to melt in contentment. She could do this every night, for the rest of her life, and never have a moment's regret.

"Happy birthday, Lily."

She smiled. "You make a heck of a birthday present."

He grunted, already more asleep than awake. She shouldn't push her luck, but . . . "Would you do me a really huge favor?"

His hand coasted down her back to her bottom. "If it's sexual, I'm your man."

She laughed, but quickly grew serious again. "It has to do with Christmas Eve."

His arms tightened. "Thank God, I'm off for a week. I'm going to unplug the phone so my mother and sister can't nag at me, then I'm going to watch television and pretend it *isn't* a holiday guaranteed to bring about depression and desperation."

Not a very promising start, Lily thought. She toyed with his chest hair and purposely misled him. "I don't get together with my family till Christmas Day, and I don't want to be alone. Will you spend the day with me?"

The seconds ticked by with no reply, and Lily wondered if he went to sleep. Or maybe she'd angered him by pushing.

Finally, he said, "As long as it doesn't involve shopping, wrapping, singing, or celebrating, then yeah, I'd enjoy your company."

She'd already done the shopping and wrapping, the choir didn't need him, and celebrating was something done in the heart, so she'd leave that up to him to work out. "Thank you."

His rock hard shoulder moved beneath her head. "I figure I owe you, anyway."

Furious, she bolted upright. "I made love with you, Parker. I didn't do you a damn favor."

Eyes glittering in the dark, he said, "I was talking about my earlier insult."

Blast. A little sheepish, she asked, "Which one?"

"Where I accused you of being a hooker."

"Oh." Lily resettled herself against him. "Now you know how ridiculous that was."

His hand slid down the length of her spine. "I dunno. I think you'd make a heck of a living selling this sweet little body."

"Flatterer." She kissed his chest and hugged him. "Seriously, after being considered a meal ticket, it's kind of nice to be viewed as a . . ." She grinned. "Sexpot, instead."

Parker swatted her ass. "Keep it up, Lily. I'm older and wiser, and have developed innovative ways to get even." His palm smoothed over the sting on her cheek, and he added, "In the morning, after I'm rested up, I'll make you pay for those taunts."

And Lily, more content than she'd ever been in her life, whispered, "Promises, promises." But already, Parker's breath had evened into sleep.

His paybacks would have to wait, because in the morning, she planned to show him how special the holidays could be. Then she planned to steal his heart. This Christmas, she wanted it all.

She wanted Parker Ross.

Chapter Four

The second Parker awoke, he knew she was gone. He sat up, saw the clock, and groaned. Noon. Jesus, she'd worn him out.

He rubbed his tired face—and smelled cookies baking.

He heard Christmas music.

He heard Lily singing again.

So she hadn't gone home. No, she'd just left his bed to bake. His heart softened.

Shit, the last thing a cop needed was a soft heart.

He felt old, damn it. What happened to the days when he could put in a long shift, make love for hours after, and still greet the morning with boundless energy?

Long gone, apparently, considering his blurry brain and gritty eyes and aching muscles.

Yet, in stark contrast, Lily was up and singing and baking.

Determined to match her, Parker threw the covers aside and stalked to the closet. But all he saw were dark suits, navy blue and brown, and they all looked too . . . dated. The differences in their lives showed even in his friggin' closet.

But . . . did he still care about that?

He sniffed the air again, smelled the cookies, and shook his head. Screw the clothes and age differences.

He wanted Lily.

Bypassing the dresser drawers that held his jeans and shorts, he walked into his kitchen—and got a very pleasant surprise.

Wearing one of his shirts and nothing more, Lily bent at the stove to remove a cookie sheet. Man. What a wake-up call.

Sneaking up behind her, his approach muffled by the music, Parker waited until she'd set the hot baking sheet aside, then slid his hands around to her belly and pulled her back against his chest. "Good morning," he rumbled.

"Hey, sleepyhead." She turned in his arms, saw his nude body, and her jaw loosened. "You're . . . naked."

"Really?" He looked down at himself and said, "Damn, I forgot pants."

She returned his teasing look. "Parker."

"Doesn't matter. You look better in my clothes than I do anyway."

Hands opening on his chest, she whispered, "Hey, I wasn't complaining," and she treated him to a killer kiss that chased away the rest of the cobwebs and gave him a lethal Jones. "Coffee?"

He shook his head and snagged her close again. *"Sex."*

Laughing, she darted out of reach. "Your hair's standing on end, you've got enough whiskers to remove a layer of my hide, and I have more cookies to bake."

Damn. Rubbing his chin, he realized she was right. He turned away, intent on one thing. "Fine. I'll be back for the coffee in ten. Finish up your cookies."

"But . . ."

"You wanted me. Well, now you've got me." He sent her a quick wink. "Wait for me in the bed."

Parker closed the bathroom door on her laughter. But he realized he was smiling, too. She made him feel lighthearted, when he hadn't thought that possible, especially during the holidays.

True to his word, Parker opened the bathroom door only ten minutes later. He spotted her sitting in the middle of the bed, and like a fantasy from a dream, he started toward her, steam billowing out around him, trailing in his wake. His stride was long and sure, his whiskers gone, his wet hair combed back.

Still naked.

Yearning curled inside her, and Lily knew it'd be so easy to stray off course, to forget her plans and wallow in the sensuality he offered.

But as much as he tempted her, as much as she wanted him at that very moment, she also wanted more. She wanted forever.

She started to tell him that they needed to talk, but Parker didn't give her a chance. He never slowed, and his steely gaze never wavered. His big hands landed on her shoulders, driving her down to the mattress, and his mouth swallowed her gasp. She found herself flat on her back, covered by hot, aroused male.

"Parker," she moaned.

"Now that I've had you," he whispered near her ear, "I want you even more."

Given his confession, there probably wouldn't be a better time to segue into a discussion on their future. Lily closed her eyes, drew a deep breath, and said, "You think you'll want me in a year? Or five? Or . . ."

He pushed back from her, but Lily kept her eyes closed, too cowardly to look at him, too afraid she'd see his discomfort, or worse, outright rejection.

His lips brushed hers, his hand cradled her face. "What are you talking about, Lily?"

Well, shoot. She'd have to open her eyes for that. She peeked, and saw he looked merely curious, a little tender, still really turned-on. Not annoyed. Not angry.

Turning her face to the side, she nodded at the large memory book on his nightstand. "I have a gift for you."

Now he frowned. "We agreed—no gifts."

"No, we agreed no singing or wrapping or . . . whatever. Besides, it's not that type of gift."

Warily, he glanced at the nightstand. "A photo album?"

"Memory book."

Both hands cupped her face. "Let's make some new memories. Starting right now." And he tried to kiss her again.

Lily pressed her head back into the pillow. "This is important to me, Parker."

"God I hate when women say that."

For that, she gave him a shove. "It could be important to you, too, if you'd stop being such a grinch and just listen."

Growling out a complaint, Parker rolled onto his back and covered his face with a forearm. "Okay, let me have it. This is about Christmas, isn't it?"

Slowly, Lily sat up. Parker looked far from receptive, but still she reached for the heavy leather-bound book and cradled it in her lap. As always, touching it, thinking about it, made her sentimental and reflective. Poignant memories brought a lump to her throat and tied her stomach in knots. "There are . . . some things about me that I think you should know. Things that might make a difference."

His arm dropped away, and his expression filled with concern. "What is it?"

Heart pounding, chest tight with nervousness because this was so important, Lily stared into his beautiful eyes. Strong, tall, protective Parker—how could he not know the difference he made to so many?

Tears welled, and Lily dashed at her eyes, trying to laugh, trying to dredge up that carefree attitude that he seemed to dislike so much.

"Oh, Jesus, honey, no." In a rush, Parker sat up beside her. He looked crushed as he smoothed her hair and kissed her forehead. "I can't take it. Please don't cry."

"I'm sorry." Darn it, she sounded like a strangling frog. "Ignore the tears."

"That's impossible." He tipped up her chin, his expression full of compassion and concern and heart-wrenching tenderness. "Is this about Christmas? It is, isn't it? I shouldn't have been such an ass. If you really want me to wrap presents, I will. Hell, I'll even help you with the cookies. Just don't cry anymore."

Wonderful, special Parker. "It's not about cookies or material gifts. It's about the holiday spirit, the kindness of strangers." She drew a deep breath. "Without that kindness, I wouldn't be here."

A strange stillness settled over him. "What do you mean you wouldn't be here? What the hell are you talking about?"

She could never think of the generosity of the human spirit without an excess of emotion. Even as she smiled, the tears trickled down her cheeks, shaming her for being such a sentimental sap, especially since she knew Parker didn't feel the same. "I would have died, Parker. My mother, too."

For several strained moments, Parker said nothing, he just breathed deep and fast, as if her statement had left him shaken. Then he pulled her into his lap, tucked her head under his chin, and said, "Okay, I'm listening. Tell me."

Hopeful, Lily opened the book. On the first page was the most important article, but she flipped past it. It was special, so she'd save it until the end.

"See this one?" The headline read, "Man Honored for Act of Heroism." Lily explained, "The woman had a seizure and her car struck a gas pump. Flames were everywhere. The people close by could see that her doors were stuck, trapping her inside."

Parker read aloud, "Phil Benton pulled Margery Wilson from her burning car, disregarding his own peril. Moments after freeing her, the gas tank exploded."

Lily sighed. "It was Christmas Day. Mr. Benton was on his way home to his wife and children. Their dinner was ruined because he spent several hours at the hospital."

"He was hurt?"

She shook her head and forced the words out around the lump of emotion clogging her throat. "No. He stayed with Margery because otherwise, she'd have been all alone. When the hospital released her, he took her home and she had Christmas dinner with his family."

In pensive silence, Parker smoothed his hand up and down Lily's back.

She turned the page to another headline. "High School Student Survives Gunshot Wound," she read. "In a true act of heroism, high school senior Dennis Clark came to the aid of his best friend during an armed attack on Christmas Day."

"I remember that one," Parker remarked quietly. "The kid protected his friend after two masked guys had beat him unconscious and tried to rob him. He got shot in the shoulder." He stared at the photo that accompanied the article. "It was touch and go for a while there."

Lily nodded. "He still has the bullet in his shoulder."

On a deep breath, Parker whispered, "And he still has his best friend."

Pleased that he'd see that way, Lily smiled. "Yes." She showed Parker one article after another. Twenty pages worth—and that was only one of her albums. She had others. Maybe someday she'd be able to go through them all with him.

Finally, after working up her nerve, she turned back to the first article and trailed her fingers lightly over the page. "This one is mine."

Parker stared first at her, his eyes seeing into her soul, his expression one of dawning comprehension before he gave his attention to the faded newsprint.

In his deep, quiet voice, he read, "Detective's Heroism Saves Pregnant Woman." He paused, tightening his hold on her. "Your mother?"

More tears blurred Lily's vision. "She was a nurse on call. That Christmas, we had almost three feet of snow, then a layer of ice. A lot of streets were closed. The salt trucks couldn't keep up."

"But she was a nurse, so she braved the weather."

"Yes." Lily laid her head on his shoulder. "Mom had just parked in the upper level of the garage and taken off her seat belt when . . . one of the road crew trucks clearing the garage lost control. It started sliding in the ice and the driver couldn't stop it or steer it away from her. It happened so fast . . ."

"Damn."

"It slammed into her car. The impact of the collision ejected her head first through the windshield. But that wasn't the worst of it. She landed on the garage floor and the salt truck rolled over her, snagging her underneath it before crashing through the guardrail. It didn't go completely over the side to the level below. It sort of just hung there, keeping her trapped."

The room grew so quiet, Lily could hear her own heartbeat and sense Parker's dread.

"Mom wasn't able to breathe. She was pretty broken up, with multiple system traumas and several fractures, including a skull fracture. And at any moment, that truck could have fallen to the parking level below." In a whisper, Lily added, "She would have been crushed. We know that."

Again, Parker's arms tightened on her, and he sounded almost as pained as she felt whenever reciting the story. "But someone saved her."

Turning her face up to his, Lily smiled. "A detective . . . like you." She turned back to the article and touched it with reverent fingertips. "The crash drew a lot of attention. Hospital staff ran out, but no one knew for sure what to do. It was such a dangerous situation. Anyone who got too close would be putting his life on the line. The detective didn't hesitate though. Knowing there wouldn't be much time left before Mom suffocated, he worked his way under the truck with a bag mask. My mother says she can still remember his calm voice commanding her to take slow, easy breaths, to hang on . . ." Lily gulped on her tears. "He told her everything would be okay— and she believed him."

His face buried in her neck, Parker asked, "You weren't hurt?"

"No." Lily gave a watery laugh. "They delivered me that day by emergency C-section, almost at the same time they were patching up Mom. I was small, but healthy."

"Thank God."

"And the cop who helped her." She snuggled closer to him. "He waited, you know. To make sure she'd be all right. To be there with her in case she needed him again. Mom says when she talked to him later, he said all he could think of was his own pregnant wife at home and how Christmas wouldn't be the same without her."

The seconds ticked by, and Lily's anxiety grew. She had no idea what Parker felt, what he thought, if baring her heart had made a difference to him.

Then she felt Parker nuzzling her hair, and he asked, "Did you feel that?"

Confused, Lily pushed back to peek up at him. "What?"

With the utmost care, he cradled her face in his hand and smiled. "The way my heart just grew ten times its size?"

Lily twisted in his lap to face him. "What are you talking about?"

He smiled gently, wiped away her tears. "Don't you remember the Grinch, when the true meaning of Christmas finally hit him, and his heart all but exploded in his chest?"

Lily started breathing too fast. "I remember."

"Well, that's what it feels like to me right now. Like my heart is so full, my ribs just might break." He kissed the end of her nose. "Damn, Lily, I've been an ass."

"You have not!"

"I love you."

She stared, stunned silly, speechless.

"Hell, I've loved you for a long time but didn't want to admit it." Parker shook his head and smiled at her. "I thought you were too young, too fanciful, and way too damn happy to suit me. All that optimism scared me, I guess because it emphasized how damn pessimistic I've become."

"You're not a pessimist. You're a hero."

He grinned at her, shook his head. "I wanted to be, but I could never tell if I made a difference."

"And now?"

"Now I'm so glad, so grateful, that you're here. That you're in my life. I make a difference to you, and that has to count for something, right?"

"You make a difference to everyone, Parker." Hope burgeoning, she bit her lip. "You really love me?"

"Yeah, I really do. It took me long enough to realize it, but I figure it has to be love. Nothing else could make me feel like this."

"And . . ." She hated to push him, but she couldn't stop herself. "You believe in the Christmas spirit?"

"You're here with me, in my bed, sharing your life. Sharing you. How could I not believe? You're my own special Christmas miracle."

Happiness bubbled inside her.

"You should be in that memory book too, because, Lily, you saved me." He turned on the bed, positioning her beneath him and getting comfortable. "It's so damn easy to get jaded, to focus on the disappointments instead of the triumphs. It's so easy to lose sight of the important things."

"Like love?"

"Like you. And sharing the holidays with friends and family."

She touched the corner of his mouth. "Speaking of friends and family . . ."

He laughed. "Maybe we should divide Christmas between my folks and yours. It'll probably send my poor mother into a faint, but I'm in a mood for her Christmas dinner. And I want to meet this remarkable mother of yours. And—"

Squealing in delight, Lily threw her arms around him and squeezed him tight. "Your heart really did grow, didn't it?"

"Enough to help you at the shelter." He kissed her. "Enough to start enjoying my job again." Another kiss, this one longer. "And enough to accept that I love you—now, tomorrow, and for the rest of our lives."

Contentment settled over her. "I love you, too."

"Let's go shopping."

Given their current position—in a bed, with her under him—Lily laughed. "You want to shop *now?*"

"Yeah. For the first time in ages, I'm in the mood to buy gifts." His gaze warmed. "For you."

"Oh, Parker." Lily turned to mush. "I have you, and that's surely the best Christmas gift ever."

SNOWED UNDER

Erin McCarthy

Chapter One

Claire Robbins was walking down Michigan Avenue trying to figure out what to buy her mother for Christmas when it hit her.

A gigantic arc of snow, that is.

Head to toe it landed, like someone had tossed a big old bucket of slushies at her. Claire gasped at the ice-cold impact as it doused her hair, slapped her cheek, slid under her cashmere scarf, and bounced off her chest. She blinked hard, wet snow falling off her eyelashes, as she turned toward the sound her brain was quickly processing.

The snowplow.

Going thirty miles an hour, its shovel aimed right at the sidewalk, shooting massive amounts of new and old snow onto every fire hydrant, every street sign, and every person stupid enough not to dodge it.

"Jerk!" she screamed after him. "Reject!" She was guessing there were notches on the side of his truck for each person he had nailed with the wet cold stuff, and she'd probably just given him number three hundred and twelve. She could imagine him cackling as he watched her in his rearview mirror.

Claire grabbed a clump of snow off her scarf and flung it toward the street at his yellow flashing lights, but he was thirty feet away already.

"Evil. Just evil." Claire set down her shopping bags and stomped a little, trying to knock some of the snow off her body. A clump fell off her knee onto her foot.

She brushed futilely at her hair and spat some snow off her lip. *"Scheisse."* Needing to swear, she did it in German, just in case a little kid was within earshot. "This stuff is cold!"

Twelve blocks from her apartment, she was going to have hypothermia by the time she got home. And she'd been in such a good mood, too, checking off everyone on her shopping list except for her mom, all while singing along off-key to the piped-in Jessica Simpson Christmas CD at Williams-Sonoma.

Claire sucked in her breath as she started trudging toward home, her feet making an ominous crunching sound. She had stupidly worn ballet flats instead of boots, and the tops of her feet were wearing a veil of snow sludge. Tapping her toes on the concrete to try and shake some off, she readjusted her bags in her hands.

Not enough cash on her for a cab, since she'd blown her last three dollars on a Godiva truffle, she pondered finding a cash machine or calling a friend to come and get her. But by then, she figured, she could have walked home.

At least she'd found her brother Derek a gift—a gorgeous pair of cuff links—and a bread maker for Derek's wife, Reese. Which reminded her . . .

"Duh, Claire!" she said out loud, mentally smacking herself. "You are half a block from Derek's apartment."

Okay, this made everything seem a lot better. She could be there in five. Derek and Reese were in New York, visiting Reese's family for Christmas, so they wouldn't be home. But Claire had a key, and she got along well enough with Reese that she could borrow some dry clothes. They wouldn't mind if she had a little hot shower either, and made herself some coffee.

Derek liked pie, and Reese frequently baked for him. Maybe Claire could even score a piece of chocolate pie.

Claire walked carefully, crunching and waddling like a blonde penguin.

Maybe she could salvage the evening, and if anyone deserved pie tonight, it was her.

By the time she got herself into her brother's apartment, after four tries shoving the key in the lock with numb, beet-red fingers, she was shaking and thinking only of warm, soft things. Bunnies. Teddy bears. Fleece. Warm Caribbean sand.

Her hair was crystallized. It was possible her earlobes had dropped onto Michigan Avenue, because she couldn't feel them. Her scarf was like a bag of frozen vegetables, crunchy and stiff. Her teeth were chattering, and her feet had turned a sickly eggplant color.

Frozen body and numb brain cells might account for the fact that she didn't scream when she stepped into the apartment and saw a man sitting on the couch, watching TV.

"D-D-D-Derek?" she stuttered, even as logic slowly told her that wasn't her brother. This was a light-brown head of hair, and her brother's was darker.

Which meant this was a stranger, and she was going to die a human Frosty because somehow she couldn't seem to make her brain command her frozen feet to turn and run.

The head turned and she decided it was worse than death. It was her brother's former coworker and her youthful crush, Justin Fairbanks. Staring at her with wide eyes.

Jumping up he said, "*Claire?* Is that you? What the hell happened? You look like you got run over by the Zamboni at the ice rink."

Oh, God, just take her out back and shoot her.

"What are you doing here?" she asked, deciding that she was lying to herself. Justin was her youthful crush *and* her twenty-five-year-old crush. He was gorgeous, her every fantasy sprung to life, with a rangy lean frame, well-defined muscles, and a crooked little smile that just screamed sex. Well, that's what it screamed to her anyway.

Of course, he had always treated her like an annoying little sister. But now that she was no longer eighteen, maybe, just maybe, he might see her as the adult that she was. Or, more likely, he would forever see her as the blonde teenage cheer-leader she had been.

"Did you fall down in a snowdrift?" Justin asked in disbelief as he walked toward her.

Oh, yeah. He still had her in the not-so-bright-blonde category.

"No!" She had an MBA, a position in marketing at an advertising agency, her own apartment, and expensive shoes. Yet all he saw was a child.

Maybe this was her chance to show Justin once and for all that she was definitely a woman, and then some. This could be a golden opportunity. To see if her fantasies about Justin and his penis size had any merit.

To have some rocking Christmas sex.

Time to take lemons and make some lemonade.

Frozen lemonade. But hopefully lemonade nonetheless.

"S-s-s-snowplow," she said.

Now if she could just stop her teeth from chattering, the attempted seduction of Justin could begin.

Chapter Two

Justin came around the couch, more than a little startled to see Derek's little sister looking like she'd been dipped in water, then strung upside down in a meat locker. Her hair was a solid three inches straight up in the air.

"The snowplow did this? Jesus." Reaching out, he peeled off her scarf, wincing when it made a sound like duct tape coming off the roll.

Normally he wouldn't have come within three feet of Claire, and touching her would have been out of the question, given that she inspired thoughts in him that could only be considered perverted. She was ten years younger than him, and just a kid.

Well, not so much a kid anymore, he had to admit, as removing the scarf revealed some killer cleavage. He swallowed hard and forced himself to look up. Into her eyes. Away from her hot, round, beckoning . . .

Damn. So Claire wasn't a teenager anymore—big friggin' deal. She was still off-limits, and he'd rather bump a beehive wearing nothing but honey than have to endure the temptation of her half-dressed, but she was in pretty bad shape at the moment.

She needed to get out of her wet clothes pronto, and to help her like a decent person would, he needed to suppress his lust. His very large, growing lust.

"Let me get your bags." He took them and set them on the floor. Unzipped her coat. Jerked it off of her by the sleeves, careful not to touch anything but the wool. Certainly not any of what was under it. Like her skin. Or her breasts.

He was a sick human being. Just absolutely nasty. It had been bad enough that he'd felt a disturbing attraction to Claire when he'd first met her six years ago, but then, he'd dismissed it as lack of sex. FBI training had cut into his social life and he hadn't been getting any.

But there was no excuse for this. He'd had sex just the week before.

Claire just stood there, arms still hovering out away from her body. "Why are you here?" she asked again.

"Oh, uh, Derek knows I'm here. I'm in town visiting my parents, but I didn't want to stay at their house, if you know what I mean. Just a little too crowded with all my nieces and nephews, so Derek offered me his apartment for a few days since he's out of town."

"How fortuitous," she said.

Forta-what? He could barely see straight, let alone process words with more than one syllable. Justin took her hands between his and rubbed gently to warm them up. They were so small, so cold. He looked her over and saw pink cheeks, watery eyes, and soaking wet jeans from the mid-thigh down. He was surely going to regret saying this, but . . .

"You should take a warm shower. Not hot, or your skin will itch from the temperature change, but warm." He let go of her hands, inspected them for signs of frostbite. They were bright red, which was a good sign. "I don't think you have frostbite, but you need to get warmed up."

"Good idea," she said, flexing her fingers before bending over to pull off her shoes.

"So, how you been, Claire? Before today, I mean. I haven't seen you since Derek got married. Man, it's been almost a year now since his wedding."

During which he'd spent the entire day dodging Claire,

telling himself he would not look at the way her silky straight bridesmaid dress clung to her nipples.

He watched her struggle with the slip-on shoes, trying over and over to tug them off, while balancing on one foot, shivers passing through her.

Christ. Rolling his eyes and praying for strength, Justin took Claire's arm. "Sit down. I'll help you."

"Thank you," she said, breathlessly, dropping down onto the couch. She stuck her foot out in front of her. "I've been great, actually. I got my Masters degree a year and a half ago, and I've been working with the Morton-Media Advertising Agency. It's a fabulous position and I'm learning a lot."

"Sounds good." Justin squatted down, braced himself, and gently pulled her shoe off from heel to toe. "You still living with your mom and dad?" He really hoped she was. It would make her seem all that much more out of reach. Remind him that with Claire he'd be cradle-robbing.

"Of course not," she said, sounding offended. "I moved out *years* ago. In my *early* twenties."

Justin was suddenly aware of how close he was to her. He was eye level with those very breasts he was trying to pretend didn't exist. He ripped the other shoe off with less precision and stood up. "Go ahead and get in the shower, Claire."

"Okay." She winced as she stood, her movements awkward. "But I seriously don't think I can get these wet jeans off." Heading toward the bathroom, she lifted her hand and wiggled it. "I can't feel my fingers. Can you help me take my pants off?"

She did not just say that.

"Uh . . . sure."

He did not just say that.

Justin moved behind the couch and plucked up a throw pillow so she wouldn't see his massive erection.

This really made no sense at all. Here he was, thirty-five years old, too old for spontaneous hard-ons, and pretty damn sexually active, thank you very much. He had a female friend, Karen, who was very happy to have an entirely commitment-free sexual relationship with him. They saw each other a couple of times a month when the urge struck either of them. Dinner, maybe a movie, then a nice piece of ass, and they were done for a while.

Worked for him.

Except that didn't explain why he was about to go off in his Levis at the thought of peeling Claire's wet clothes off.

She smiled at him, the first one since she'd walked in the door. "Don't worry, I won't get embarrassed or anything. I'm not shy."

Wonderful. Just what he'd been worried about. Her modesty. Ha.

Justin dumped the pillow back on the couch and pictured Derek reconfiguring his face if he touched Claire.

"So, what have you been up to, Justin?" she called over her shoulder as she headed for the bedroom. "Still living in Dallas? Working? Girlfriend? Vacations to exotic locales?"

"Yes, yes, no, and no." He walked very, very slowly. Maybe by the time he got there she would be stripped all on her own.

Wait a minute. That didn't sound like a good thing for him to discover either. He stopped so fast he had to grab the wall for balance.

Her head popped around the corner of the door frame. "What do you do for fun then?"

"I go to the firing range."

She laughed. "No, seriously."

He was thirty-five years old. What did she think he did in his downtime? "I have a boat. I work out. I cut the grass in my backyard. I go to the movies with scads of beautiful women."

"All at once?" she asked. Then she winked.

She fucking winked at him. What the hell was that? And emerged from the bedroom with a bundle of clothes in her arms, which didn't hide the fact that she had peeled off her sweater.

He could see bare arms and hot pink satin peeking around at him. With those little shiny stones trimming it, the things that sparkled and reminded him of Vegas showgirls and Victoria's

Secret ads. The name of the stones wasn't coming to mind, maybe because his mind was on coming and nothing else.

"I'm a man of many talents," he told her.

"Oohhh, sounds promising." Claire brushed past him and dropped the clothes on the floor in the bathroom. "Let's see if your talents extend to taking off wet jeans. Damp denim has a super-glue quality to it."

She reached into the shower and turned it on, stretching and arching and showing him all that pink satin thrust forward straight at him.

It was a very, very small bathroom.

Knight and his wife weren't particularly neat either. Their toiletries burst out of the medicine cabinet and covered every spare inch of counter space. No place to lean there. The burgeoning hamper was filled beyond the brim with towels and what looked like the legs of jeans. No way he could sit on that.

The only place to be was exactly where he was—a foot in front of Claire.

She made a futile attempt to undo her jeans. She managed the button and half the zipper, and pink popped out at him. He broke out into a sweat. That damn shower was heating the room, steam swirling all around them, and he could see her pink panties. See how satin was hugging what was right behind it.

"That steam feels so good." She rolled her neck, loosening her shoulders. "I've never been so cold in my whole life."

Justin understood the concept. He was freaking frozen to the floor.

Another attempt at her jeans and she only got them an inch down. "Help," she said with a laugh.

Yeah. Real funny. He was just cracking up here.

Alright. He pushed on his fist and popped all his knuckles. He was going in.

Her skin was cold and clammy, and she shivered when he made contact right above the waistband of the jeans. Justin jerked back. "Sorry, are my hands cold?"

He blew on them, bent over, and gripped the front pockets of her jeans.

"No." Her voice had grown a little husky, and Justin panicked. He knew that sound. That was a sex sound.

Which shouldn't be coming from little Claire's mouth, especially not when his mouth was half a millimeter away from her navel and his hands were jerking down her pants.

He wasn't gentle or subtle in his attempt to get the task over with, which only served to turn right around and bite him in the ass. He pulled so hard, the jeans went down her thighs, but the movement ricocheted her forward. So that her pink panties popped him right in the mouth.

It lasted only a second before he leaped away, but it was long enough for him to process the smoothness of satin, the contrast of warmth there where the rest of her was cool. The smell of damp, and perfume, and something that seemed entirely like arousal to him.

But that was probably wishful thinking, sack of shit that he was, so he let go of the jeans at her knees and stumbled backward.

"There you go. You should be able to get them the rest of the way."

Then he took his demanding dick and ran, slamming the bathroom door behind him.

Claire grabbed the countertop for support and allowed herself a little whimper. So close, yet so frustrating.

She didn't understand it. His face had been virtually in her crotch, and yet, nothing. He was either a man or steel or he had no interest in her whatsoever.

Which would totally and completely suck, because not only had she been wanting to jump his bones for half a decade, she had now managed to get herself a little hot and a lot bothered.

His face had been in her *crotch*. His breath had blown across her stomach. Of course she was going to get turned on. Not to mention it had been eighteen months since she'd had sex. And even then her boyfriend Brian hadn't been all that great at it. Straight shooting he could do, but the man didn't know what a tongue was for.

Claire kicked off her jeans violently and stopped her thought train before it wrecked. The last thing in the world she wanted to be thinking about was Brian's oral techniques, or lack thereof.

What she wanted to know was Justin's take on tongue action.

She also wanted to rip his sweatshirt off and try her own tactile tricks.

Maybe she just needed to be a little more obvious so he wouldn't have any doubts about what she was offering.

Unless he really didn't want it.

Popping her bra off, she commanded herself to chill out. Only she couldn't prevent a gasp of utter horror when she looked in the mirror.

Maldigalo, she silently cursed in Spanish. No wonder Justin didn't want anything to do with her. She looked like hell.

Touching her wet, stiff, lopsided hair, she groaned. She looked like one of those freaky, maniacal porcelain dolls her grandmother collected. "I'm like Bride of Chucky!"

With a Rudolph red nose, scarlet cheeks, cotton candy pink ears, and a strange magenta streak across her neck. She was the whole flippin' family of reds.

"Nice. Just fabulous." Ditching her panties, she stepped in the shower.

"Aaahh. Oh, yeah. Okay, everything's better when you're warm." That felt so good. The water soothed her, running all through her clammy hair and down her red face. After washing her hair twice, and cranking up the heat, she leaned back in the hot stream. She forcibly relaxed her muscles and used large amounts of Reese's shower gel to massage her shoulders, arms, inner thighs.

She lingered between her legs with characteristic optimism, hoping she'd need enticing mango shower gel scent there because Justin would be inhaling it.

Of course, picturing him doing just that while her slippery hands slid over her skin had her hitching her breath and reaching out for the shower wall for support.

That was it.

"Screw this." Turning off the faucet, she flung back the shower curtain. Squeezed water out of her hair. Stepped out onto the bath mat.

Time to go for broke.

"Justin?" she called. "I forgot a towel. Can you bring me one?"

Chapter Three

You know, he was trying to do the right thing.

But it was so damn hard.

Justin pulled his sorry ass off the couch with a sigh and opened the linen closet in the hall.

Why couldn't Knight's sister be old, married, crabby? All of the above would be even better.

The closet wasn't in any better order than the medicine cabinet. Six towels fell on his head when he tried to extract one. Studying the pile, he carefully found the biggest one and rammed the rest back in. This blue one was good. It was like a towel and a half. It would go down to Claire's knees and up to her chin.

He knocked on the bathroom door. "I have a towel for you."

"Come in."

It occurred to him as he pushed the door open that the shower wasn't running any longer. And if the shower wasn't running, she probably wasn't in it. And if she needed a towel, that meant she didn't have one . . .

It was too late to retreat.

The door was open and Claire was right in front of him.

Naked.

"Oh, my God," he said, even as his eyes raced over her body at warp speed.

The view he had was in profile, but it was still a hell of a view. Her hands were in her hair, squeezing it into a ponytail. The movement arched her back and raised her breasts enticingly. Her creamy, pink skin had water rivulets running down it, and every inch was covered in a glossy damp sheen.

As he watched, a droplet hovered on the tip of her nipple for the space of a breath before falling off. He almost moaned, and barely managed to prevent himself from diving to catch that droplet with his tongue.

Claire's ass was tight and high as she reached up, with enough curve that his hand itched to race over it, squeeze, slap.

"Thanks." Claire turned and held her hand out, like there was nothing out of the ordinary happening. Just a stroll in the park here. Naked.

Justin shook the towel open, frantic. "Claire!" He held it in front of her like a tarp, tucking it under her armpits and pushing her arms to her sides so it would stay in place. "Cover up, for God's sake."

"Oh, calm down, *por favor. S'il vous plait.* Don't be such a prude, Justin." She shook her hair back and tried to unpin her hands.

He held fast. No way was he letting that towel drop. A man only had so much self-control, and his was just about shot.

"A prude? So you think it's okay to just stand around naked in front of anybody? You might give a guy the wrong idea, you know."

She rolled her eyes. "You mean like I'm interested? That I would like to have sex with him?"

"Yes!" Naked pretty much screamed sex to him when you were with a member of the opposite gender and it wasn't a visit to the doctor.

"Then I'm doing it right."

"*What?*" His ears started ringing. His legs went numb. "What is that supposed to mean?"

"Where have you been? I've had a crush on you since I was eighteen." She licked her very red lips and gave a sensual smile. "I was hoping you would see tonight as the opportunity I do— to see if I've been justified in wanting you all these years."

"What exactly are you suggesting?" Justin was feeling very, very confused. He'd been to a holiday luncheon at his grandmother's nursing home that afternoon. Maybe the eggnog had been bad and he was hallucinating.

But it felt all too real when Claire lifted her arms, taking advantage of his slack hold on her. Two-fisted, she grabbed that towel and jerked it away from her body, and tossed it to the floor. Then leaned right up against him, her hands on his shoulders.

Justin shot his arms out like airplane wings so he wouldn't be tempted to touch.

"I'm suggesting that we spend the night together. In bed. 'Tis the season to give, after all, and what I want . . . is you."

"Don't you want an iPod instead? That's what everybody else wants."

"I already have one."

Then he was out of arguments.

Maybe he could think better if her breasts weren't pressing into him, and her hips weren't brushing against his. If she wasn't all snuggly and sexy and rubbing just a little in all sorts of interesting places.

But there was nothing going on upstairs. He was Odie, the dog from *Garfield*. Drooling and excited.

So when she kissed him, he didn't even try to stop it.

As far as fantasies springing to life, this was a pretty damn good one. Claire was totally naked, wet in more ways than one, and kissing Justin Fairbanks, federal agent and first-class hottie.

While never a timid sort of girl, even she was a little surprised by her boldness. But hey, if you wanted something badly enough, you had to reach out and grab it. Literally.

And she really wanted Justin. At least once.

Too bad the kiss only lasted a microsecond. One glorious second during which he kissed her back, and the earth tilted, the heavens burst forth, and a bunch of other metaphorical crap that Claire had thought was made up until her mouth touched his. In that instant, she realized it was—*ta da*—all true. Then he ruined her girl moment by yanking his lips away and grabbing her forearms. Setting her away from him.

Claire sucked in a breath, disappointed, and waited for him to explain, though she wasn't at all sure she wanted to hear what he was going to say. He looked pained, and not the least turned-on.

Which was bad. Because she was standing there totally and completely naked, and if he rejected her, she was going to stick her head in the sink bowl and drown herself in sheer horror.

"We can't do this. I'm old enough to be your father," he said.

Her knees sank in relief. Okay. Much better than an announcement he was secretly married, gay, or thought she was the most unattractive naked woman he'd ever set eyes on. Better than all of the above, true, and yet so much more incredibly stupid.

Claire leaned back against the counter, the cool marble hitting her backside. She propped herself up with her hands and sucked in her gut, determined to give this one last shot before she slunk off and put on her brother's sweatpants.

"Wow, you must have been a really mature third grader then."

"What do you mean?" Justin looked at the ceiling. At the floor. At a piece of wallpaper that was peeling by the door frame as he kept picking at it. Anywhere but at her.

Dummy. "I mean you're like nine years older than me! That's a little young for fatherhood, even for aggressive kids."

He finally looked at her. Shook his head like he wasn't buying it. "I'm thirty-five. I had a birthday last week."

"Happy birthday. And I have a birthday *next* week. I'll be

twenty-six. See? Nine years. And I'm old enough to know what I want, and I want you. If you're not interested, if you don't find me attractive, then just say so." So she could put her panties on and go home and put an end to her crush once and for all. "I'll live. Just say, 'I'm not interested, Claire.' "

But he didn't say that. He gave her a smoldering look, gaze dropping down to her breasts. "Oh, I'm interested. And I find you more than attractive. You're downright sexy. You're hot as hell."

Oohh. This was working. "And?"

"And I've thought that since the day I met you, all those years ago, when you were way too young for me to be having such nasty thoughts about you."

Even better. "I was in college, I wasn't that young. But that's irrelevant now. The important thing today is that we're both adults. I *am* old enough, and ready and willing to do anything you want to do. Since you're interested."

Damn, she was getting herself excited. Claire squeezed her legs together tighter and tried to mentally will Justin to move toward her.

"Anything?" he asked in a low voice, looking like he had a few choice ideas in mind.

She nodded, pushing her breasts out a little farther.

"We really shouldn't . . ." he said, and she knew she had him.

"All right," she said. "That's cool." And reached for the pile of clothes she had put on the toilet seat. "I'm going to get dressed then, I'm getting cold."

"Wait." He grimaced. Ran his fingers through his short hair. "Shit."

"Yes?" she asked innocently, turning to look over her shoulder, well aware he must have an up-close and personal shot of her butt.

"I don't want you to get dressed." He said this like he was begrudgingly admitting to wearing a toupee. With reluctance and shame.

"Justin." Claire suddenly felt like laughing. "You are making such a huge deal out of this. It's okay, I promise. We're consenting adults who have a sexual interest in each other. There's nothing wrong with that."

He just brooded.

"It will be painless. You don't even have to do anything. You can just lie back and I'll do all the work." She gave him a saucy smile.

She meant for him to laugh, but he just frowned.

"I don't get it," he said. "I feel so out of control when I see you. It ticks me off that I want you this much, that I'm so out of control."

Claire stood back up, thinking that personally she liked the idea that she made him lose control. "You've just had a lot of time to want me, that's all. Just like I have with you. That's why I'm doing things I would have never dreamed I would do—like standing here stark naked having an entire conversation. But I have an idea."

"What's that?"

"Go back in the other room. We're going to start this all over." Now that he was reconciled to the idea of sleeping with her, Claire wanted Justin comfortable, feeling in control, even if it was a total illusion.

But the key to a successful seduction was understanding your target. And she had Justin pegged.

Time to let him take the lead.

Chapter Four

Justin should have taken off when he had the chance. Just gotten the hell out of there when Claire sent him into the living room to wait while she stayed in the bathroom.

Because she had emerged looking cute and squeaky clean, her hair in a ponytail, and wearing huge sweatpants and a fleece sweatshirt. It was almost worse than naked because now she looked like a woman after sex. Like she could be his girlfriend and this could be their apartment.

Which meant he must have caught senility at the nursing home, because he had lost his ever lovin' mind.

"Have you eaten dinner?" she asked, acting like nothing unusual had just transpired at all.

"No." He had been contemplating microwaving popcorn for dinner when she had burst into the apartment like a living Popsicle.

"You like pasta? I can throw something together. I'm starving. All I ate was a chocolate truffle when I was shopping."

Justin followed her into the kitchen, not exactly sure what to say. He could tell her to go home. He could let her stay.

He could enjoy what she was offering. Dinner, conversation, sex he was sure would be hot.

Was there really any choice there?

The question was better put—How dumb was he?

"Pasta sounds great."

He wasn't that dumb. He didn't need the action—he had Karen for his physical needs—and Claire wasn't a candidate for the wife/future-mother-of-his-children he was looking for. Claire was something he didn't understand, someone he wanted in a way that was illogical, that had spanned miles and years and some hard living in between.

So it didn't make sense. So it couldn't be anything more than one night.

What was the harm in enjoying just that one night?

Down that road of logic lies the dark side, but Justin was willing to risk it. Claire was right. They were adults. She wanted him, and it was Christmas. In the spirit of giving, he should do this. Better to give sex than to receive it.

Geez, he was a sick bastard.

Justin moved up behind Claire as she filled a pot with water and set it on the stove, turning the burner knob on. He ached to lift that sweatshirt and taste her skin. To suck her nipples into his mouth and to wiggle his fingers into her hot flesh. To have what he'd spent six years wanting.

"It will have to be jarred sauce. Reese and Derek aren't exactly known for having a stocked pantry." She stretched up to reach the cabinet and Justin shook his head.

The hell with it.

"You know, Claire?" Justin gave up. He was going to choke on his lust if he didn't satisfy it. "Let's just hold off on that pasta for a minute."

"What? Why?" She turned and almost collided with him, given that he was hovering a half inch behind her. Startled, she fell backward against the stove and grabbed at her chest. "Jesus, you scared me."

Now that he had made his decision, he couldn't imagine why he'd ever resisted. She looked delicious. All pink and warm and glassy-eyed in the cozy kitchen. Justin cupped both of her cheeks and pulled her mouth to his.

Oh, yeah. He let his eyes drift closed. This was much better than the first time, when he'd been half-stupid with shock. Make that fully stupid.

Now he was all there and all willing to take what he wanted. He tasted her thoroughly, in and out with long, luxurious kisses. She had a full bottom lip, and Justin sucked it between his, letting go when she shuddered.

"Is that all you needed?" she asked on a shaky breath, her fingers gripping his waist.

"Nope." The sweatshirt she was wearing was loose and soft, a nice, inexpensive Hanes Her Way kind of shirt. Justin turned it inside out as he ripped it over her head.

She hadn't bothered to put a bra back on, for which he was extremely grateful. Leaning back just a little to savor the anticipation of touching her chest, he dropped her shirt to the floor. "I need to be inside you. If you've got a problem with that now is your chance to speak up."

Claire fiddled with the button on his jeans, not trying to undo it, just touching it, brushing, playing with it. "No problem at all. You know, I'm not the kind of person to pine over a guy, but I have to admit, in your case I've pined."

Justin cupped her breasts with his hands, enjoying both the feel of her warm, full flesh and the soft moan of encouragement she gave.

"I prefer to call it 'occasionally thinking about with longing.' Same thing, but less adolescent than pining."

"So you did that? Thought about me with longing?" she asked, her head lolling back a little as he moved his thumb over her nipple.

"A number of times." Probably more times than he was willing to admit. Every time he heard Derek's name or saw him, he automatically had thought of Claire. Which would always morph into a disturbing sexual want.

"Mmm, that's sexy, Justin. Now I'm going to stop talking."

"Good plan." Justin bent over and flicked his tongue over her tight nipple.

Instead of moaning or begging or gripping his head like he

expected and hoped for, Claire pushed at him. "Bugger! Hold on. Hold on, hold on."

Justin froze, mouth open, ready to suck her nipple in. No, no, *no*, she did not just say that. "Why, for God's sake?"

"I have to get a condom. I'm not on the pill or anything." Claire shoved his head hard and started across the kitchen, topless. "Just two seconds. Reese and Derek have condoms *everywhere*—they, like, define sexually active."

He needed to know these things?

But he had to admit he was grateful for Derek's sex drive when Claire did, in fact, return two seconds later with a box of condoms, waving them triumphantly. Later, when his conscience had returned, he would ponder the ethics of using Derek's condoms to screw Derek's sister, but right now he was too busy screwing Derek's sister to worry about it.

Or he would be if she would just stand still. Now Claire was bent over the stove, still topless of course, turning off the burner she had set the pan on. Then she was in the refrigerator— what could possibly be in there that they needed?—clanking around. Finally, she emerged with a bottle of water and blinked at him.

"What? You're looking at me like I'm a freak."

"What are you doing?" Besides testing every ounce of willpower and patience he had.

"Getting water. I have a tickle in my throat."

He'd give her a tickle in her throat. When he rammed his tongue down it.

Justin ripped off his Henley shirt and closed the distance between him and Claire. Her eyes went wide. Grabbing her by the waistband of her sweats, he pulled her flush up against him. Her breasts bounced against his chest, her damp ponytail swinging back and forth.

Claire had a tight body, firm skin over elongated muscle. She was thin, but with some back. Justin kissed her, his hands clamping down over that perky backside and grinding.

"Ooohhh," she said when he gave her a split second for air.

But he didn't leave her a chance to say or do anything else, before he had his tongue sweeping into her mouth, his desire roaring with urgency. Every cell in his body was screaming. Must. Have. Now. There was nothing polite or tepid or skilled in his advances as his hands raced all over Claire, gripping and grabbing and squeezing.

He couldn't get her pants off fast enough. Shoving at them, he made a happy discovery. "Damn, Claire." She wasn't wearing any panties.

His hand was skimming over smooth flesh, and he worked his way around to the front, movements not following any plan of attack other than *gimme, gimme.*

Claire's answer was to kick her sweatpants down to her ankles and spread her thighs for his hand. Justin couldn't resist that kind of invitation. He reached to cup her mound and was shocked to find nothing but soft folds beneath his touch. Unable to form the question, he just glanced up at her.

She gave a sly shrug. "Bikini wax. A habit for bathing suits and low-rise jeans. And I'm blonde . . . thin hair to begin with. Didn't mean to flip you out."

"I'm not flipped out." A little startled. Shocked. Turned-on. Justin didn't normally date women who had anything waxed, let alone that, and he had to admit he was impressed. Anyone who could handle that kind of pain was one tough chick. "You're very soft." He teased his finger between her folds. "And wet."

Definitely wet. Justin slid his finger down deep inside, enjoying the way she felt, reveling in the jerk she gave.

"Justin," Claire whimpered. She held onto his shoulders, her knee turning out, body rocking toward his.

He understood the feeling. Popping the snap on his jeans, he got rid of them in hard, fast movements, and reached for the condoms. Stroking her clitoris in sensual circles, he slipped down and pressed his thumb into her hot flesh. Claire squirmed, her breath frantic little pants.

"*Scheisse*, I'm going to come and I don't want to this soon," she said, even as her hips ground against his touch.

Justin let her go, and she stumbled, crying out in disappointment. "Don't stop!"

"What? I need two hands to put on the condom." He demonstrated, trying to look innocent, but he couldn't prevent a grin.

"Tease," she said without much heat, her eyes trained on his cock as he rolled down the condom. "Need any help?"

"Got it. What does *scheisse* mean?"

" 'Shit.' I have a habit of swearing in other languages. It's more polite, I think."

He wasn't feeling polite. Justin put a foot on her sweatpants to hold them in place. They were puddled on the floor, still around her ankles, and he wanted them off. "Get over by the wall."

"Excuse me?" She stepped out of the pants, obviously guessing his intentions, but looking dubiously at the kitchen wall, where a calendar of sailboats was hung on a bulletin board.

"Put your back against the wall," he said slowly and clearly, giving her a nudge to get her moving. He was done. He had to have her yesterday, and every second of foreplay was killing him.

Glancing over her shoulder as she turned, she took a slow step, a smile on her lips. "Bossy, bos—"

He cut her words off by moving up behind her. Traced his fingers down her arms, lifting them, placing her palms flat against the wall. Kicked her ankles apart, blood pounding in his head, mouth thick, body hot and tight. Spread her folds with his right hand, while rubbing his palm over her clitoris.

"Sorry, but you were taking too damn long." Justin entered her from behind with one hard thrust, groaning as her vaginal muscles clamped around his cock.

The velocity forced Claire forward, smacking her into the wall, and Justin thought he should apologize, ease up, but it felt so fucking good, and his eyes dropped shut. Just a second to savor, just a second, then he'd see to her comfort, her pleasure.

Except Claire was frantically reaching back for him, her hands grabbing at his waist. "Oh, damn it, Justin, move. I'm going to . . . I'm coming."

He felt her muscles contract around him at the same time her shoulders jerked. A high-pitched yell ripped out of her mouth. Instead of thrusting, he quickly reached around and stroked his thumb over her tight, swollen clit.

She shuddered her way through an orgasm, hips grinding back against him, before she went slack, resting her forehead on her arm. "Oh, crap, sorry."

He wasn't. Justin kissed the back of her neck, enticingly exposed because of the ponytail. Her skin was dewy, flushed. "Do not apologize. I'd be a freakin' idiot if I were upset that you came when I was inside you."

"It was just . . . so big . . . so there, all of a sudden . . . you got so aggressive, and just . . ." she sighed. "Yum."

And then some. "Hold onto the wall, baby."

There was nothing capable of stopping him now. He sank deeper into her, moaning at the tight, hot fit. Her ass bumped up against his pelvis, and he held onto her thighs, pulling her back further to get them as close as possible without actual fusion.

The angle strained his calves, but he didn't notice the burn, just felt the pleasure, the gut-wrenching waves of it that rippled through him with each stroke. He felt the tightness swelling, the sharp bite of ecstasy digging deeper, harder. It was safe to say that when he let out a rebel yell and came, it was with an abandon he hadn't experienced since age sixteen.

Which, as he had tried to explain to Claire, was a hell of a long time ago.

About an hour or two later, he finally stopped shaking and groaning and pounding, and collapsed against her and the wall. He knocked the bulletin board off in the process.

"Jesus," he said as the corkboard crashed to the vinyl floor with an offensive smack. "Look what you made me do. I'm wrecking the joint."

"*I* did?" Claire said, though her words were muffled, given that he had her face squashed into drywall.

"Yes. *You* did, Miss We're Both Adults, Let's Fuck Like Animals."

She laughed. "I've figured something out about you."

Wow, he couldn't wait to hear this. Ten bucks said it wasn't flattering.

"You blow everything out of proportion. You exaggerate to the point of hilarity. Good thing I'm the rational one in this relationship."

The R word. Justin broke out in a sweat and pulled out of her so fast he almost gave himself whiplash. "We don't have a relationship, Claire."

He could practically hear her eyeballs rolling back into her head. "Oh, *mon dieu,* don't ruin a perfectly good postorgasmic moment by being an idiot. I wasn't implying anything, so just chill out."

Ouch. Okay, maybe that hadn't been the smartest thing to say.

She rolled across the wall so she was facing him, hand out. "Now give me my pants."

"No." It was asinine and ornery, but he didn't like that their moment of perfect closeness had been ruined by his stupidity. So he was going to make it worse.

"Fine. I'll cook the pasta naked. See if I care." She turned the water back on and walked across the room, head in the air, pausing only to shake out her legs a little like they were sore.

He stood there, condom still on his dick, and debated. "Claire."

"Hmmm?" she said, face buried in the cabinet.

"I want to get married." When she dropped a two-pound box of pasta on the floor, he realized what that had sounded like. "I mean, I want to get married soon, eventually here, not so far in the future, to a woman who wants to marry me, and is ready to have children, and a house, and, and, shit like that."

Justin rubbed the flat of his palm into his forehead and winced. "I'm ready for that, and I'm on the lookout for that woman."

Claire just stared at him. "Well, if I see a likely candidate for the position of Mrs. Fairbanks I'll let you know."

Now he was at a loss. "Uh . . ." Hands on his hips, feeling like a fool, he turned to the stove. "So, what can I do to help?"

And maybe it was time to put his pants back on. Claire looked like her storefront sign had switched from OPEN to CLOSED.

Hell.

Chapter Five

Men.

Couldn't live with them, couldn't get away with killing them.

Claire tossed pasta in the pot and slapped a lid on harder than was necessary.

Why did guys have to ruin everything by leaping ahead and throwing up roadblocks when they were *miles* from that turn in the road? Justin had taken them from first-time lovers to The End in less than an hour.

The sheer arrogance that she would even want a relationship with him had her blood boiling like those noodles. Had she asked for that? She didn't think so.

She was half-tempted to just go home, but one look out the window had her rethinking that. It was cold out there. And dark. And she still didn't have any money for a cab, and since Reese was a shoe size smaller than she was, she would have to wear wet ballet flats with sweats for ten blocks.

It wasn't in her nature to huff all night anyway. She was a direct person and liked to resolve problems right from jump.

So while Justin hung the bulletin board back up, she stirred the red sauce from a jar, and sighed. Relaxed her shoulders. "Justin?"

"Yeah?" He sounded wary.

As well he should. Dummy.

"You do know that what you said to me about marriage was rude, don't you? Like, hey, you're good enough to sleep with, but nothing more."

"I didn't mean it that way. I was just trying to be honest." He came up behind her, rubbed her forearms slowly, the fleece underlining of the sweatshirt she was wearing comforting on her skin. She believed him. Justin wasn't a cruel person at all. Just dense.

"I respect you, Claire, which is why I've spent six years dodging the urge to do what we did tonight."

There was a compliment in there somewhere. "Don't go warning me off a relationship before I ever said I wanted one, okay? It's like telling me your house isn't for sale when all I said was that it was a lovely home. I can admire something, enjoy it, and that doesn't mean I want to own it, you know what I'm saying? Ownership requires a lot of time, money, maintenance. I'm more in a rental phase in my life."

Of course, that was something of a total lie. She was renting when it came to other men. With Justin, she did want to buy, settle down for the long haul. If not a whole house, at least a *condo*, but she didn't want to scare him. But neither did she want him to make assumptions about her. He was anticipating that she wanted a relationship and that she was falling for him.

Which she was. Or always had been. But even more so now that he had looked at her like that, with longing, touched her with intimacy. She really did feel those silly fluttering feelings. Like given the chance they could morph into bigger feelings. Forever feelings. But he didn't need to know that. Yet.

He turned her around so she was facing him. "You do realize why men like me reach the age of thirty-five without getting married, don't you?"

It was a mystery to her. He looked especially adorable right at the moment, his short hair sticking up as much as it could and his brown eyes soft and serious.

"Because you enjoy your bachelorhood?"

"Because we're stupid."

Claire laughed. "Oh."

"I try to do the right thing, and it's always the wrong way. I'm great on the job, but in relationships, I'm not so solid. It takes me a while to work things around in my head."

"But you're ready for something permanent? Marriage?" The stove knob was digging into her backside, but Claire didn't care. She wanted to stand here in this warm kitchen in Justin's arms until she had a dent in her butt and he had figured out that they could have a relationship.

"I'm ready to share. I was never ready to share before—too selfish. Wanted to keep all my time and my toys to myself. But now I'd rather have someone to come home to than a bunch of electronics, only I can't seem to put my finger on who the right woman is. I figure one day soon, a woman is going to just slap me upside the head and announce that we're getting married, because that's probably what it's going to take for me to recognize it."

Claire shivered in Justin's arms, a weird sort of tremor that rippled through her at his words. She wanted to be that woman Justin shared his life with. It felt like until that moment, all her relationships had been practice, a training ground for the one that mattered. The man who had always been in the back of her mind.

Justin should just consider himself slapped.

She was going to be that woman he married.

Justin was feeling slapped. Stunned. Strange.

Claire had managed to produce a decent dinner, and they'd eaten and talked. Then they'd gone into the living room and talked.

Watched two movies back-to-back and talked.

It was three in the morning and they were still snuggled up on the couch, the lights on the Christmas tree blinking in the dark room.

"That's the tackiest tree," Claire said, leaning against his chest, feet tucked under her legs. "It looks like Derek and Reese bought everything from an entire aisle at WalMart and put it on there."

It was a little over the top, but Justin thought it suited Derek better than his first wife's sense of style. Dawn had done some kind of Victorian theme with songbirds and candles on the tree. Justin had been kind of appalled by it. Reese's slap-dash style was more in tune with Derek.

"I like the way the star has chaser lights." He tilted his head. "Maybe they were going for a garland record. There is no green left visible at all."

"What does your tree look like?"

"I have a live tree, probably dropping needles on my floor as we speak. It's got mostly red and gold balls on it, with white lights. Plain."

"I have a live tree, too, with mostly blue and silver balls on it. Plain."

Justin wondered if taste in Christmas decorating could indicate compatibility. He was feeling pretty compatible with Claire at the moment. He'd had the most relaxing, fun night with her, and he should be tired but he didn't want the tranquility in the apartment to end. The peaceful, yet somehow edgy feeling he had. Like everything was good and could stay that way if he just did the right thing.

Of course, he didn't know what that was. He never did.

Give him insurance fraud to investigate and he was on it.

A woman and he was clueless.

"Do you like Christmas movies? You know, like the sentimental classics they show every year?"

"No," Claire said. "It's like visually consuming sugar. Too sweet for me."

Amen to that. "I'm with you. I always feel pummeled by moral lessons. I like cartoons better for moral lessons. Got to love Frosty and Rudolph."

"Oh, my God, I love those shows. And when Frosty gets locked in and melts in the greenhouse, it's just like the most horrible thing ever. I used to cry every time."

"I used to wonder why Frosty didn't just throw a chair at the door and bust himself out. I mean, the whole building was *glass*."

She laughed. "That was the future federal agent in you."

Claire used the remote to turn the stereo on. She surfed until she found Christmas music. Bing Crosby. "I was feeling like Rudolph earlier, with my bright red nose. I probably scared the crap out of you."

"Not what I was expecting tonight, that's for sure." Justin slipped a hand under her shirt and rested it on the warm skin of her stomach. "But I'm really glad you got nailed by the snowplow, because I'm having a great time."

"Me, too," she said.

But Justin wanted her to say more. He suddenly realized he wanted her to suggest they see each other again.

Which meant he was an ass. He couldn't expect Claire to say anything of the kind after he had delivered his Wife Wanted speech.

It was up to him to take that next step if he wanted to see her again. Which he did. "So, it's Christmas Eve already. How are you spending your day? I've got family to see. Babies to kiss. You know, the usual."

"You kiss babies?" Claire shifted to look up at him.

"Doesn't everyone?" You saw a big fat baby cheek, you blew on it. It was human nature.

"No." She shook her head slowly. "No, they don't."

Claire looked so pretty, so solemn, so sweet, that Justin leaned down and kissed her. A soft, worshipful kiss that explained his feelings better than words could, because he was likely to screw the words up. He had a handle on the kiss thing.

She responded with a sigh, before pulling back and looking up at him, searching. "Justin?"

He knew the question she was asking in that one word. Was there any sort of future for them?

Claire was ten years younger than him, at the beginning of her career, while he was settled into a routine at the FBI, living two thousand miles away in Texas. But in all his thirty-five years, he'd never felt this attraction to a woman, and he had to find some way to explore it.

Starting with now, under Claire's sweatshirt.

"I don't leave until two days after Christmas. Think you can spare some time for me?" he asked, even as he worked her shirt up.

Claire sat up so she was next to him on the couch, facing his way. Her shirt fell back down much to his disappointment. "I told you what I want for Christmas is you, so I think I can squeeze you into my schedule."

The sassy little thing reached out and stroked the front of his jeans. "You're a great present—much better than an iPod."

Predictably, Justin swelled beneath her touch. "I'm the gift that keeps on giving."

She gave a sexy, husky laugh. "Oh, I like the sound of that. We should tie a ribbon on you. Right here." She squeezed him.

Justin clenched his teeth. "That's not going to happen."

"You're no fun."

"That's completely untrue. I can be a riot." Justin flipped Claire onto her back and had her pants down in about three seconds.

She blinked up at him.

"See? Isn't this fun?"

And he kissed her right on her clitoris, flicking over her with his tongue.

Chapter Six

Claire had cussed in at least six languages by the time Justin lifted his mouth from her, his lips shining.

She was half sitting up, every muscle in her body tense, every nerve firing. Her breath came out like a buffalo snorting when he left her teetering on the edge yet again, for the third time in as many minutes.

"Having fun yet?"

"I'm going to kill you if you don't finish what you started."

He took a long leisurely lick up one side, down the other, while she shuddered. "They'll throw you in jail for that, you know."

Arching her hips up to press her point home, Claire knew she'd never doubt his tongue talents again. Holy cow, happy crap, mucho delicious, he had her boneless, brainless.

"You know, if you don't want to put your tongue back— you know, like if maybe you're tired—you could always put something else there."

"Like what?" He was licking a path up past her navel, a tickling wet trail that had her squirming, her inner thighs feeling betrayed even further. "What could you possibly be talking about?"

He didn't think she'd say it. He was wrong. She had no

qualms about calling a spade a spade. Especially when she wanted it. "You know. Your big, hot cock."

Justin's eyes went wide with shock. Then he made a sort of growling sound down in his throat. "Damn, Claire, you weren't kidding when you said you're not shy. I'll never make that mistake again."

"Am I woman enough for you?" She was teasing, but at the same time, she wanted to know that he could see her as an equal, not Derek's kid sister. Reaching down, she felt his thickness with her hand, stroked up and down.

"Oh, yeah." Justin kissed her, his salty lips pressing hard on hers. "The only woman I want."

While she was swallowing the sudden grapefruit-size lump in her throat, he pushed into her with a smooth shift of his body over hers. Air rushed out of her lungs and her eyes pricked. She stared at him, shocked. It was love she was feeling, this strange hyperexcitement. This giddy sense of wonder.

How absolutely freaking ridiculous.

But Justin slowed his strokes down, locked eyes with her. "Claire . . ."

"Yes?" she whispered, suddenly afraid. Nothing had ever mattered to her quite as much as the words Justin was about to speak.

"I . . . I think . . ." He closed his eyes briefly. Then took a deep breath. "How crazy would it be to say that I care about you? That I want to . . . be with you."

"Not crazy at all." Claire grabbed his shoulders, hauled him down for a searing kiss. "I think maybe when you have a six-year crush on someone, it's really been more than a crush all along."

Then she clamped her legs around his thighs and shoved him, hoping to roll him on his back so she could really feel him deep inside her. Except in her haste, she'd miscalculated. That they were still on the couch.

For a brief precarious minute, they hovered, before crashing to the carpet in a heap of naked body parts. Justin's head cracked the floor because he reached out and held onto her, cushioning her fall. The little chivalrous cutie. Claire grinned in pure giddiness.

"Oops."

"Yeah, I'll oops you," he grumbled, adjusting his shoulder. "But somehow we managed to stay together. That's pretty damn impressive, don't you think?"

It felt pretty damn impressive. Claire wiggled a bit to gain her balance, than started slow up-and-down movements on him. "Mmm, yes, I do think it's very impressive."

"Do you think that means something? Could we qualify for an award or anything? *Guinness Book of Sexual Stunts?*" He assumed an announcer's voice. "Even wild tigers couldn't rip them apart."

Claire was laughing so hard she couldn't get her rhythm right. She felt like she was dancing off beat.

"What's the matter with you? Got an itch?" he said in mock bewilderment, eyebrows going up. "You'd better hurry up and get moving. I'm old. I can't keep it up forever."

That had her laughing even harder. "Stop that. I can't concentrate when you're making me laugh."

"Told you I was a riot." But before she could reply, he rolled her on her side and thrust hard up inside her. "You don't have to do all the work. Just meet me halfway, Claire."

His words were gruff, but she heard their meaning. She pushed her hips to meet his, a small groan leaving her lips. "I can do that. I can definitely do that."

They moved together, bodies joined tightly, legs intertwined, her heart racing and her head resting on the carpet. Justin's breath mingled with hers, and his eyes drove inside her, taking and claiming.

When he came, she let go and went with him, digging into his skin, slick with sweat. As she burst, she realized that she had never thought it could be like this, so elemental, so raw, so real. So right.

"You're beautiful," he said. "Just beautiful."

And she was suddenly the one who felt slapped. Slapped with pleasure, and an eager hope.

Chapter Seven

Claire didn't think about answering or not answering the phone when it rang. She just reached for it automatically. "Hello?"

"Who is this?" a suspicious woman's voice cut through the sex-and-sleep induced fog Claire was in.

"It's Claire, Derek's sister," she said, remembering that she was at her brother's house. In his bed. With Justin.

Taking a peek over her shoulder, she saw Justin was still sleeping, the sheet up to his waist.

"Claire? What are you doing at my apartment?"

It was Reese, her sister-in-law, and Claire couldn't help but blurt out in a whisper, "Reese! Oh, my God. I slept with Justin. And I am totally and completely in love."

"You and Justin? Hey, that's been a long time in coming, hasn't it? Cool. So did you just come over and jump him or what?"

She knew she could trust Reese to see her side of things. "I got iced by the snowplow, and I was right around the corner from your place. Justin being here was a happy surprise. *Then* I jumped him." Or coaxed him into doing the jumping.

"Hang on." There was a rustling on the other end as she covered the phone. "Justin," Reese said, her voice a little muffled. "So what? Calm down, Knight, she's a grown woman." Reese uncovered the phone. "Your brother's having a heart attack."

Reese didn't sound too worried about it.

"I owe you guys some condoms. And you have no food in this apartment. It was a struggle to pull together pasta."

"We're in New York, why does there need to be food in our apartment in Chicago? And don't worry about the condoms— we don't need them anymore. It turns out your brother has knocked me up. We're very happy, but Knight's a little nervous about the whole thing."

"Are you serious? A baby?" The thought made Claire feel all warm and fuzzy. "That's so awesome! I'm going to be Auntie Claire."

"Yeah, well, the poor kid isn't exactly getting a domestic goddess for a mother . . . hey!"

There was a scuffle on the other end before Derek's voice came over loud and clear. "What the *hell* do you think you're doing, Claire?"

Curbing the urge to stick her tongue out at the phone, she said, "I'm having sex with Justin. Now let's talk about you. Congratulations! Reese says you're going to be a daddy. Is she okay? She sounds kind of tense."

"She's just a little nervous. She grew up without a maternal influence, you know. But I know she's going to be an incredible mother. I'm not the least bit worried. I'm ecstatic." His voice softened, and Claire felt tears pricking her eyes.

"I'm thrilled for you, Derek."

There was a pause during which he cleared his throat, then said, "Thank you. Now don't change the subject. Put Justin on the phone."

Claire rolled her eyes. "That's not going to be helpful."

"Put him on the phone. Now."

This could go on for hours, so Claire decided to just get it over with. "Fine. Chill."

She turned and found Justin staring at her, still on his back, but very much awake. Wild-eyed, in fact. Intense.

"Totally and completely in love?" he asked.

Oops. She'd never been all that good at whispering. Tucking

the phone into sheets, she raised her chin. "Yes. I am in love with you." No point in lying about it after the fact.

Justin had experienced a woman telling him she loved him before. He'd even thought once or twice that he returned those feelings.

But nothing, nothing, had prepared him for the intensity of having Claire speak those words. She was rumpled from sleep, wearing one of her brother's oversized T-shirts, her expression defiant, like she expected him to balk.

That wasn't what he wanted to do. What he wanted to do was take her in his arms and make love to her, slowly and sweetly. Show her how much it meant to him that she felt love for him. That quite possibly he felt the same.

But first he had to talk to her brother.

His mouth was gritty, chin stubbly, muscles stiff, head itchy. He hadn't had enough sleep, and he was about to get bitched out by Derek. Yet he felt fantastic. Like he could run a 20K without breaking a sweat.

Like he was in love.

"I'm in love with you, too. Now give me the phone."

Her mouth dropped open, a little "uhh" coming out. Then she handed him the phone without a word.

He sat up and put the phone to his ear. "Hey, Derek, congrats on the baby." Justin took the aggressive tack.

"Don't give me that, Fairbanks. I give you a place to stay and you . . . take advantage of my sister."

Justin pictured Claire naked in the bathroom, casually holding her hand out for a towel. Yeah, he'd worked real hard to get her out of her clothes. Please. "Your sister is an adult, and anything between us is mutual."

"She's young, and you're too damn old for her."

That had been his very own argument, but it seemed so irrelevant now. "You know, Claire is the same age Reese was when you met her. And yet I'm a year younger than you were at the time."

"You're scum, Fairbanks."

But there was no heat in the insult. Justin knew Derek was a reasonable guy. He'd come around. He was just trying to protect his sister.

"If you hurt her, I'll kill you. I mean it."

Justin glanced over at Claire, whose cheeks were flushed pink, her blonde hair tumbling over her shoulders. "Got no plans to do that, Knight. Now how about you worry about your wife and baby, and I'll worry about your sister from here on out."

"You're serious about her?"

"Very serious."

"God, where are my antacids?" Derek sighed. "Alright, I guess I can think of worse guys than you to have around all the time. Now Reese called because she wanted to know if we got a fax. She's expecting something for work."

"No fax."

"Okay, I'll talk to you later. Tell Claire I expect to see her when we get home the day after Christmas."

"I'll let her know."

After he hung up, he told Claire, "Your brother expects to see you when he gets home."

She rolled her eyes. "It's because he's so much older than me, you know. And before our mom married my dad, after her divorce from Derek's dad, he had to be the man around the house, you know? It makes him overprotective."

"He says he'll kill me if I hurt you."

"He probably means it. But you don't plan on hurting me, do you?" She leaned closer to him, let her eyes drop to his lips.

"Not if you love me."

"No, I don't plan on hurting you. And about that. Loving you." Justin snaked his arm around her waist. She was warm, and smelled good, like vanilla. "What do we do now? Freak out? Have a cow? Call the media and announce it?"

"We'll do what all people in love do. I'm going to move to Dallas or you're going to move back to Chicago." She snuggled up against him and squeezed his biceps. "We're going to spend lots of time together. Then in a year or two we're going to married."

"Oh." Justin leaned against the headboard, pulled her flush up against him. He stroked her back, feeling ridiculously happy. "Good thing I have you to explain these things to me."

Claire's fingers moved down, down, down, until they hit pay dirt. She loved Justin's body, all its hard planes and angles. "Some men need a firm hand guiding them."

He groaned. "I think I'm one of those."

She laughed and pulled back a little. "Thanks for waiting for me to grow up, Justin. It wasn't right when I was eighteen, but it is now."

Justin traced his finger over her lips. "You were meant for me, Claire. Here's to a Merry Christmas."

"And a Happy New Year, of course."

"You change your mind about buying a house?" His eyebrows went up and down. "Come here, let me show you my FOR SALE sign."

Claire kissed his finger and laughed. "I think I'm going to rent-to-own."

And she rolled onto him to prove it.

Ms. Humbug

Jill Shalvis

Chapter One

Three days before Christmas, City Planner Cami Bennett looked at her reflection in the Town Hall employee bathroom mirror and gave herself the silent pep talk. *You can do this. You can do something besides work your tail off. In fact, having fun is just like work, only . . . better.*

Probably.

Oh, who was she kidding? She liked the big O's—order and organization.

Orgasms would have been a nice addition to that list, but due to being a little uptight—and, okay, *a lot* anal—those kinds of O's were few and far between.

Now the big city hall annual Christmas party was later tonight, a masked ball where "fun would be had by all," and she was required to go.

Oh, goodie.

It wasn't that she was the female equivalent of Scrooge, but more that everyone at work always seemed to go on and on about the holiday ad nauseum—decorations, gifts, travel plans. Somehow, they'd all built themselves personal lives as well as careers, something Cami hadn't managed to do, and Christmastime just emphasized the failure on her part. She hated the pressure of the parties, the expense of buying her family gifts they didn't need or want, and, most especially, the loneliness.

Until now she hadn't had much time to think about it, not with the huge town shake-up that had involved the mayor and his very pretty boyfriend's private sex tapes being stolen and posted on the Internet for perusal by anyone with $29.95. It'd been the biggest scandal Blue Eagle had seen in decades, and no one yet knew how the rest of the town's staff was going to fare when all the cards finished falling.

Especially since the now-*ex*-mayor's boyfriend had turned out to be two weeks shy of legal age *and* the son of the D.A.

Ouch.

The front page of the *Sierra Daily* had showed a picture of Tom Roberts, stripped of his mayor's title, being led out of his office in handcuffs.

Talk about airing your dirty laundry in public.

A couple of councilmen had been dragged through the mud as well, one with a paternity scandal and the other with a bank scandal. Both accusations looked false, but were ugly nevertheless.

Morale had never been lower in Blue Eagle.

A soft sound came from one of the bathroom stalls, a sort of . . . mewl. "Excuse me," Cami said to the closed door. "Are you okay?"

The only answer was a whimper.

Concerned, Cami moved closer. "Do you need help?"

"Oh, God. *Yes!*"

Cami bent down and looked beneath the stall. She could see a pair of Jimmy Choo black toeless pumps, the ones Cami had drooled over in Nordstrom's but had not bought, choosing instead to pay her mortgage for the month.

Facing the opposite direction of the Choos was a pair of men's black leather dress shoes, equally expensive, and Cami went still. She knew a man who wore shoes like that. Ned Kitridge. He was a city councilman, and her casual date for the past two months.

Embarrassment warred with fury.

Fury won.

Before her eyes, the woman's pumps lifted off the ground and vanished. There was a thunk against the stall door, and a long female sigh of pleasure.

And then the sound of a zipper.

In shock, Cami watched as an empty condom packet hit the floor.

Steaming, horrified, she staggered back. Even the bathroom was seeing more action than she.

And with Ned, *Ned*, a man who hadn't made a move on her, not once in six dates!

As her ego hit the floor next to the condom wrapper, Cami grabbed her purse and exited the bathroom, nearly blinded by an unhealthy mix of anger and mortification. But could she just slam out of the building? *No.* She couldn't abandon her compulsive, organized, anal routine. Hating that she couldn't, she meticulously shut off her adding machine and the light over her drawing board, glancing at the new sticky note on her computer.

Cami,
    I need to talk to you before the ball. Meet me in the conference room at 7:45.

                                    Ned

Yeah, she just bet he needed to talk to her! Only a few moments ago, she had assumed—hoped—he'd actually pick her up at her place so they could go to the ball together. For eight weeks now, he'd driven her crazy with his need to take things slow. Slower than a-snail's-pace slow. Slower than icicles-melting slow. So-slow-she'd-been-losing-interest slow.

And yet in that bathroom, he hadn't seemed to be taking anything slow.

Don't think about it.

The others on her planning team—Adam, Ed, and Lucy,

usually all too happy when things were going bad for her—had told her to be patient with Ned because he was a great guy.

Well, Ms. Choos apparently thought so, too. Damn it, even more than tearing Ned apart, she wanted some sexual action.

She wanted the man-induced orgasm.

As she left the building, steam coming out of her ears, she didn't see another soul. This deep into the year, the nights fell early in the Sierras. In pitch blackness, she made her way through the parking lot, the icy air cooling her off. With a few hours before she had to be back for the dreaded Christmas ball, she should hit downtown and knock off the list of gifts she needed in order to make a showing at her parents' house for Christmas dinner.

After all, she hated an undone to-do list.

But she was too shaken from the Ned-screwing-in-the-bathroom scene to stop. Plus, it was snowing lightly, just enough to dust all the windows on her car, hampering her vision. She pulled out her ice scraper from beneath her driver's seat and attacked her windows, but the ice stuck stubbornly. Giving up, she got into her frozen car and cranked the heater, which fogged the windows, adding to the visibility challenge. Things kept getting better and better. Forced to roll down her window to see, she stuck out her head.

But the falling snow blocked her view. So did her own iced-over car. Damn it. She put the car into reverse and slowly eased off the brake—*wait.*

Had she seen movement back there?

Again she stuck her head out the window, but all she could see was snow flurries. Hell. Luckily, she knew she was the only one in the lot, so with another light touch on the gas, she crept out of the parking space and—

Crunch.

Oh, God! Oh, damn! Jerking her car into park, she leapt out of the car with her heart in her throat and came nose to nose with a man—scratch that. Nose to broad chest. "I'm *so* sorry!" she said, trying to blink the white flakes from her eyes to see past the man's long dark coat and hood. "I—"

"You weren't looking."

"I couldn't see—"

"I honked."

"I'm sorry—"

"Are you in *that* much of a hurry to get to the Christmas ball?" he asked.

It suddenly sank through her agitation that she knew that frustrated male voice. Craning her head back, she lifted her gaze past broad shoulders and stared up into a pair of slate-gray eyes filled with annoyance.

Oh, no. *No, no, no.*

Not him. Anyone else on the planet but *him.*

The *him* in question pushed back his hood, his dark hair glistening with snowflakes, making him seem even more fiercely intense and devastatingly handsome, if that were possible. Cami imagined even the most hardened of women would sigh over those chiseled features and that rock-hard body.

But not her. Nope, she was entirely unmoved.

Because in addition to the fact that he stood on her last nerve, he was the newly appointed mayor.

Her boss.

Her nemesis, Councilman Matt Tarino. They'd worked together in planning for two years before he'd moved on to councilman six months ago, and in their time together, they'd done nothing but gone head-to-head. He was the bane of her existence.

And now he was mayor. That he was tough as nails and cowed to no one when it came to getting fair share and equal housing for the lower-income population—her pet project—didn't matter. Nor did the fact that he'd been an excellent city planner, an advocate for all that she herself fought for.

Not when he was everything her orderly, organized, rule-loving brain couldn't fathom. He had no patience for precedence, rules, or expectations, and adding insult to injury, he seemed like sin personified, possessing a charismatic presence that conquered worlds, parted seas—and women's legs—with a simple smile.

It drove her crazy.

Logically she knew that these feelings were coming from the little fat kid inside of her, the one guys used to cruelly call Whale-Tail, but she didn't care. He was just far too perfect. Everything about him made her want to gnash her teeth into powder.

And now, Merry Christmas to her, because she'd crunched his front fender and taken out his right headlight, and quite possibly ruined her life and her career—which *was* her life. Closing her eyes briefly, she opened them again and looked anywhere but into Matt Tarino's frustrated face. That's when her gaze landed on his feet.

Specifically, his black leather dress shoes.

Not Ned in the bathroom with Ms. Fabulous Choos, but . . . *Matt?*

And just like that, her humiliation vanished, and so did the ball of nerves lodged in her throat. "It was *you*," she breathed. "You were the one in the women's bathroom!"

He blinked. Snowflakes fell from his long, dark lashes. "What?"

It made perfect sense. Women were always talking about him, sighing over him, drooling over him . . . "I heard you two in the stall," she said in disgust, crossing her arms. "Now, I'm sorry I ran into you, but truthfully, you'd distracted me. Get a room next time, sheesh!"

A slow shake of his head. "I can assure you, I don't frequent the women's bathroom."

She didn't believe him, of course, but his denial did mean that she had to take full responsibility for her own stupidity. Damn, she hated that. Sighing, she rubbed her temples. "Okay, fine. You're being discreet. I get it. I'm sorry about your headlight. I'll have it fixed. Just let me get my insurance information—" She turned toward her car, but he took her arm and pulled her back around.

He was always doing that—*that* being whatever he wanted. In fact, she figured if she looked up "alpha male" in the dictionary, she'd find his picture there.

"You're looking like a Popsicle," he said. "It can wait until tomorrow."

Unexpected decency. That, too, made her self-righteousness difficult to maintain. She wished he'd be an ass about this, but even she had to admit that while Matt defined stubbornness and mule-headedness, he also possessed integrity in spades. She'd seen it in action, when he ran town meetings, maintaining the voice of reason, even if it had a sarcastic edge.

She also knew him to be wild, daring, and a complete rebel at heart. So much so that no woman had ever tamed him.

Cami had never even considered trying, especially since she was too competitive to give him the upper hand, in or out of bed.

After all, he was unlike any man she'd ever been with, or wanted to be with—not that she had much to go on. He was just a little uncivilized, just a little politically incorrect. Not afraid of a battle.

And she so wanted to say *not* decent.

But he was still holding onto her arm, guiding her off the icy asphalt and into her car.

"Matt?" The female voice came from the pretty blonde sticking her head out of the passenger side of his car. "What's taking so long?"

Cami rolled her eyes and muttered beneath her breath to Matt. "Probably you should have stayed in the women's bathroom."

"Her car wouldn't start. I'm giving her a ride home."

"And don't forget the ride in the bathroom."

"I wasn't in the bath—"

"Whatever." She tried to pull her door shut, but his big body was in the way.

"Are you going to be careful?" he asked.

"Move, or lose a body part."

"Just don't hit reverse until I get out of your way, he said with a smirk, wisely stepping out of her way just as she slammed the door.

Chapter Two

Matt's evening could be going better. He could be at his brother's house nursing a beer and a pizza while watching the Lakers game.

Instead, he had to forgo his favorite evening wear—jeans—for a tux. In less than half an hour, he was going to be standing around, smiling at ridiculous small talk about the weather, eating tiny little hors d'oeuvres of questionable origin that never filled him up, all while being scrutinized by every single guest there, even by people who'd known him for years.

This was because he had a big old bull's-eye on his back, courtesy of getting the mayoral position unelected.

Never mind that there had been a city hall vote that he'd won by a vast majority. Never mind that he'd never done anything but great things for the town of Blue Eagle. Never mind that he was exactly where he wanted to be—for now—when it came to work.

Until he figured out who the hell was messing with the town's reputation, there would be rumors and doubts and questions. Frustrated over that, he left his house. Still snowing, which meant good skiing this weekend. The roads would be icy. Not so good. He got into his car and headed back to Town Hall for the ball. His starched shirt scratched him every time he so much as leaned forward to adjust the radio. His shoes were making his feet unhappy campers.

And a mile from his house, the rest of his headlight fell out. Nice, and yet the irritation faded as he remembered what Cami's face had looked like when she'd realized she'd hit *his* car.

Frazzled.

The thought made him grin because Cami frazzled was an amusing sight. A sexy one, too. It was her eyes, so brave, so huge and expressive, that made him inexplicably hungry, and not just for melting chocolate.

But more than just her eyes got to him. She had one of those bodies that women complained about and men loved, curvy and lush despite the yoga she did with her team for relaxation— useless in her case because she was incapable of relaxing, he'd discovered.

In fact, it was the office joke—she was so tightly wound, she squeaked when she walked.

Most men would be put off by that, and given her dating record, they had been put off but good. But he had a feeling that beneath all the organization and planning and general analness beat a wildly passionate heart. He saw it when she was lost in a project at work, when she stood in front of the council and argued for that project with all her might. How many times had she made it her personal goal to pit herself against him for any of a million reasons?

And each and every time, the air between them had crackled like lightning.

The truth was, whether she admitted it out loud or not, they'd been dancing around the sexual issue for two years. She was an amazing opponent, sharp and intelligent, ruthless, with a single line of focus that he'd seen in only one other person.

Himself.

Beyond that, they were polar opposites, she with her love of order and rules, he with his utter disdain of both. And yet somehow they'd made an incredible pair, and during their two years of mutual city planning, they'd improved the quality of life in Blue Eagle and its growth rate more than any other team in the city's history. It was something to be proud of, and he was.

But he'd moved into the council now, and they no longer worked side by side. In fact, she worked for him, a phenomenon he was quite certain drove her crazy.

And made him grin some more.

He pulled back into the parking lot and looked at Town Hall. The building had been built in 1890 and was, in fact, a historical monument. It had once been an icehouse, a storage unit in the days before refrigeration. Truckloads of ice had been shipped from here to San Francisco on demand. It'd been renovated three times since, and now white lights were strung across the front, anchored by groups of holly and pine branches, backlit by the bulbs. In front, on either side of the walkway, were small Christmas trees, decorated earlier in the week by the local elementary school children.

At the sight, some of Matt's spirit picked back up. So he was in a tux. So he'd have to drink champagne instead of beer. So he was going to miss time with his brother watching the game. Things were pretty darn good for him, and he was thankful. He'd go inside, smile and make merry, and maybe even figure out who was wreaking all the havoc for the town staff members. Not that Matt condoned the ex-mayor's crime of seducing minors, but whoever had exposed Tom, as well as lodged the accusations against the two councilmen, had done so publicly for a reason.

Someone was having a grand old time screwing with the town council.

Turning off his engine, he reached for the required mask. It was black, with an elastic string to go around the back of his head so he wouldn't have to hold it up to his face all night. Putting it on, he stepped out of the car and into the falling snow. Inside, the decorations were overly festive, bordering on gaudy, but that might have been due more to the badly played rendition of "Jingle Bells" coming from the high school band.

The room was already filled with staffers dressed to the hilt in their Christmas finery, all wearing masks, some elaborate, some looking like Tonto.

Mostly guys looking like Tonto.

Matt thought he saw Ed and Adam from his old team in planning. Couldn't miss Ed's carrottop or Adam's double-fisted drink habit. Plus they both waved, so he waved back, and grabbed a flute of champagne from a passing waiter.

"Matty," murmured a soft feminine voice from behind him. Turning, he came face-to-face with a woman in a tiny, sparkly silver dress and mask. Hannah Pelinski. He'd dated her once and had been put off by her relentless pursuit of a diamond ring. He smiled at her but tried to keep moving, only she started dancing right in front of him, blocking his way.

"Join me," she coaxed, making sure her breast brushed his chest.

"I'm sorry, Hannah. I have to . . ." Do anything rather than see the desperation in your eyes. "Go upstairs for a sec."

"Well, find me when you come back down."

He smiled rather than lie, and as quickly as he could, moved across the large room, past the elevators, to the stairwell, which was dark. Having worked in this building for so long, he could find his office blindfolded, so he didn't flip on any lights as he made his escape. On the second-floor landing, he turned left.

Halfway down the hall, he heard a soft thud. So he wasn't the only lurker tonight. He caught a flash up ahead, coming from the conference room, where there was a long wall of file cabinets, filled with years and years of information on everything from town council meetings to amendments to the city plan. Matt had no idea what, or if anything, someone would want from those files after hours, but as things had gotten crazy lately, he intended to find out.

He peeked into the dark room, smelling the pine of the small Christmas tree in the corner. The windows let in a glow from the string of lights on the outside eaves. He could make out the outline of a woman, sitting in the window well on the far side of the room. Knees up, her arms around them, she stared out into the night. Her dark hair was piled on top of her head, tendrils escaping along her neck. Her shoulders and arms were bared by her dress.

She didn't have on a mask, but even if she had, he'd have known it was Cami by the set of her narrow shoulders, as if they carried the weight of the world on them.

His little snooper had left a few file drawers open, some files sticking up. He was dying to know what had drawn her, what she was looking for, but felt even more curious about what was making her look so . . . sad.

She didn't look at him as he stepped into the room. "You're late," she said softly.

Was he? He glanced down at his watch. A quarter to eight. No, he wasn't late at all.

Which meant she was talking to someone else.

"Oh, Ned," she whispered, and hugged her knees tighter. "I need to talk to you, too."

Ned. *Ned?*

Still looking out the window, Cami stood. "I want to understand something."

Her profile was tight, grim. Unhappy. And suddenly he wanted to see her happy, even lost in laughter. Better yet, lost in passion, with him. He wanted her in his arms, his name on her lips.

"You like me, right?" she whispered.

Apparently more than he'd thought. "Yes."

"Then why don't you ever kiss me?"

Matt blinked. That hadn't been what he'd expected, though, in truth, he didn't know what he *had* expected. He knew she was talking to Ned, not to him, but he still stepped closer, so close that he could have bent his head and put his mouth to the nape of her neck. Her scent came to him, soft and lovely and incredibly sexy.

So sexy.

Her skin seemed to glow in the pale light. She tended to dress conservatively, and he supposed the cut of her black velvet dress was modest enough, but it molded and hugged her body, dipping both in the front and the back in a clean, sensual line.

"Ned?"

Christ, he wanted her to stop saying some other man's name. He wanted to hear *his* name.

She sighed then, a lost sound, a sorrowful sound, and unable to take it, he wrapped his fingers around her arm and turned her to face him. Before she could decipher the fact that he had a good four inches on Ned, he hauled her up against him and did as she'd asked. He kissed her.

Chapter Three

Cami sank immediately into the kiss. She couldn't see a thing in the dark room, but she didn't need to. Ned's mouth was firm yet warm, and tasted yummy. Then his tongue touched hers, and a bolt of desire zinged her from her roots to her toes, hitting all the good spots in the middle.

Oh, did he know how to kiss. Thankfully. She'd been worried because not once had he swept her up in his arms like this, against his body, inhaling her as if she was the greatest thing since sliced bread, and she loved it. Loved also the obvious hunger and passion he had bottled up.

For her.

Not to mention the delicious hardness of his chest, his belly, his thighs . . . in between. *God.* She hadn't been kissed like this since . . . she couldn't remember.

It didn't matter, she was being kissed now, and she couldn't believe how amazing it felt. Her bones melted, along with her reservations about Ned being the right one for her, and she ran her hands up his chest, winding her arms around his neck to pull his head even closer to hers.

His hands moved, too, at first grazing up and down her back in a seductive motion that drew her in even closer, molding her body to his. Up and down, further each time, over the skin bared by her dress, until he cupped her bottom. The intimate touch shocked her, and aroused her beyond belief. He squeezed, the thin material of her dress and her new thong the only things separating his hand from her flesh. A brave departure for her, but she'd needed something drastic tonight, had needed to try something different. She'd loved the way she looked when she'd caught her reflection in the mirror. Sophisticated and glamorous—so unlike her usual self.

Now she was glad she'd dared, though his fingers on her, with so little barrier, felt shocking. One hand left her bottom, gliding back up her body to sink into her hair, dislodging a few carefully placed pins as he palmed her head, holding her in place while he decimated her with a kiss so deep and sensually charged, she could only whimper and let him take her where he would.

"Mmm," rumbled from deep in his throat, the hand still on her bottom urging her closer, rocking the softest part of her to the hardest part of him. Oh, God, this felt good, so good. If she let herself think, she might have admitted it was difficult to reconcile this deep, wet, hot, shocking erotic connection with the mild-mannered Ned, the one who was so nice and kind he often let people walk all over him rather than face a disagreement or handle a contradiction.

But she didn't think, because the rough growl that reverberated from deep in his throat made her weak. So did his sure and talented mouth, his steady and knowledgeable hands, both of which were driving her crazy. So did his mouth as it made its way to her jaw to nibble her throat. In fact, she had to clutch at him to remain standing. "You feel good."

In an odd reaction, he went completely still for a beat, then pulled back and stared down at her, the mask covering the upper part of his face but not the heavy rise and fall of his chest as he breathed erratically.

That's when it hit her. Ned wasn't this tall. Or broad. Or built.

Then she caught the glittering of his eyes.

Not dark brown, but . . . steely, stormy gray.

Oh, my God.

Not Ned. Not Ned, but— Reaching up, way up, she grabbed his mask. She wasn't tall enough to yank it off over his head, so she pulled it down and stared into those glittering eyes. *"You."*

"Me," Matt agreed utterly without repentance or apology.

Stepping back in horrified, humiliated shock, she came up against the window just as his mask, caught by its elastic string, slapped him in the chin.

Without a word, he ripped the thing off and stepped toward her.

"Don't," she choked out, her every nerve ending still pulsing with hopeful pleasure. She lifted a hand to hold him off, but he just took her fingers in his and came up against her, trapping her between the window and his body.

The window was icy cold. But not Matt. Nope, his hard body radiated heat and strength as he cupped her jaw until she was looking him right in the eyes. "Well, *that* took me by surprise," he murmured.

"What are you talking about? You knew exactly who you were kissing!"

"Yeah, but I didn't expect to be leveled flat by it."

"You expect me to believe that *you* were laid flat? *You,* the man who's kissed every single woman in a hundred-mile radius?" God, she was a fool. She'd known better, a small part of her had known from the moment he'd touched his mouth to hers—Ned would never have taken her like that, kissing hard and deep and unapologetically fierce—but her body had surged with such heat and need, and a desire so strong, she was still shaking from it.

And yet, the pathetic truth was, Matt had just been playing with her. It burned, she could admit, and burned deeply. All her life, she'd been the outcast. She'd been a chunky, nonathletic, clumsy kid in a house full of lean, coordinated, beautiful people. She hadn't improved much as a teenager, and though her frenetic exercise and dieting had finally worked, leaving her much fitter now, the stigma had never left her. Inside, she was still the left-out, laughed-at, fat kid, the girl who was the object of a wager among the boys of the varsity basketball team—the winner was to be the first boy who could get a pair of her "granny panties" to hang as a prize in their locker room—the woman who even now men tended to keep their distance from.

The remembered humiliation still burned.

She heard the footsteps coming and turned toward the doorway just as another man appeared, also in a tux. Mask in hand.

Ned.

And in that flash, from a distance of twenty-five feet or more, Cami wondered how she could have ever mistaken the two men. Ned wasn't as tall or built as Matt, instead a comfortable height for looking straight into his eyes, a nonthreatening bulk that brought to mind a scholar rather than a tough boxer or basketball player, as Matt's physique did.

And that wasn't the only difference between them.

There was the fact that the nice, kind, sweet Ned would never have taken advantage of a dark night and a mask, kissing a woman simply because the opportunity presented itself.

"Sorry I'm late," he said, and moved into the room, eyeing Matt inquisitively. "Tarino."

"Kitridge." Matt turned back to Cami. "Enjoy the ball."

Enjoy the ball? She'd enjoy kicking his butt, that's what she'd enjoy, but before she could tell him, he was gone.

When they were alone, Ned smiled curiously at her but, true to form, didn't ask. There was no reason why that should annoy the hell out of her, but it did. Her dress was wrinkled across the front where she'd been mashed against Matt, her hair was half up and half down thanks to his busy fingers, her mouth was still wet from his.

And Ned didn't appear to think anything of it. Frustrated, she grabbed her mask from the window seat and went to move past him, noticing that his tux was wrinkled, too—sort of en- dearing, really—and that his shoes—

Oh, my God.

His shoes were still black leather, identical to the ones Matt had worn, and still identical to the ones in the bathroom stall from earlier. Lifting her gaze to Ned's face, she was further disconcerted to find him blushing slightly. His usually perfectly groomed hair was standing up on end, and he still wasn't meeting her eyes. "You're late," she said slowly. "But you're never late. You're wrinkled, but you're never wrinkled. You're blushing, your hair is a mess . . ." She stared into his guilty eyes. "It *was* you in the bathroom. You've been making out with someone else."

Ned shifted from one foot to the other, jamming his hands into his pockets. "Technically, it's not someone *else*, if you and I have never made out."

"But . . ." No, she refused to ask why not her, why it was never her.

"I'm so sorry." His voice was rough with the apology she hadn't gotten from Matt. "I didn't want to hurt you."

"Wait." She couldn't think. Funny how her brain could work on an entire city plan, formulating for population and roads and more, and yet now, here, she couldn't process a thought. This wasn't supposed to happen this way. *He* was the office geek. *She* was the prize here!

"Cami, *Jesus.*" He squirmed. "I don't know what to say. It's just that you . . ." He lifted a shoulder. "You scare me."

"*What?*"

"And Belinda—"

"Belinda. Belinda Roberts?" The daughter of the ex-mayor and a city mail clerk? Who was still in college and giggled when a guy so much as looked at her?

"She's sweet and caring," Ned said defensively.

Which, apparently, Cami was not.

"She makes me cookies," he said. "Oatmeal raisin, because of my cholesterol."

Cami could have done that. Probably. If she'd even known he had cholesterol issues.

And if she'd known how to work her oven.

"She doesn't argue or disagree with me at work," Ned said. "Or make me feel as if my ideas are stupid."

"I don't—" But she did. She couldn't help it. Many of his ideas *were* stupid. And she had little to no tolerance for stupidity.

"I'm really sorry," he said again, softly, with surprising thoughtfulness. "I really didn't intend for you to find out like this. I wanted to come here and talk to you like adults."

"Right," she said. "Because *adult* is screwing the file clerk in the women's bathroom."

"Again, very sorry." He looked desperate for a change of subject. "I intended to tell you tonight, but then I found you in here with Matt. What did he want anyway?"

"Uh . . ." *Ms. Pot, meet Mr. Kettle.* "Nothing." If *nothing* meant the hottest, wildest kiss she'd ever experienced.

"Okay, then. Well . . ." More shuffling, this time accompanied by a longing look at the door. "I hope this isn't going to be awkward."

She just laughed.

Ned's flush lit up the dark. "You look really great tonight. Your dress—"

"You can go now, Ned."

"Thank you." In a cowardly blink he was gone.

Men. Cami kicked a file cabinet closed as she left.

It turned out Cami was grateful for the masked part of the ball after all—who'd have thought—because it allowed her to stay virtually "hidden" for the hour she forced herself to stay and smile and make nice. Trying to forget the kiss, she danced with Adam and Ed from her department, and she danced with eager-beaver Russ from the Permit Department, though surely her feet would never recover. She danced with a few others as well, mostly because it meant less talking.

And then she made her escape, leaving the festivities that had been meant to boost everyone's low morale. She drove home reliving the mortifying portion of the evening. In her quiet condo, she decided to grow from the experience. And then she buried herself in the work she'd brought home because, as it turned out, work was all she had.

The next morning, she went into her office early, and to protect herself, she put a sign on her door that said STAY OUT OR DIE.

But apparently the new mayor couldn't read because half an hour later, Matt stuck his head in, wearing one of those wicked smiles that had always annoyed her in the past but that now inexplicably scraped at a spot low in her belly.

"Hey," he said. "Busy?"

Just looking at him reminded her of last night. Of his bone-melting, heart-stopping kiss. Of how he'd held her as if he could do nothing else. How he'd gotten hard and rocked her hips to his. She'd dreamed about that part in particular, damn it, and remembering brought the heat to her face. She shouldn't be picturing the mayor with a hard-on. She especially shouldn't get hard nipples at picturing the mayor with a hard-on. "If I say yes, I'm busy, will you go far, far away?"

His grin spread.

Good God, could the guy be any more gorgeous? Or annoying? Or sexier? Now it wasn't just her nipples going happy, but things were happening between her thighs, too. "Didn't you read the sign?"

"Yes." He pulled a pen out of his pocket. Clicked it on. Eyed her with a mischievous lecherousness.

"Don't even think about it," she warned, gritting her teeth when he underlined the STAY OUT part. Then shut the door—with him on the wrong side.

He smiled.

She did not. But she wanted to, damn him, so she got up, walked around her desk, and reopened the door, silently inviting him to leave.

"Ah," he said. "Someone forgot to eat her Wheaties this morning."

"And someone forgot he was an ass—"

"Still mad, I see." He nodded as if this was perfectly acceptable to him. "How long do you plan on pouting?"

She gaped. "I am not pouting. I never pout."

"Then what's this?" He rubbed his thumb over her lower lip, which was indeed thrust out petulantly.

The touch electrified her, and she struggled with her reaction. If his expression went smug, she was going to have to kill him.

But he didn't look smug at all. He looked as shocked as she felt.

In the startled silence, a woman walked by her office. Danielle was a city clerk but looked like a stripper, and when she saw Matt, she stopped and smiled. "Hey there, big guy. Nice dancing with you last night." She made some promises with her bedroom eyes and body language before moving on.

"*Big guy?*" Cami shook her head. "Never mind, I don't want to know. Please just go away."

"Yeah." He looked at her for a long moment. "But only because I have three meetings, all scheduled at the same time."

"I'm in two of them with you. Oh, and I hope *you* ate *your* Wheaties because at the first one, for the proposed amendments to the town plan? I'm planning on nailing you."

His eyes heated. "Promise?"

She felt her insides quiver at his expression. "Get out."

"Okay, but first I wanted to talk to you about last night."

"No. No way."

"I had some trouble sleeping," he said, all kidding aside. "I was thinking maybe you did, too."

"Slept like a baby." Yeah, if babies had wet dreams.

"You slept like a baby," he repeated.

"You betcha."

He didn't believe her. "Then why are you in such a big hurry to get rid of me?"

"Because I don't like you."

He grinned. "Liar."

"Oh, just get out!" To make sure that he did, she shoved him, then closed the door firmly on his grinning face.

She felt her own reluctant smile and was just glad she'd shut the door before he could see it. The last thing she needed to do was egg him on.

"You still there?" he asked through the door.

"Where else would I be?"

"Just wondering if you've managed to bite back your smile yet."

She threw her pen at the door, then rolled her eyes at his soft laugh.

The next day, the local newspaper broke a story on one of the public officials in the Public Works Department. It turned out the official had once been charged with extortion in Florida, a charge no one here had known about.

The article went on to raise the question of whether such a thing could happen right here in Blue Eagle.

The official resigned, leaving everyone in every department unsettled and nervous. Cami's haven—work—had become a nightmare.

In a hastily called meeting, Matt stood before all of them, cool and calm, effectively outlining a plan of attack to face the public and an inner plan of attack to find out what the hell was going on. Afterward, he stayed around talking in his easy way, making everything seem okay, when Cami knew it wasn't.

She had to admire how he handled himself, how he eased everyone's mind with just a few words. Which didn't explain why she didn't feel eased, but . . . revved. Every time she inadvertently caught his eyes, her body hummed and zipped, like it had when he'd touched her. She was a walking-talking live wire, and any minute now she was going to snap. It was hard to maintain her composure like that, but she was the master of control, so she managed to fake it.

After the meeting, she stood in the break room, waiting for

the coffee to brew, ignoring the mistletoe some poor sap had hung over the doorway in hopes of getting lucky. To keep her hands busy, she was compulsively straightening up, putting the filters and mugs in their places, refilling the pitcher of drinking water on the counter. Not that it would all stay that way, but the motions calmed her. Organizing always did.

It was the kiss that was unnerving her, she knew that. Just thinking about it infuriated her because there were so many other things to be obsessing over—the newest scandal, the fact that there were only two shopping days left until Christmas, that she didn't have a boyfriend to shop for . . .

She poured herself coffee and stood there stirring it, wishing things could be different. But Matt had only been playing with her, she *knew* that. She must have just imagined how good it'd been, how hot—

"I could show you again."

With a gasp, she lifted her head and looked into Matt's amused, aroused eyes.

"Yeah," he told her. "You said it out loud."

Groaning in embarrassment, she brought her hands up to her hot cheeks, but he pulled them away. "Don't," he said in that voice that Cami was certain could coax a nun out of her virginity. "Let me show you that you didn't imagine a thing."

"No. No way."

"Okay, then." His hands slid to her hips, and her body quivered hopefully. "Then how about *you* prove *me* wrong?" he murmured, and pulled her close.

Chapter Four

It was sick of him, he knew, but Matt loved the way he could shake Cami's composure. Loved even more the way she shoved her nose so high in the air she became in danger of getting a nosebleed.

"Don't be ridiculous," she said in a frosty voice he was coming to realize meant her control was slipping as well. The interesting thing was she didn't push him away. "I'm not going to kiss you again just to prove there's nothing between us." She added a laugh that didn't fool him any more than her voice had. "We're grown-ups. We're professionals. We're—"

"Hot for each other," he said.

When she only glared at him, he laughed. "You know I'm right. Come on, admit it. You're dying to kiss me again. You're thinking about it. Hell, you're talking to yourself about it—"

"I am not going to dignify that with a response."

Leaning in until their noses nearly touched, he grinned right into her eyes. "I double-dog dare you."

"Please," she said with a sniff. "I don't feel the need to take every single dare that comes my way."

"Then I win by default."

Steam nearly came out of her ears at that, which was fun,

too. So was the sparkle of life in her eyes. Never mind that it
was an angry sparkle—he liked it. He liked her.

A lot, as he was discovering.

Then, the break room door opened. Adam walked in, took
one look at the two of them in such close proximity, and raised
a brow as he reached for a mug. "I didn't realize you two guys
were knocking it out."

Matt went from amused to pissed, and so did Cami by the
looks of her.

"Probably it's why you approved Cami's open-space amend-
ment for North's Landing," Adam said, oblivious. "Too bad I
don't have a vagina, or I could get my own agenda passed, too."

Before Matt could say a word past the red haze now blocking his vision, Cami stepped toe-to-toe with Adam, tipping her
head back to glare into his eyes. "Watch out," she said very
quietly. "Your knuckles are dragging."

Adam snorted as he walked past her and sat at the employee lunch table. "All I'm doing is calling it like it is. Now I
know all I have to do is sleep with Matt."

Matt took a step toward him, not exactly sure what he was
planning on doing, but his fingers itched to encircle Adam's
neck. Cami beat him to it, picking up the pitcher of water on
the counter and emptying it into Adam's lap.

Adam yelped and surged to his feet, doing the cold-water-
in-the-crotch dance.

Cami shot a glare toward Matt, making him very grateful
he hadn't been the one to place the last straw on her back.
Then she swept from the room.

Matt leaned back against the counter, arms crossed, watching Adam yell and swear and hop around like an idiot.

"Uptight bitch," Adam griped, sagging back to the chair.
"My balls are wet."

"Adam?"

"Yeah?"

"If you ever pull anything like that again, insinuating that

Cami is anything less than a lady, or that I'd accept bribes, you won't have any balls to worry about."

Later, Matt worked his way through the stacks upon stacks of work on his desk, trying to prioritize the various fires. When he looked up again, he realized the hallway was dark, the place silent.

It was nearly eight o'clock.

So much for getting a couple of ski runs in before dark. The cons of his new job he knew. His time was not going to be his own for the remaining portion of his term. But after that, when he'd made his mark, when he'd done what he wanted to do for the town, he could happily walk away. Sure, he was only thirty-five, but that was the beauty of retiring young—he'd be able to enjoy it.

He and his brother had had it planned since their wild and crazy and completely uncontrolled childhood. There was much about that time that they didn't want to ever revisit, but one thing they agreed on—the freedom had been great. Eventually they would get back to that, using their winter days to ski themselves stupid and the summer days to travel, or whatever suited them, but Matt couldn't get there until he worked out the mess here—

In the utter silence of the building came an odd scraping.

Matt left his office and walked the dark hall, looking for the source of the sound. The receptionist's desk was shaped like a half circle, with a wall of filing cabinets behind it. The computer was dark, as was the little fake Christmas tree with more lights than faux branches that Alice had in the corner. Everything looked completely normal . . . except that the chair moved slightly, the wheels squeaking against the plastic runner.

Only no one was in the chair.

Matt came around the half circle of the desk and stopped short.

"There's a good explanation for this," Cami said from her perch on the floor beneath the desk.

Matt leaned a hip against the wood and casually crossed his arms. "Really."

"Yeah." Staring up at him, she bit her lower lip, her mind no doubt whirling.

She wore a black-and-white-checked wool skirt and white silk tank top. Earlier she'd had on the matching checked jacket, but it was gone now. Her skirt had risen high on a pale, smooth thigh, her tank snug to her most lovely curves. He'd noticed the outfit earlier in the day because her black heels had been so sexy he hadn't been able to take his eyes off them, or her legs. Or any part of her, for that matter. She was such a delicious contradiction, so tense and uptight about work, and yet there were these little hints of a wildly passionate side.

He wanted to see more of it.

"Would you believe I lost an earring?" she asked, coming up to her knees. She wasn't wearing those sexy heels at the moment.

Was it him, or had her nipples just gotten hard, pressing against the thin material of her tank? "You never lose anything."

"Well, then . . . I forgot to get my phone messages earlier."

"You *purposely* forgot to get your phone messages."

"Fine." She blew a strand of hair out of her face. "I came to leave a message for Alice."

"Let's try something new," he suggested, still leaning casually against the desk. "Like the truth."

A sigh fluttered out of her lips. "I'm snooping."

"For?"

"For the same thing you're interested in—finding out which one of us is trying to screw up Blue Eagle's reputation beyond repair, and why."

Pushing away from the desk, he crouched in front of her. On her knees, staring up at him, it struck him how unintentionally erotic her position seemed. "How do I know it's not you?" he asked.

Her eyes were clear and right on his. "The same way I know it's not you."

That surprised him. "I figured I was at the top of your list."

"I know you better than that," she said.

"Really? What do you know about me?"

"That you're incredibly cocky." She sighed. "But you're good at what you do, damn it, so you get away with it. And that's not a compliment," she said, pointing at him. She sighed again. "I suppose it can also be said that you have a code of honor. You don't cheat. It's why you never have just one woman in your life. If you did, you'd have to give up all the others." She lifted a shoulder. "You can be trusted."

"Thank you," he said wryly. "I think."

She lifted her shoulder again and then began to crawl past him.

He grabbed her ankle. "For the record," he said when she looked back at him. "It's not that I can't deal with only one woman at a time, but that the right woman hasn't come along."

She snorted and crawled free of the desk, then stood up and walked off.

Matt took the time to enjoy the sight of her nicely rounded ass before following her. He was struck by how petite she was without her shoes. She barely came to his shoulder.

She didn't appear to notice the discrepancy when she stopped, turned, and poked him in the chest. "Who are you looking at?"

"You."

Her eyes narrowed. "Why?"

"Ever look in the mirror? You're not so bad to look at."

She stared at him, then shook her head. "I don't have time for your lines. I want to be home before midnight." With that, she wheeled away, moving down the dark hall again, her bare feet silent, her hips swinging gently, mesmerizing him with her attitude and utterly accidental sexiness.

"Why do you have to be home before midnight?" he asked.

"I'll turn into a pumpkin. Here." She entered the mail

room. "I was thinking maybe someone is reading incoming mail."

"There's only one mail clerk."

"Belinda," she muttered.

"She's young, but awfully sweet. I don't think—"

"If she's so sweet, then why aren't *you* dating her? Why aren't *you* doing her inside a women's bathroom stall?"

He eyed her carefully. "You keep mentioning the women's bathroom."

She sighed, rubbing her temples. "You know what? Never mind."

"No, I think I want to hear this."

She strode over to the mail sorter's desk and the computer there. Someone had forgotten to turn off the radio, and "Santa Claus Is Coming to Town" strained lightly over the airwaves. Cami's hair was wild now, from her own fingers, and he loved the way she walked, full of authority and temper, her ass tight and tempting.

"I walked in on her having a fun time in the bathroom," she said, booting up Belinda's computer and chewing on a nail while she waited, silent and stewing.

He also loved watching her sizzle, but this was more, there was sadness, too, and he moved closer. "Fun. You mean sex?"

"I just never thought he had it in him—" Computer booted, she began clicking on the keys, but something in her tone had him taking her arm, pulling her up and around to face him.

"I don't want to talk about it," she said, looking at a spot somewhere over his shoulder.

Cupping her jaw, he waited until her eyes met his. And in them he found his answers. "*Ned*," he said softly. "That asshole."

"Yes, well, you're right about that," she said in a lofty tone that didn't fool him one bit. He remembered the night of the party. She'd thought he was Ned. She'd asked him why he never kissed her.

And now she was doubting herself. "You are far too good for him, Cami."

"Really? Then why does no one else want to date me either? Why do I have to beg men to kiss me? Oh, forget it— Oof—" she said when he tugged her back against his chest.

"I do not want a pity kiss," she choked out, hands flat on his pecs.

"That's good, because you're not getting one." With one hand anchored low on her spine, the other slid into her hair at her nape. Watching her, he lowered his head. "This is the real thing," he murmured.

"Matt . . ."

"Shh." When their mouths connected, he felt it reverberate through him. Like coming home, he thought.

With a surprised murmur, she pressed even closer, tentatively touching her tongue to his. He lost it. Growling low in his throat, he dug in, losing himself in the feel and taste of her, pulling back only when she put her hands against his chest and pushed.

He stared down at her, and she stared right back, not trying to break free, just breathing like a lunatic and blinking those huge, expressive eyes at him, as if coming awake from a long sleep. "I don't think—"

"Perfect. Don't think." And he took her mouth again, savoring her soft little whimper of pleasure and the way she fisted her hands on his shirt, anchoring him close. He had no idea how long they went at it this time before they had to stop again to breathe. He'd pressed her back against the desk, and had one hand on her sweet ass, the other toying with the strap of her tank top, a muscled thigh shoved between her softer, more giving ones. Her nipples were boring holes into his chest, and he was so hard he couldn't see straight. "God, you look good here."

"In the mail room?"

"In my arms."

"I don't need pretty words, Matt. I'm not the kind of woman a man fusses over."

"Then you've been with the wrong men."

"Agreed."

He looked down into her flushed face. Her lips were full, and still wet from his. Her eyes were luminous, and shining with so much emotion she took his breath. "I could be the right man," he said quietly.

She laughed, then her smile faded when he didn't laugh back. "You're . . . not kidding."

"No." This wasn't just play, or just a kiss. This wasn't just lust, although he felt plenty of that right this very minute.

It was the real thing.

But she shook her head. She didn't believe him. Hell, he couldn't blame her, given his life and the way he'd lived it— one day and one woman at a time. He wouldn't have believed him either. "I want to be with you," he said, and though it might have sounded rash, it wasn't. It'd been building for a long time. "Exclusively."

"What?" She shook her head, as if certain she'd heard him wrong. "What does that mean?"

"You might have heard of it. It's called dating."

She gave him a long look. "I wasn't under the impression that you understood the word *exclusive.*"

"I understand more than you think." He kissed her just beneath her ear, enjoying the way she clutched at him and shivered. "Watch out, I just might convince you to believe in this. In me."

"Don't hold your breath." Pushing away now, she turned to the computer. Then, after a moment, she glanced back at him, looking uncertain. "What I'm going to do here is a bit of an invasion of privacy. You might want to go home and pretend you never saw me here tonight."

"You're going to look through people's e-mail files. Specifically, the e-mails sent to the newspaper."

"Yes."

"You really think someone is stupid enough not to have deleted the correspondence?"

"I'm banking on it."

He smiled. "E-mail files here at the city offices are public records. So technically, there's no invasion of privacy, because there is no privacy. Scoot over."

She looked surprised. "It might take a while."

"I realize that, Sherlock."

"Don't you have a date or something?"

"Two things, Cami. One, not all men are scum. Two, I just told you I wanted to date *you*. And only you."

She never took her eyes off him as she absorbed his words, looking so bewildered. And so heartbreakingly unsure, as if no one had ever made her such a promise.

Hell, he'd never made such a promise himself. *He* should be the terrified one. And there was some of that, but also an inexplicable sense of hope. "Scoot over," he said again, gently.

After a moment's consideration, she made room for him at her side. Just where he wanted to be.

Chapter Five

By two A.M. they'd gotten through half the offices and had found something both shocking and morbidly interesting. There wasn't just one employee e-mailing information to the newspaper, but a spattering of them, none from the same department, and none who had any obvious connections to each other.

Was everyone in this building losing their minds?

They were missing something big here, Cami knew it, and because she did, she refused to give up.

Oddly enough, so did Matt. He'd benefited from what had happened to the town council more than anyone. He'd become mayor because of it. It would be further to his benefit to leave it all alone.

And yet he stayed, brow furrowed in concentration, fingers clicking across the keyboards as fast as her own, concentrating intently on everything they went through.

He was on her side.

They'd been on the same side before, and they'd been on opposite sides. He was a fierce competitor, she knew this.

And also fiercely loyal.

The combination, the dichotomy of him, fascinated her, when she didn't want to be fascinated.

And now he'd said he wanted to date her. Imagine that. She

and Matt. The problem was, she *couldn't* imagine it. So she organized her thoughts like she did everything else and put them out of her way for now, to be obsessed about later. Far later.

Matt suggested they wait until they finished going through all the rest of the computers before making their findings known, which would take at least one more night, possibly two. They went to the employee break room for food, and Matt came up with a package of donuts. "Probably stale, but chocolate is chocolate."

Cami stared at the donuts, mouth watering as she went to war with her old fat self.

Eat them, that old fat self begged.

You might as well just spread them over your hips, sneered her new, thinner self.

"Split them with me?" He was already breaking into them, sending the scent of sugary sweet chocolate wafting across the room.

Her stomach growled. "Um . . ." *Get some control, woman.* "No, thanks."

"Sure?" He shoved one in his mouth and moaned unapologetically. His tongue darted out to catch a crumb off his lip. "Nothing like the rush of sugar at two in the morning."

He was smiling, his eyes filled with pleasure. He found pleasure in everything he did, whether it was working, laughing, arguing . . . She imagined he'd be like that in bed, too. Her belly tightened.

He caught her looking at him and smiled. "Change your mind?"

Had she? He was cocky, edgy, at times arrogant, and then there was the fact that she couldn't outwit him like she could most others. Which in effect meant she couldn't control him, or how she felt about him.

Just like she couldn't control the urge for donuts.

"Cami?"

"No, I haven't changed my mind. Not about anything."

Without looking too disturbed, he popped another donut into his mouth and brushed the sugar off his hands. "Your loss."

It didn't matter to him either way, she knew that. He'd probably already forgotten he'd said he wanted to date her. *Exclusively.* Men like him said stuff like that all the time just to get laid.

At least she hadn't fallen into that trap.

"You have a thing against stuff that's good for you?" he asked.

"The stuff you're referring to is *bad* for me."

"I wasn't talking about the donuts."

"Neither was I."

He laughed softly, and again the sound scraped at a spot low in her belly. "All work and no play . . ." he began.

"Makes me feel worthwhile."

"Do you ever let up on that self-control?" He looked genuinely curious. "Just to enjoy yourself?"

"I don't like to deviate from a plan."

"Don't I know it," he said with feeling, reminding her of all the times they'd gone head to head over one of her "plans."

"If I'm driving you so crazy, why are you here?" *Using words like exclusive?*

He stepped close. "Oh, you're most definitely driving me crazy."

"Then why—"

He put a finger to her lips, his touch making her heart race, reminding her how much her body craved him. "You're also making me feel things I haven't felt in a long time," he said. "I like you, Cami. A lot, I'm finding. Now, about deviating." He cupped her face. "Buckle in, because this is a big step off the planned path for the evening."

"Matt—"

He kissed her. It was another of those soul-deep connections that had her hands lifting of their own accord, anchoring her to him as her fingers dug into the hard muscles of his shoulders. A soft little murmur escaped her, horrifying in its dark neediness, but there it was. Undeniable.

She wanted this more than the donuts, and that was saying something. She held on tightly, purring in pleasure when his hands roamed up and down her back, squeezing her bottom, her hips, up to her breasts. His thumbs made a pass over her nipples, and when he found them hard, he let out a rough sound that rumbled from deep in his throat.

She let out a matching moan when she heard it, and the desperation behind it, and she pushed at him.

He lifted his head, looking hot and bothered and extremely sexy for it.

She staggered back against the refrigerator, feeling drugged. And achy, deliciously so. "That's . . ." Words failed, so she just fanned the air in front of her hot face.

He wasn't breathing any more steadily than she was. "I see what you mean about planning." His voice was husky and aroused. "If we'd planned that, maybe I wouldn't feel as if I've just been hit by a bus."

"There's no plan in the world that can prepare you for *that*."

"Which proves that it's okay to wing it once in a while."

"I can't argue with you when my brain is fried." She poured herself a large, cold drink of water. It didn't cool her off. "I need to do something organized right now," she decided.

"Right now?"

"*Right now.*" She opened the drawer by the sink. A mess. Perfect. She began to straighten the forks and spoons and pencils and matches, pulling out a Christmas CD that someone had shoved in and forgotten.

Matt leaned against the counter. "Let me get this straight. You can face the entire town council and argue a point until their eyes cross, but you can't face me?"

She stilled her fingers, hating her weaknesses. "You're right. I should do my own office first." She marched out of the break

room and into her office. "Go home," she said when he followed her so closely she couldn't get her door shut without
taking off his nose. "Get some sleep."

"I'd rather watch you organize your already perfectly organized office."

Jaw set, she went to her desk, pulling her top drawer open.
Damn if every single thing wasn't already in place.

"So you're obsessive-compulsive as well as anal," he said
conversationally.

"I organize when I'm nervous or upset. It's no big deal. I'm
sure you do something for your nerves, too."

"Sure. Face the problem."

She whipped up her head, met his gaze.

"Talk to me," he said softly.

She looked down at the pencils and pens carefully set in
their proper slots. She had one for erasers, too. And her tape.
Her stapler. Everything was perfectly aligned.

"Cami."

In spite of his sincerity, she still hesitated. This wasn't an
easy admission. "I used to be fat," she finally said. There. She
said it out loud for the first time. "All throughout my childhood and school years. I was the fat kid in a fit, active, successful family. They were all perfect, and I wasn't." He wasn't
running for the hills yet, so she went on. "Then I left home and
went to college, out of the reach of my parents and brother
and sister. I lost fifty pounds and got control of myself." She
straightened her shoulders. "Being in charge and organized
and controlling is who I am, and I realize you might see it as
neurotic, but being this way makes me feel good about myself."

"You *should* feel good about yourself."

She didn't dare look at him or absorb his approval. "Once
in a while I let myself relax, I let myself cheat. So I am warning
you now, the next time you offer me donuts, be prepared to
lose your fingers."

He didn't laugh or mock her. He didn't even smile. Instead,

he stepped closer, lifting her chin with a finger. "We grew up in the same town, remember? I know how you used to be."

"You know I used to be fat?"

Now that finger traced her hairline. "I played basketball with your older brother. You came to the games."

Yes, she remembered. She'd stand at the concession stand and eat.

And eat.

"I don't care what you used to look like," he said softly, tucking a strand of hair behind her ear.

"Come on, Matt. Look at you. Your reflection probably sighs in bliss every morning. You're telling me appearances don't matter to you?"

"I'm telling you life experiences matter. Listen, my brother and I grew up with a teenaged mom who didn't know the first thing about being on her own, much less about raising two boys. We had no rules, no authority. Hell, we had no roof over our heads half the time. I worked damn hard to be who I am now, and I want someone who understands that, who has her own experiences to draw on. I want a woman who can talk to me, who can understand my world, who can be both serious *and* fun-loving. And if she just happens to be easy on the eyes, and believe me, you are extremely easy on the eyes, Cami, well then . . . lucky me."

She stared at him for signs of deception and saw nothing but open honesty in his gaze. "I don't know what to say to you. I think I should go home now." She turned off the lights.

Her office settled into darkness, but it wasn't complete. From the windows came the glow of the seasonal lights, twinkling merrily, casting shadows across the desk and floor.

Matt put his hands on her. She didn't protest as he drew her in. The soft night fell over them—hypnotic, lulling, sweetly silent—and when he touched his mouth to hers, she settled into the soft, gentle kiss.

"Night," he whispered, and stepping back, he slipped his hands into his pockets, leaving her wanting more, damn him.

The man was smart, she'd give him that, knowing when to push and when not to. If he'd kissed her senseless and then asked her to go home with him, would she have gone?

Of course not.

Oh, crap. She'd have gone in a heartbeat, and not because he kissed like heaven, but because he'd seen her at her compulsively organizing worst and hadn't gone running. Grabbing her purse, she made the mistake of turning back to him.

There was passion and heat swimming in his eyes, and something more—affection.

Oh, God, but that got her. How often did a man look at her like that? Never. How often did she feel this way, sort of quivery and . . . desperately horny?

Double never.

Maybe . . . maybe she needed a New Year's resolution—live life to its fullest, even if that means occasionally deviating off the known path. She could mark the deviating on her calendar for, say, once a month.

Starting now. She dropped her purse on her desk. "Matt?"

"Yeah?"

"Do you carry condoms?"

He blinked. "What?"

"I assume a man like you carries." She put her hands on his shoulders. "I've never made the first move before—"

"Cami—"

"Not because I'm a prude or anything, but because there's never been anyone I wanted badly enough to risk the rejection."

His eyes went dark, so very dark, as his hands came up to her waist. "I want to be clear, very clear," he said. "This is you coming onto me, right?"

"Yes." She swallowed hard. "It's a New Year's resolution sort of thing, a week early. Be kind, okay?"

"Cami, I plan on being everything you ever wanted." He lifted her against him and set her on the desk.

"Here?" she asked breathlessly, her heart in her throat, her body on high alert, beginning with her nipples and ending with a dampness between her thighs.

"Oh, yeah, *here*." His big, warm hands settled on her thighs, pushing them open, and before she could decide how she felt about that, he stepped between them.

"Wait," she gasped.

He went still. "Really?"

Do it. Do *him*. "It's okay. It's a good kind of wait." Twisting around, she swept an arm across her meticulously neat desk, knocking everything to the floor in one fell swoop—her phone, her desk pad, her notes.

"Nicely done," he said approvingly.

She stared at the mess on the floor, chewing on her lower lip. The urge to pick it all back up nearly overpowered her.

Matt's mouth was solemn, but his eyes full of humor. "You want to take a moment and clean it up?"

That he'd read her mind so easily was a little disconcerting. "No, I'm . . . good."

He tipped up her chin, away from the mess. "Sure?"

"I want to be in the moment, damn it! Just once!"

"In the moment is just where I want you." His other hand slid down her spine to her bottom, tugging her closer.

Pressed up flush against him, she could feel every inch of him. He was hard, and it made her heart beat faster, heavier.

"Yeah, right here," he said softly, his mouth only a fraction of an inch from hers. "Just tell me if you need to stop to obsess about anything."

"No, I'm fine." Sort of. Pretty much. Oh, my God, he was big.

His smile was slow and warm and sexy. "Yeah, you're fine." And this time when he kissed her, she sank her fingers into his hair and kissed him back, thrilling to his firm, quietly demanding mouth, which stirred instincts long suppressed. Living life to the fullest. In the moment. *God, in the moment tasted good.* But there were too many barriers between them—his clothes, hers . . . Impatient, she pulled his shirt from his waistband, sliding her hands beneath to touch his heated skin, stroking up his smooth, sleek back, loving the feel of his muscles, bunched and tight. Letting out a little sigh of pleasure, she shifted to touch his flat abs, feeling him tremble. For her.

He knew her now, or he was starting to. He knew the real her, and he was still here, still wanting her. She could feel that wanting in his kiss, in the way he touched her, and the knowledge was so incredibly empowering and arousing, she gave herself up to it. To him.

She wasn't alone, not tonight, and marveling over that, too, she touched his mouth, feeling him smile beneath her fingers, his tense jaw, the muscles bunched beneath the wall of his chest. "I'm still fine," she marveled, giving him a breathless update.

He smiled and nibbled his way to her ear. She shivered, which he soothed away with his hands as he lifted her tank top. Looking into her eyes, he peeled the material over her head. Oh, God. Her inner fat girl surfaced for a brief flash.

He danced his hands from waist to ribs, palming her breasts. "Okay?" he murmured, his thumbs rasping over her nipples.

"O-okay," she managed. *Don't think about him seeing your body, don't think about it, just enjoy.*

"You're so beautiful," he said, banishing her inner fat girl for another day.

Somehow she stripped off his shirt as well, looking at him in the low light. The man had a body like a pagan god, and she wanted to touch it.

Before she could, he dipped his head, forging a path of hot, open-mouth kisses down her shoulder as he unhooked her bra, baring her breasts.

The heat within her spread. Fat girl stayed banished.

"Still okay?" he wanted to know as he bent to a breast. Licked. Sucked. *Bit.*

She panted for breath. *"Yes."*

"Good." His hands curled around the hem of her skirt, skimming it up her thighs. Then his fingers hooked into her panties.

She stared into his hungry eyes. "Um . . ."

"Tell me you're still hanging in," he said, his voice not so light now.

"Y-yes. Hanging in."

"Good. Now hold on." He stepped back, tugged, and her panties vanished. Cold air danced over her legs, but then he was back between her thighs. With his usual bluntness, he looked down at her sprawled out for him like some sort of feast, letting out a hungry sound she felt all the way to her womb.

Torn between the erotic sexual haze he'd trapped her in and a vulnerable embarrassment, she squeezed her eyes shut. Not as experienced as she'd have liked, she didn't know the protocol here, or what to do with her hands. He'd told her to hold on, so she gripped the edge of the desk for all she was worth, struggling to remain calm. Should she say something? Tell him she didn't often climax with a man because it was hard for her to give up her control? Or should she just smile sexily and fake it?

Or do what she was already doing, which was panting for air because she could hardly breathe.

He took the decision out of her hands when he sank to his knees and stroked his fingers over her.

Her body jerked in surprise, in pleasure.

"Shh," he murmured, and with another rough sound of hunger, leaned in and tasted her.

Reality had no chance then, no chance at all. At the first stroke of his tongue, she became incapable of smiling sexily, or even of blushing, incapable of doing anything except holding onto that desk and gasping for air between little whimpers of pleasure. Oh, God, this felt good, this felt *amazing*. She could actually— She was going to— "Matt!"

"I know. It's okay. Come for me, Cami."

When she did come—*exploded*—with a shocked, breathless cry, he murmured his approval and did it again.

Did *her* again.

"Oh, my God," she panted when she could speak. She was flat on her back, blinking at the bright stars dancing in her vision. "I think I've walked into the light."

His face appeared above her as he braced a hand on either side of her head. He wore a grin, albeit a tense one. "Those are the Christmas lights outside the window."

"Oh." She smiled sheepishly. "That was . . . holy cow. You have no idea."

"Been a while?"

"*You have no idea*. There's more, right?"

"Oh, yeah, there's more." He unzipped his pants, put on a condom from his wallet, a task most pleasurable to watch, Cami thought dimly, her brain not quite connected, her body still pulsing.

"Still with me?" he asked.

"So with you."

"Good." Draping her thighs over his forearms, Matt gripped her hips and slid home, filling her to bursting, a feeling intensified by the low, serrated sound of desire that ripped from deep in his throat.

She could feel her toes curl as he breathed her name in a husky, destroyed voice. "*Cami.*"

She couldn't respond, because within a few strokes she was clutching at him, panting, whimpering. *Dying.* Between the delicious friction and the expression of need on his face alone, she flew high, trembling, quivering, suspended on the very edge, until with a rough, guttural groan, he shattered. He was still in its throes when she took the leap with him.

Again.

Chapter Six

Cami told herself that she was fine, that she'd escaped from the experience in her office with Matt relatively unscathed. She told herself that all the way home, and all the way through her hot shower, and all the way through the next three hours in her bed, until her alarm went off at six A.M.

Just a torrid affair, like she'd always wondered about.

The after part had been a little rough, she could admit now—the coming-home-alone part. Matt had wanted her to go to his place, but she'd been unable to fathom repeating the whole mind-blowing experience and then walking away.

Once had been hard enough.

When her snooze alarm went off again, she got up and dressed. *Christmas Eve.* Most people wouldn't be going into work, but she was going to. Dedication at its finest, she supposed.

And a telling way to hold at bay the memories from last night. Or the loneliness she knew would hit her any minute now. The Christmas loneliness. She could try to forget, she could try to pretend it didn't exist, but it always came.

She entered her office and stopped short at the sight of her desk. The scene of her indiscretion, so to speak. Her momentary lapse in good judgment. Last night, she'd straightened it all up, she'd had to, but she didn't need to see all her things on the floor to remember what Matt had done to her there.

Pulling out her chair, she sat down and tried not to look at the blotter, which now contained an imprint of her butt. She dug into work, feeling very mature for doing so, but by mid-afternoon, she gave up. She had to get out, or lose her mind, so she headed downtown, where she wandered the long row of art galleries and unique gift shops to find her last-minute family Christmas gifts. Determined to be chipper and in the spirit, she hit them all.

And found nothing for her picky parents or impossible-to-buy-for brother and sister.

All around her, the trees and streets were lit with seasonal lights. Each storefront had been decorated, and Christmas music and delicious scents surrounded her. So did people. Everywhere. Couples, families, friends . . . everyone talking and laughing and having a ball, all in the holiday spirit.

No one seemed to be alone.

Except her.

She ended up back at her car, arms empty. *Damn it*. Determined, she sat there waiting for the defroster to work, wracking her brain. Finally it came to her. Ski-lift tickets. Her parents would love the excuse to dust off their skis, and her siblings would think the present original and cool. Cami let out her first smile of the day, because she just might have hit upon the perfect gift *and* the perfect way to impress her impossible-to-impress family on Christmas morning.

Congratulating herself, she drove the seven miles out of town to Eagle Ski Resort. There she purchased the tickets, and had just put them in her purse when someone said in her ear, "Well, look at that. You tore yourself from work."

The last time she'd heard that voice, he'd been standing between her sprawled thighs whispering wicked-sexy-nothings to her. Turning, she faced one Matt Tarino, dressed in black board pants and jacket, wearing a Santa hat and aviator reflector sunglasses, and holding his snowboard. He should have looked ridiculous. Instead, he looked fun-loving and carefree, not to mention incredibly sure of himself, and sexy as hell for it. Belatedly, she remembered his brother owned this place, so of course he'd be here. Or, maybe not so belatedly. Maybe she'd known—hoped—to see him. Disconcerting thought. As she stood there staring at him, wondering at the odd ping in her belly—and between her thighs—two women skied by and sprayed Matt with powder from their skis, laughing uproariously, flirting with their smiles and eyes.

Cami dusted herself off, surreptitiously watching Matt as he waved back, turning down their offer to join them. Instead, he moved closer to Cami and brushed some powdery snow from her cheek. "So. What brings you here?"

Now that they'd had raw, wild, animal sex on her desk, he made her feel even more off balance than usual, and she was painfully hyperaware of his every move. Even her nipples were hard. It was ridiculous, and to counteract the phenomenon, she stopped looking at him. "I came by to purchase some lift tickets for my family for their Christmas gifts."

"Nice gifts."

Let's hope they think so.

"Enjoying your Christmas Eve?"

"Sure." Less than she would a cruise to the Bahamas, but more than, say, a root canal.

Matt shoved up his sunglasses to the front of his Santa hat. "You're looking pretty uptight for someone who's enjoying herself. Come join me for a few runs before the slopes close."

She looked down at her long maroon skirt and sweater. "I couldn't."

"What's your preference, skis or board?"

"Skis, but I'd planned on going back to the office to finish going through those computers—"

"I'll help you after."

"But I don't—"

He tugged her close. She stared resolutely at his chest.

"Was last night so awful, you can't even look me in the eyes?" he asked quietly.

Surprised, she lifted her head. "No. No," she said again into his rueful and, damn it, hurt gaze. "It was . . . well, you know what it was. It was incredible."

His eyes smoldered. "So let me show you another good time. On the slopes."

She looked at him for a long moment, because she knew herself. She was falling, and falling for a man—especially him, the one man to make her feel things, the one man to get inside her and care about her—was dangerous. It gave him all the power he needed to hurt her. Scary, scary stuff.

On the other hand, it was only a few runs on a ski hill, something that was shockingly tempting . . . "Maybe for a little while."

With a smile that melted her resolve and very nearly her precious control, he led her inside the small lodge. "My brother runs the show here," he said, waving at yet another group of women who called his name from across the large room. "I just help out when I can. We'll get you all set up."

The next thing she knew, he had her in borrowed gear and on skis from the demo shop. And then out on the slopes.

Having a ball.

Truthfully, much of her fun came from just watching Matt. The man was sheer poetry in motion, all clean lines and easy aggression, with a wild abandon that aroused her just looking at him. Who'd have thought such a sharp-witted, politically driven man could move like that?

After last night, she should have known.

She wondered what *he* thought of last night, but they didn't talk about it. They just took the slopes with an easy camaraderie and laughter and . . . fun, and by the time the lifts closed two hours later, she felt chilled to the bone but exhilarated. For a few hours, she'd been like the people she'd seen in town, not alone . . . happy.

"Thanks," she said when she'd turned her equipment back in and he'd put his board in his locker. "I really needed that."

Standing in the lodge, he stroked a strand of hair off her face and smiled. "You're cold. I have a cure for that, too."

"I think you've cured me enough."

"Come on, Cami. What's the worst that could happen?"

That he would offer to warm her up, maybe in his bed, and she might be just weak enough to let him. And then she might not want to ever leave.

"Do you trust me?" he asked.

She stared into his eyes. She'd seen them stormy and furious; she'd seen them soft and heated. They were somewhere in between now, filled with an honesty and affection that took her breath. Did she trust him? She knew she didn't want to. "I wouldn't follow you off a cliff, but at work . . . maybe I trust you there."

He laughed. "A start, I suppose. What about personally? Do you trust me outside of work?"

Back to that jumping-off-a-cliff thing. "That's more complicated."

"Ah." He nodded agreeably, then shook his head. "Why, exactly?"

"Well . . . you like women."

"I believe that's worked to your benefit."

She blushed. "You like *lots* of women."

"Yeah." His smile faded. "I suppose that's the rumor mill you're referring to. You know, a lot of that is exaggerated."

"How much of it?"

"What?"

"What percentage of all the women I've seen drooling over you is exaggerated?"

He paused. Considered carefully. Ran his tongue over his teeth.

"Thought so." She searched her purse for her keys.

He reached for her hands to still them. "Should I judge you for your past?"

"No, but I haven't slept with every single man in the free world."

"Neither have I," he said, and tried a grin. When she didn't return it, he sighed. Rubbed his jaw. "Okay, listen. I've had a good time with life so far. I'll admit that much. But I'm not afraid of commitment. Can you say the same?"

"Yes." Maybe.

Probably.

Fine. Commitment made her nervous, a fact that was undoubtedly tied to her need to control every little issue. But she'd like to think she wouldn't let that stand in the way of a real relationship.

"I really don't see the problem here," he said softly.

He wouldn't. "We're so fundamentally different."

"You mean you being uptight, anal, and overly organized?" She crossed her arms. "I would think people would love that about me."

"Maybe I'll love you in spite of it."

She went utterly still. "What?"

"Not here," he decided. "We're not doing this here. Come on."

He led her back through the lodge, across the icy parking lot, to the far side of the property where a couple of cabins faced the mountain vista. There was a driveway between them, and in it sat a truck and Matt's Blazer.

"My brother's," he said, pointing to one cabin. "And mine," he added, pointing to the other, opening the door, revealing a small but lovely living room accented all in wood. One wall was all windows, overlooking a white-capped peak, and another was filled with a stone fireplace. He had a Christmas tree in the corner, tall and beautifully simple, with white lights and red bows, but somehow it held more holiday spirit than anything she'd seen.

His couch looked like an old favorite, overstuffed and well used. A football lay on the floor, along with a pair of battered running shoes, a stack of newspapers toppled over, and a very neglected fern. Leaning against the far wall were several pairs of skis, two snowboards, and two pairs of boots. Warm and homey but definitely lived-in. Her fingers still itched to at least straighten the newspapers.

Or jump Matt.

"I'll start a fire," he said, putting an arm around her and pulling her in close to his big, warm body. "Come get comfortable."

She couldn't. Shouldn't.

"I promise not to bite." He rubbed his jaw to hers. "Unless you want me to."

"You've lost your mind." But she looked into his eyes and melted a little.

A lot.

It was official. He hadn't lost his mind—she'd lost hers.

Chapter Seven

"I shouldn't come in," Cami said in a last-ditch effort to save herself. "You don't want casual company tonight. It's Christmas Eve." She stood in his foyer, uncertain, and desperately trying to hide it from him. "I'm sure you have better things to do."

He just looked at her with amusement and something more, seeming tall and sure and so damn sexy. "Tomorrow my brother and I are going to watch college football and exchange fond insults, but until then, I'm all yours."

Until then? She swallowed hard. She was attracted to him, so so *so* attracted, but deep inside she knew she might not be able to control that attraction if she let him touch her again.

"You're thinking waaaaay too hard," he said lightly, taking her hand as if to make sure she couldn't run off.

"Bad habit, thinking too hard." She took a deep breath and stepped into the living room. "I still want to go back to work and search the rest of the computers . . ."

"I know." He moved to the fireplace and lit the already laid-out fire. "Come closer to the heat."

She did so slowly, hugging herself tightly, throwing him a smile that she hoped seemed confident, not shaky.

He went into the kitchen. She heard him moving around, and her heart went into her throat. He was planning her seduction. Probably lighting candles, finding music, hunting up condoms.

Her thighs tightened.

Bad body. No more sex. She'd had her fling. She'd had her fun. Time to hunker down now—

He came back into the living room with cheese and salami and cut-up apples on a plate. She stared first at the food, and then at his face. "You're . . . feeding me?"

"It's dinnertime. I figured if I took the time to make something, you'd vanish on me. But we're going to need fuel if we're going back to the offices—"

"It's just that I—" She cleared her throat. "I thought you were going to try to seduce me."

"Oh, I plan to," he said easily. "Just not until after we work, or you won't relax. And I want you relaxed, Cami. Really relaxed."

She stared at him. "You actually understand me. I mean *really* understand me."

"I'm trying."

"Matt?"

"Yeah?"

The hell with it. She tugged him close and kissed him.

"Mmm," he said in surprised pleasure, but after a minute, he pulled back and pushed the food in front of her. "Eat. Then the office. And then, Cami, then this. I'm going to take you to bed. *Mine.*"

His. God. How bad off was she that she thrilled to that idea?

The offices were dark and chilled, but Cami turned determinedly toward the department they hadn't yet gone through— her own.

The first three computers were clean, including hers. One office left. She stood in the doorway and looked at Ned's desk.

"We're committing equal opportunity privacy invasion," Matt said quietly. "We have to look."

"Despite the Belinda fiasco, he wouldn't hurt anyone, not this way."

"Let's just be absolutely positive."

"Okay."

To Cami's utter shock, they found several e-mails addressed to the newspaper, in Ned's sent file, one of which suggested the fire chief of Blue Eagle might be an arsonist. "Oh, my God," she whispered, looking up into Matt's grim face. "It's him, too." She couldn't believe it, didn't know what to think.

"You all right?"

It just made no sense. But she was all right. What Ned did didn't reflect on her, didn't mean anything except that Ned was an ass. *She* was okay. She was really okay, and it'd all started with that New Year's resolution to go for it, to deviate from the plan once in a while. To live life to its fullest . . .

And Matt was it. He was her "go for it," her "step off the path."

He was the way to live life to its fullest. And not just a one-time deal. "Matt?"

At her soft, extremely serious tone, he stroked a strand of hair from her face. "What is it?"

"Maybe you should sit down," she said a little shakily. "This is going to be a doozy—"

The office door creaked open behind them, and someone stopped in surprise at the sight of them.

"Hey," Matt said, but the figure standing there whirled to run.

"*Shit.*" Matt surged up, just barely snagging the person by the back of the jacket.

Cami leaped for the light switch, then gasped in shock when the fluorescent bulbs sputtered to life and she found a gun in her face.

"Belinda," Cami gasped.

Belinda tore free of Matt's grip. Tall and willowy, with her long blonde hair piled on top of her head, she was wearing black, studious-looking glasses and a tight red suit, none of which hid her beach-babe figure. "You two scared me to death," she said. "What are you doing in here?"

"How about we talk about the gun first?" Matt asked, gesturing carefully to the weapon still in Belinda's hand.

Belinda looked at it, flushed, but didn't lower it. "You scared me. I thought you were a burglar. I was just protecting myself."

"Well, it's just us," Matt said. "So you can put it down."

The gun wavered slightly, but remained cocked and aimed, now at Matt's face. "Why are you snooping in Ned's computer?"

Matt didn't so much as look at Cami as he slowly turned toward the computer in question. Belinda's aim followed.

"We were looking through everyone's e-mail files," Matt said.

Belinda didn't look happy as she followed him to the computer. "Why?"

"We were looking for the person leaking those vicious rumors."

"They aren't rumors if they're true," Belinda said, leaning in to read the screen. "And it was all true, no matter what anyone says."

"Really?" Matt's fingers flew over the keyboard as he turned his body completely away from Cami now.

So did Belinda.

He was turning Belinda away from Cami. Trying to keep her safe. *Oh, my God.*

"How do you know it was all true?" Matt asked Belinda.

Belinda stared at him.

He stared right back, calm and cool, despite the gun only inches from his face.

"You already know," Belinda guessed softly. "Don't you."

"What, that you were the one who did the e-mailing from all those different computers?" Matt nodded. "Yeah. Just figured that out. So now what, Belinda? Because up until right now, you haven't committed a crime that would land you some serious jail time. The gun changes that."

Belinda looked at the gun.

"Don't be stupid," Matt said softly.

Cami felt frantic. The foolish man was baiting her! Heart in her throat, she took a step toward the wall, where Ned had plans of his latest pet project, a bike trail along the river. They were rolled up in a canister and weighed a good ten pounds. Hoisting them up, she took a slow step toward Belinda's back.

"What were you trying to do?" Matt asked Belinda. "You got your own father kicked out of here."

"He deserved it! He was cheating on my mom. With a *guy*." Belinda shuddered. "And everyone here acted so self-righteous about it."

"So you hurt them, too?"

"Yes! And maybe you were next."

Matt shook his head. "You couldn't have gotten me, Belinda."

"Why not?"

"Because I'm smarter than you are."

Cami couldn't believe it! Didn't he see the gun right in his face? She could scarcely breathe for fear it'd go off by accident.

Belinda's hand wavered, probably with rage. Jesus. Cami took another step and raised the tube of plans. Matt looked up, and so did Belinda, at the same time lifting the gun, just as Cami closed her eyes and brought the plans down on Belinda's forearm, hard.

The gun flew into the air, then hit the floor, and with a frustrated, rage-filled howl, Belinda whipped around to face Cami.

"I figure I just saved you a long prison visit," Cami said. "You can thank me later."

Belinda let out an enraged scream and took a step toward her, but instead of strangling her, as Cami half-braced for, Belinda ran out of the office.

Matt strode to Cami and hauled her against him. Tense with fear and fury, he ran his searing eyes over her. "Are you all right?"

He was looking at her as if she was his entire world. She

loved that. She loved him. "Of course I'm all right. You were the one with the gun in your face, you stupid, stupid man!" She tugged his face down and kissed him. "Hell of a time to realize I love you. We have to go after her."

He gripped her arms, lifted her up to her toes. "What?"

"I said we have to go after her—"

"The other thing."

"Later." She was shaking. "We have to—"

"Say it," he demanded.

"I love you."

He leaned in and kissed her, one hard, warm connection. "I love you, too. So damn much."

The words filled her, warmed her. She was in shock. And she was in love. Heady combination.

"I wanted to be your hero," he said. "But you saved yourself."

She ran her hands up his chest, feeling his heart pounding beneath her fingers. It steadied her. *He* steadied her. "It's okay. It's all part of that New Year's resolution. I'm going for it, remember? At all times."

"But you always go for it."

"At work, yes. But I'm expanding to other areas. Like my personal life."

His eyes shined with emotion. "You going for me, Cami?"

"Yeah, I guess I am. How does that feel, Mr. Mayor?"

He glanced at his watch. Two minutes past midnight. "Like the best Christmas present I've ever had." And he pulled her close.

I'll Be Home for Christmas

Kathy Love

For Perry Como, Sting, David Hyde Pierce, and Kate Duffy. (Betcha never thought you'd see that group of names together, did ya Kate?)

Chapter One

"Christmas sucks," Rob Marsten muttered as he pulled the sleek silver Palm Pilot out of the side pocket of his leather briefcase. He plucked the stylus from the holder along the top and punched the small machine to life. A few more rapid taps, and he was looking at his whole life for the remainder of 2005.

According to his schedule, he should have landed in Portland, Maine, at six thirty-five P.M. He glanced at his Rolex.

Seven fifty-two P.M.

Well, that wasn't going to happen.

He picked up his carry-on bag, slinging the strap over his shoulder, and joined the throng of harried and irritated travelers surrounding the help desk.

"Okay," called the airport employee from behind the tall counter. "All flights out of Boston have been canceled this evening."

The crowd muttered and groaned, swarming the agent.

Hence, the reason for the height of the counter, Rob noted. So passengers couldn't easily crawl over it in revolt.

"I'm sorry," the attendant said automatically, with no real sorrow in her voice. "The nor'easter was expected to go out to sea by early evening, but it has settled over the tip of New

England instead, and it isn't forecasted to leave until early tomorrow morning."

More grumbles.

"Some Christmas," a man beside Rob complained.

Rob nodded his agreement. But this served him right for even considering this trip. He didn't have the time to take away from work, not now with his promotion almost clinched. But his sister had worn him down.

"He's your very first nephew. And it's his very first Christmas," she'd said.

"Mo, you know how busy I am."

"No, I don't. I don't see you or talk to you enough to know *what* you're doing. You haven't even seen Stewie yet. Do I need to remind you he was born in April?"

"I remember. But please tell me you aren't going to call that child Stewie his whole life."

"What's wrong with 'Stewie'?"

"Nothing—if you're looking for an adjective for something that is or has the qualities of stew."

"Whatever. Just come home. Mom and Dad miss you. I miss you."

Rob had finally agreed. He hadn't been home in a couple of years, but he simply didn't have time. A man didn't get ahead in life being forever on holiday. But he knew he should see his nephew, if only to make sure the poor kid got a better nickname.

He checked his Palm Pilot again. Assuming he got the first flight to Portland in the morning, he'd have about forty-one hours to spend with his family. And that was if the storm cleared when predicted.

He left the angry mob and looked out the terminal window. The snow was definitely falling, but he noticed the airport vehicles were getting around in the several inches with no difficulty.

A woman in the blue-and-white uniform of the airport staff rushed by him.

"Excuse me," he said.

The woman stopped, her expression irritated as she turned. Her eyes quickly roamed from his face to the perfect cut of his clothing to his face again. The strained expression immediately disappeared.

"Can I help you, sir?"

He forced a pleasant smile. Women always responded to one thing. Money.

"Yes, you can. I was wondering which way to the car rentals?"

Her eyes drifted back down to his tailored suit. Kenneth Cole. A limited edition. Very expensive. From the glimmer in her blue eyes, she could tell.

Being able to impress with his clothing and his expensive accessories had once pleased him, but lately he found himself annoyed with people's shallowness.

"They're on the lower level. Follow the signs for baggage claim, and you'll find them. Although I'm not sure there will be many cars available. A lot of travelers have opted to drive tonight rather than wait out the storm. Not a fun way to spend Christmas Eve."

"No," he agreed. But then again, he never enjoyed Christmas Eve. Not for years anyway.

"Thanks for your help." He nodded to the woman, then started out to the main concourse, following the signs.

When he got to the lower level, he was surprised to see it was relatively deserted. Strange, given how many people were stranded tonight. He couldn't be the only one willing to risk driving in the storm.

Then he realized several of the rental agencies were closed. He approached the desks, which held signs that said they were closed because they had no more rentals available.

He walked farther down the hallway, noticing a man standing at a counter. As he approached, he saw it was a rental agency, and they were actually open.

162 / Kathy Love

Hire a Heap.

He grimaced. That didn't sound too promising, but at this point he couldn't be choosy, could he?

"There you go," the clerk behind the counter said to the man, handing him a set of keys. "The last car. Good timing."

"Thank you. And Merry Christ—"

"You don't have any more cars?" Rob strode up to the counter, ignoring the fact that the other customer was still talking.

The clerk, a young guy with a bad haircut and grease under his fingernails, shrugged. "That was the last one. Sorry."

Great. Rob immediately turned to the other customer, who regarded him with a distinct look of annoyance. "I'll give you a hundred dollars for the car."

The man, in his thirties with short-cropped blond hair and small, wire-rimmed glasses, immediately shook his head. "I have a wedding tomorrow in Portland. We have to get to Maine tonight."

Rob frowned at the guy. Who the hell got married on Christmas Day? He started to ask as much when a voice behind him stopped his words cold.

"Good, you didn't leave without me." The voice was light. He could tell the speaker was smiling even without seeing her.

Rob remained still. He didn't move to look at her. He didn't need to. He knew that voice. That lilting voice was as familiar to him as the first notes of a favorite Christmas carol.

But the man in front of him did look at the speaker and smiled broadly. "Of course we didn't leave you."

"Thank goodness! Or I'd be spending my Christmas Eve sleeping on one of these airport benches." She laughed, the sound just as Rob remembered, brilliant and rich.

His heart seized in his chest, and he struggled to take in a breath. Slowly, he managed to turn.

She'd stopped at one of the benches nearby and was rooting around in her large satchel purse. Her face was in profile, but he could see the slight upturn of her small nose and the wide, lush set of her mouth.

Damn, he'd loved that mouth. The way it turned up at the corners when she laughed. The way just one side quirked down when she was concentrating. The way it had felt against his, soft and velvety and warm.

He forced his gaze away, trying to cast aside the memory of those lips pressed against his. Pressed to his skin. But try as he might, he couldn't keep his eyes off her.

Her golden curls were pulled into a messy knot on top of her head, several tendrils escaping, caressing her cheeks and the neck of the red turtleneck sweater she was wearing. Her profile as beautiful as a delicately carved cameo.

It was Erica. His Erica.

Suddenly he was seeing her profile, not now, but from a night years earlier.

The doorbell rang.

He'd been pacing the worn braided rug in his parents' living room, hoping, praying she wouldn't change her mind. That she would come like they had decided.

He opened the door, and she stood on his front stoop, her profile illuminated by Christmas lights glittering off the falling snow.

"You're here." He could hear the relief in his voice, but there was no reason to hide it. Erica knew how desperate he was for this night. He'd dreamed of this night. He burned for it.

"Yes." She'd turned her hazel eyes on him and smiled. The red of her sweater brought out the pinkness in her cheeks and her mouth, making her more stunning, more beautiful.

They had planned this night, knowing that their parents

would both be attending the Cochrane's annual Christmas Eve party. Knowing that they would be alone all evening.

Rob stepped closer to her, nervous and unsure. Unsure of everything except the fact that he loved Erica and he had to touch her.

"Are you sure you're ready?"

She nodded. He could see the certainty in her eyes. That certainty made him feel more confident. He pulled her against him, her breasts pressed tightly to his chest. The rapid beat of their hearts answered one another.

There on his front doorstep, under the falling snow and the pristine quiet of Christmas Eve, he'd kissed her. He'd kissed her before, many times, but tonight was different. Tonight, their kiss felt perfect. It felt earth-shattering. Tonight, they were going to make love.

Rob squeezed his eyes shut, both to block out the memory and the woman before him. When he opened them again, he half-expected Erica to be gone, like some apparition sent to torment him and then vanish.

But Erica still stood before him, still rifling through her purse. Still unaware that he was there, his body wanting her as much as it had that Christmas Eve when they were both just seventeen.

"It's here somewhere," she muttered.

"Don't worry," said the man beside him, the man Rob had actually forgotten was there. "We can sort it out later."

Erica started to lift her head, a smile on her lush lips intended for the man beside Rob. But at the last minute, several of the items that had been threatening to fall out of her purse did. She squatted down to pick the objects up.

Rob turned his eyes to the man beside him. A nice looking guy. A guy who was on the receiving end of Erica's smiles. And a guy who was getting married tomorrow.

Rob's gut clenched. Was this guy marrying Erica? Was he marrying the woman that Rob once thought he'd marry?

"Donny, I don't want you to . . ."

Rob stopped gaping at the man and turned back to Erica as he heard her sentence come to a sudden halt.

She gaped at him, the items she'd dropped held forgotten in her hand. She blinked, perhaps thinking she was seeing a ghost, too.

Finally, she managed to breathe. "Rob? Is that really you?"

Chapter Two

Erica knew she was gaping at him like an idiot, but she simply couldn't believe it. Rob. This was really Rob.

"What are you doing here?" Then she immediately laughed at the silliness of her question. "Well, you're obviously getting a car. But are you heading to Maine?"

"Trying," he said with a slight, wry smile. The small movement of his lips hinted at the dimple in his left cheek.

The dimple. He'd been able to wrap her around his little finger by flashing that baby. She forced her gaze up to meet his. She'd forgotten how dark his eyes were, like strong, hot coffee.

She took a few steps toward him, her first inclination to hug him. To touch him. To make sure he was real. Only his cool demeanor stopped her. But it didn't stop her eyes from eating up the sight of him. He looked more gorgeous than she remembered, than she could have imagined. Of course, she hadn't factored in the haircut that made his unruly waves look fashionably messy, or the stylish suit that fit his broad shoulders to a tee, or the fact that his eyes seemed even darker and more smoldering.

Her gaze dropped to his sculpted lips. Did they taste the same? Had that changed? Her lips tingled at the thought of sampling his. She immediately forced her eyes back up to his unreadable gaze.

"Erica, you know him?" Donny asked.

"Yes, this is Rob." And she'd once known him better than anyone on the earth. But now, now he was little more than a distant acquaintance. In fact, she'd stopped really knowing him long before they'd actually broken up. And they hadn't seen each other since.

That had been . . . seven years ago. Seven years ago this very night.

"Come back to Rhode Island with me." Erica reached over and pulled the book from Rob's hand. "Your classes don't start until a week after mine."

He blinked up at her as though he barely recalled she was there. She ignored his indifferent attitude, snuggling against him on his parents' age-softened tweed sofa.

"I already told you, I can't. I have to get ready for my classes. I have a heavy class load this semester."

He had a heavy class load every semester. And he rarely came to see her at her school anymore, even though they were only an hour away from each other.

"Couldn't you come for just a couple days? I miss you." She leaned closer, her lips brushing his ear. "I miss having you all to myself."

She glanced around to make sure his parents weren't nearby. Then she pressed an opened-mouth kiss to his neck and slipped a hand up under his shirt to stroke the hardness of his belly.

He closed his eyes, his breath coming faster as her fingers teased over his skin, the tip of her finger dipping into his shallow belly button.

"I can't, Erica." He caught her hand and removed it from under his shirt. "I need to stay focused. I need to keep my grades up."

His rejection hurt and confused her. Although, over the past year, his brush-offs were becoming the norm. Just like his obsession with school.

But she didn't tell him that, instead pointing out, "You always get all A's. You did in high school, and you do in col-

lege." She laughed, but the sound was filled with pride. She touched his cheek. "You're a genius."

"No, I need to study," he insisted. "Some of us don't go to a school where they do arts and crafts all day."

Erica shifted away from him, shock and hurt clenching her chest. "What do you mean by that?"

"Exactly what I said. I need to work. I need to study. I can't slap some paint on a canvas and get an A."

"Is that really what you think of my art? Of what I do?"

Rob hesitated for a moment, then grabbed his book back from where she'd placed it on the coffee table. "You just need to understand that I have commitments. I have goals and dreams."

"So do I. And those commitments and dreams and goals include you as well as my art."

He grunted, stating very eloquently what he thought of her aspirations. He flipped open his book and started to read.

She sat there for a moment, staring at him, seeing his familiar features. His dark, wayward locks, which she knew would curl around her fingers if she touched them. His face, which she knew as well as her own.

But she didn't know Rob anymore. She didn't understand him.

"Robby, you've changed," she finally said, hoping if the words were said out loud, he'd maybe recognize the truth and see the difference in himself.

He looked up from his book. "You're right. I'm growing up."

She knew that was another dig. "You are letting go of everything that was you. That made you alive and fun. Everything that made you smile and laugh. Everything you enjoyed and loved. All because you think only success matters."

His eyes locked with hers, and for just the briefest moment, she thought she'd reached him.

"You don't understand," he finally stated, his voice flat.

"But if I am letting go of everything I loved, then I suppose it would make sense to let you go, too."

His words shocked her to the core. "Are you?"

He glanced down at his book, then back at her. "It might be for the best."

Numbly, she rose from the sofa. She went to the front door, pulled on her boots and her parka. She looked back at Rob, but he wasn't looking at her. His brows were drawn together, his attention returned to the book in his hands. The Christmas tree lights colored the foil words on the cover. Investment Banking.

She walked out of the Marstens' house, the heavy storm door slamming behind her.

The memory of that sound and Donny's voice startled her out of her recollections.

"So, are you going to Portland, too?"

Rob stopped gazing at her and turned to Donny. "Yes, actually, I am."

"You could catch a ride with us."

Erica immediately stepped forward. "Is that such a good idea? I—I mean, the car is going to be pretty crowded with all our luggage and everything."

Not to mention, she didn't know if she could handle being in the closed confines of a car with Rob for several hours. Her head might remember how he'd broken her heart all those years ago, but her body had no recollection of it whatsoever.

Rob raised an eyebrow as if he knew exactly what her excuse had really been about.

"There aren't any more cars available," Donny told her. "I think we can all crowd in."

"Oh," Erica said, distressed—and a little excited at the same time.

Donny cast a look around the lower level. "Alex should be back with those coffees. Let me go see if I can help. I'll be right back."

Erica watched almost desperately as Donny disappeared up the escalator to find his friend.

When she looked back, Rob was standing right next to her. So close she could feel the heat of his large body even through her sweater.

"Surely, it isn't a big deal to give an old friend a ride home," he said, his deep voice like crushed velvet, brushing over her skin.

"No. I—it's just . . . It's fine."

"I won't tell him we were lovers."

Erica frowned. Why *would* he tell Donny? She'd just met Donny and his significant other, Alex, today herself. They had been chatting while their plane was delayed, realized they were going to neighboring towns in Maine, and decided to travel together.

"Okay," she finally said, having no idea how else to reply.

"But maybe *you* should. After all, it's only fair to the guy to let him know you did intend to get married once before."

"I don't really think he'd much care." She gave Rob a bewildered look. "But I suppose I could."

Rob regarded her with those smoldering eyes. "He isn't the jealous-type?"

She started to reply that she didn't have any idea when he reached out and brushed a strand of her hair away from her face. His fingers grazed her cheek, just a faint whisper against her skin, but she felt the caress throughout her entire body, sizzling over her skin, bringing her blood to a sudden boil.

A small gasp escaped her, and she gazed up at him, her eyes wide, startled, both by the fact that he'd touched her and by how she'd reacted to him.

"Would he be jealous if he saw me touching you like this?" His voice was low and a little gruff as he cupped her cheek, his thumb making a slow, breath-stealing sweep over her lower lip. "Would he be angry if I kissed you?"

Before she realized his intent, before she even deciphered

his words, his mouth came over hers, moving over her lips, strong, coaxing.

At first she didn't respond—couldn't. Shock held her frozen. Then his tongue teased the seam of her closed lips, hot and hungry, demanding a response. And she helplessly gave it to him, opening her mouth. His tongue darted in, mingling with hers.

He tasted just as she remembered—like melted dark chocolate, sweet and sinful on her tongue. She moaned, deep in her throat, and opened her mouth wider to him.

Lord, no one on earth kissed like Rob Marsten. No one made her feel like she was about to explode right there in his arms with nothing but his lips seducing her.

She whimpered, overcome by the ache in her breasts, between her thighs. She had missed this, and she wanted more.

Then suddenly, those lips and arms were gone.

She gazed up at him with confusion. Her eyelids felt heavy, her vision unfocused. Her chest rose and fell in harsh pants.

Gradually reality returned. And so had that cool, inscrutable expression Rob had worn when she first saw him. Aside from his breathing being a little uneven, Rob looked totally unaffected. The scorching heat that crackled over her nerve endings and in her veins iced over, leaving her cold and solitary.

She pressed her fingers to her lips, which no longer tingled. Now they only felt swollen and far too sensitive.

Finally she whispered, "Why?"

Why had he done this? She'd worked so hard to forget this man. All the attraction. All the need. And all the ache, both in her body and in her heart.

And with one kiss, he'd brought it all back.

Chapter Three

Rob couldn't answer her. He didn't understand all the strong emotions churning within him. He prided himself on being a composed guy. A person who didn't raise his voice. Didn't lose his cool. He'd learned long ago that success required him to be focused and circumspect. He couldn't afford strong emotions distracting him from his goals.

Yet from the moment his lips had touched hers, he wanted nothing more than to throw her on the floor and make love to her right there.

He breathed in deeply through his nose, trying to calm the overwhelming need that was still chanting for him to go for it. Make love to her. Strip away her layers of clothes and touch the perfect golden skin that he knew lay beneath.

No. He didn't lose control. He didn't. Not to mention the fact he was not the type of guy who touched, much less kissed, another man's woman. And Erica was now someone else's. His Erica was someone else's.

A wave of possessiveness swirled through him, turning the blaze in his veins into an inferno.

He was being crazy. It had been years since they'd broken up. It was ridiculous to think that a woman like Erica hadn't found another man.

His eyes locked on Erica's face, her flushed cheeks, her reddened lips. She looked that way because of him, because of his touch. And damn him, the other man didn't matter. Only one goal, one dream, existed, and that was Erica.

Then he met her eyes, and her wounded, confused expression was like a sucker punch straight to his gut. What the hell was he doing?

He rubbed a hand over his face in a lame attempt to squelch all this burning desire, to banish his possessive thoughts. His fingers shook as he pinched the bridge of his nose.

Finally, still not feeling the least bit calmer, he met her eyes again. "I shouldn't have done that. I'm sorry."

The words sounded unruffled, but inside, his libido still raged, shouting over and over that he absolutely should have done it, and he should do it again.

She pressed her lips together, then nodded. "It's okay. But it can't happen again."

He nodded, too. She was right, of course. Although one part of his anatomy wasn't listening, didn't care, and was quite merrily throbbing in his pants.

"Here we are," Donny called from the down escalator.

Both Rob and Erica jumped and took a step away from each other.

Donny approached them with a paper coffee cup in each hand. Beside him was a tall, muscular blond man with two cups in his hands as well.

"Rob," Donny said with an affable smile. "This is Alex. Alex, this is Rob."

Alex smiled at Rob with blindingly white teeth. "Donny says you're joining us on our blizzard adventure."

Rob nodded. "If that's okay?"

Alex eyed him up and down, then smiled again. "Sure. Here." He offered Rob one of the cups. "We picked you up a latte. Although you look more like a double espresso kind of guy to me."

"Thanks," Rob said, not exactly sure what that meant. He accepted the cup and added, "I really do appreciate the lift."

"Not a problem," Alex said adamantly.

Donny rolled his eyes, and Rob wondered if maybe Donny had somehow sensed that he and Erica had a past. Rob certainly sensed it—the air crackled with awareness.

"Well," Erica said, her voice a little higher than normal, which Rob knew happened when she was nervous. "Let's get this show on the road."

They stood around the rusty, dented, almost white sedan, all four pairs of eyes sporting the same skeptical look. To call the car a "heap" was being generous.

"Well, I guess we can't be choosy. It was the last one," Donny said with a shrug and unlocked the trunk. He tossed his bags in. Alex followed suit. Rob watched as Donny got in the driver's seat and left Erica struggling with a large army-style duffel bag.

What a guy, Rob thought disgustedly.

Rob reached around Erica and took the bag from her, trying to ignore the scent of her perfume, light and citrusy, which drifted around him over the smell of the exhaust-filled parking garage. With more force than necessary, he tossed the bag on top of his Armani suitcase.

"Thanks," she murmured, slipping around him to the back door on the passenger's side.

She was sitting in the back? With him? Then he noticed that Alex was already riding shotgun. Donny and his pal really were quite the gentlemen.

"The door is stuck," Erica told him over the roof, tugging on the handle to demonstrate. "I'll have to slide across."

Rob watched as she pitched in her coat and her huge purse on his side. Then, rather than sit down on the seat and scoot over, she crawled. The faded denim of her jeans shaped the rounded curve of her hips and her ass, and the seam, slightly darker, ran straight between her thighs like an arrow pointing the way to the place he most wanted to touch.

He fought down a frustrated groan and the urge to grab her hips and thrust himself against her. But he couldn't fight down the erection that had calmed but now strained against the confines of his pants.

"Are you coming?" she asked once she was situated on her side of the backseat.

His cock pulsed eagerly at that question. But he just nodded and bowed his tall frame into the small quarters, wincing. In the best of situations, the crowded backseat would have been uncomfortable. At the moment, it was like trying to curl into a ball with a giant metal pole in his trousers.

He groaned, but managed to get himself inside and slam the door.

"Are you okay?" Erica asked.

"Yes," he muttered, his voice tense.

She peered at him a moment longer, then fell back against the seat.

Donny started the car's engine, which rattled to life with a sick cough. "Into the tundra we go."

Once they got outside of Boston and onto Interstate 95, it became very clear why all flights had been cancelled. Snow covered the highway with no lanes visible, just a flat swath of white ahead of them. The road signs were caked over with flying snow, and they had to creep along, the old car creaking with every gust of wind.

But the blizzard raging outside was nothing to the desire tearing through Rob. The backseat was little more than a sensual torture chamber. Every time Erica moved, he felt it. The accidental bump of her knee. The brush of her arm. The nudge of her shoulder. Even the rhythm of her breathing seemed to circle around his body, over his skin. Around and around.

"Come on. Get in."

Erica bit her lip and regarded him dubiously. "There isn't enough room. Your legs will be cramped."

He shifted himself back in the small car shaped like a rocket, demonstrating all the room. "You can fit in front of me."

She hesitated a moment longer, then with a laugh crawled in, sliding down in front of him. He laughed, too, as she wiggled around trying to find the right fit.

Once she was settled, her narrow back against his chest, her bottom tight against his groin, he reached forward and secured the worn black seat belt around the two of them.

"See, perfect," he declared, wrapping his arms around her midriff, pulling her still tighter against him.

She nodded, laughing again. Her blonde curls tickled his chin. He sank his nose into her hair, breathing deeply the fresh scent of her shampoo.

The bell sounded, and the tiny rocket began to orbit, rising up in the air, high above the fairgrounds, through the brisk autumn night.

Rob moved his hands then, once they were above the whole world, catapulting through the air. He slipped them under her jean jacket, under her sweatshirt, until he found her warm, soft skin. Up over her belly, spanning the delicate ridges of her rib cage, until he cupped her small, perfect breasts. Her head fell back against his shoulder, her back arching up to press his hands firmer against her.

He circled her pointed nipples, which prodded hungrily against the satin of her bra. Squeezed them with gentle twists, until she moaned. He groaned, too, at the pressure of her pressed against him. A need that pounded through him.

And even though he desperately wanted to have her completely, to lose himself in her tight heat, it was just as thrilling to touch her, to please her. And to know that she was his and that she loved him.

Slowly, they descended back to earth, and the small car shook to a halt.

Erica didn't move, even as his hands slipped out from

under her clothes and back to her waist. Even as the other passengers exited the ride. She remained against him, her eyes closed, a small, knowing smile curling her lips.

"So that was your plan all along?" she finally murmured.

"Mm-hmm," he agreed with no remorse. He nuzzled her neck.

"You're bad."

"Mm-hmm," he agreed again.

"Let's go again," she sighed.

He laughed and squeezed her. This was what life was about. This was all that mattered. Erica.

"Who sings this song?" Donny asked, snapping Rob out of his memory.

Erica leaned forward, the length of her leg pressed against his. "I can't hear it. I don't think the speakers back here work."

Alex turned it up, and a Christmas tune filled the small car.

Erica tilted her head slightly as she thought. Golden curls clung to her cheeks.

Rob stared at those curls, longing to touch them. To smell them like he'd once done whenever he wanted. Wishing . . . Wishing he had the right. That he'd never given up the right.

"Oh, that's . . . It's on the tip of my tongue."

"It's Sting."

Alex glanced over his shoulder at Rob. "That's it. How could I not remember that? I love, love, love Sting."

"We know," Donny muttered.

Rob frowned at the two men's exchange. Then Erica shifted back beside him, and all he could think about was her leg pressed against the length of his leg. And if that wasn't distracting enough, her hand brushed his where it rested on his knee.

"Sorry," she said, snatching her hand away.

He nodded, not trusting himself to speak.

She finally settled back, keeping her hands and her legs to herself. But she began singing along with the Christmas music.

A soft, sweet sound drifting over him—making him crazy. Good lord, even the sound of her voice was enough to make him horny as hell.

"Do you have to do that?" he suddenly barked.

She straightened, her eyes wide. "Do what?"

"Sing!"

Chapter Four

Erica frowned at Rob. She'd only been singing to get her mind off the fact that she was practically being forced to sit on the man's lap. A fact that was slowly driving her overexcited body insane, and was conjuring lots of very vivid images of doing more than sitting on him.

But she was trying her best to be polite, so he certainly could try to do the same.

Instead of telling him so, she said, "Yes, I can stop singing."

"I think you have a nice voice," Donny told her.

"It was good," Alex agreed.

"Thank you." She appreciated her new friends' support.

"Perhaps not as good as Sting," Donny added pointedly.

"Did I say that?" Alex snapped.

Erica, ever the peacemaker, promptly shifted forward on the seat to stop the two men's bickering. "I think you sort of look like Sting, Donny."

"I do?" The man seemed pleased.

She nodded, scooting further up on the seat. Suddenly, Rob's large hands gripped her hips, his fingers holding her still.

"Stop," he hissed, his mouth right next to her ear.

She could feel his hard body close behind her, and despite the earlier rudeness and the irritation she now heard in his voice, her body reacted. Her nipples hardened, an excruciating rasp against the lace of her bra.

Annoyance rose in her, both at his demand and at her reaction to his touch. "Stop doing what?" she hissed back, not keeping her voice quite as low.

"Stop wiggling."

She could hardly wiggle with her hips braced between his huge, strong hands.

"*My, what big hands you have.*" Erica giggled as she squirmed away from Rob.

He caught her ankle and dragged her back across the sheets toward him. She continued to giggle until the hand that had clasped her ankle slid slowly up over her calf, over her knee, up her inner thigh, until it reached the triangle of curls at the apex of her legs.

He shaped his palm to her mound and murmured in a deliciously evil voice, "Better to touch you with."

She propped herself up on her elbows and watched as Rob's fingers parted her, stroking her damp, sensitive flesh. With slow caresses, he teased her clitoris, each sweep and swirl of his fingertip exquisite torture.

When he pushed the length of his finger deep inside her, she fell back on the mattress, writhing against him. "Rob!"

He smiled at her, the curl of his wide mouth and the deepening of his dimple sinfully sexy.

"Come for me, Erica."

She moaned, as his hand worked magic, plunging her toward release. Colors whirled behind her closed eyelids. Shades of red and pink. The colors of her passion.

Then his thumb increased its speed against her clitoris, and his finger bent inside her, stroking the spot only he knew how to find. Instantly, the reds and pinks exploded into bursts of brilliant orange. She cried out as wave after wave of release crashed over her.

She barely registered Rob's hands leaving her until she felt his thick penis sliding into her, filling her to her womb. The orange intensified, the waves pounded.

But he didn't move inside her, once she was full of his hard flesh. Her muscles pulsed around his erection, gripping him, hungry to stroke him. But still he didn't move.

She opened her eyes to find him levered over her, his weight braced on his arms, the muscles of his shoulders and biceps bulging.

He smiled down at her, a strained half-smile.

She smiled back, bobbing her hips, stroking his penis as much as his pinning position would allow.

His smile faded, and he groaned deep in his throat.

She did it again, searing, wet flesh fondling hot, rigid flesh. This time he groaned loudly.

She flexed again. "My," she said, her own renewing arousal making her voice breathy, "what a big penis you have."

He grinned then, his dimple deep and so very sexy. "The better to do this with."

He pulled his erection almost completely from her body, then thrust it back in.

She moaned, arching up against him, feeling him throughout her whole body. Yes! Definitely better. The best. The very best.

Erica whimpered as the memory and his hands holding her now made her nipples throb and her loins ache. She couldn't handle this.

She tried to wriggle out of his grip. How dare he hold her like this and boss her around like some caveman. And how dare she find it arousing. This was madness.

"I'm not kidding, Erica," he said, his voice low, his hot breath on her ear. "If you keep moving, I swear . . ."

"You swear what?" She managed to keep her voice steady and to not lean back against his muscled chest like her body was urging her to.

"I swear, I'll pull you right onto my lap and kiss you senseless." The hands on her hips tightened, shooting aching need straight to the pit of her belly and lower. "And I don't give a damn if your fiancé is in the car to see it."

"Fiancé?" the two men in the front seat cried out in unison. The car slowed sharply, then fishtailed. Then the Hire a Heap spun, revolving in a large, almost graceful circle in the center of the empty highway, before sliding to a jarring halt in a snowbank.

Erica slammed against Rob with an *oof*. His arms came around her, pulling her against that solid, muscular chest that she'd been trying to avoid. Shockwaves that had nothing to do with the accident vibrated through her.

"Are you okay?" he asked, his voice sharp, but this time with something that sounded distinctly like concern.

She pushed away from him, even though the car was tipped at a slight angle, which made sliding up the slippery vinyl seat difficult.

"I'm fine." Her voice held all the irritation his had lost.

"Are you two all right?" he asked the men in the front.

"Yes," they both breathed. Then the car fell silent as if no one knew how to react to the chain of events.

"Listen," Rob finally said, his voice quiet and full of remorse. "Donny, I had no right to say what I did. Erica and I have a past, and seeing her again brought back a lot of emotions. But I—I wish the two of you every happiness. You have yourself a wonderful woman."

"Rob," Donny started, twisting in his seat to peer over the headrest.

But Erica interrupted. "Let me out!"

She needed air. She needed to get away from this situation. It was ludicrous, but it was also—infuriating!

When no one moved, she said it again, her angry voice deafening in the now-quiet car. "Let me out! Now!"

Rob obeyed, opening the door and holding it open against the gusting wind so she could slide out.

The cold air and clinging, icy snow felt good on her flushed skin. She stepped past Rob and leaned against the snowbound car, pulling in deep breaths, trying to calm her anger, her hurt, and her desire.

"Erica, I never meant—"

She spun toward him.

"Do you have any idea what you've done to me?" she shouted, the wind stealing away some of the volume.

"I know," he said.

She laughed bitterly. "You don't have a clue."

"I—"

"No!" She didn't want to hear his words, his hollow words. Words apologizing for something that hadn't actually happened. Words that completely ignored what had.

She marched toward him, her heeled boots slipping in the snow. "You come back into my life and, within minutes, turn it completely upside down. Do you know how long it took to forget you? To push you into a dark, faraway corner of my mind where I could no longer see your face or hear your voice?"

He opened his mouth to speak, but she didn't let him.

"But I did it. I moved on," she said, her voice breaking. She blinked, but the tears froze in her eyes. She forced her voice to remain even as she continued. "I've made a new life for myself, and you have the nerve to think you can waltz back in and destroy that?"

"I hope you—and Donny can forgive me," he said, the wind tearing at the low words. But she heard him, and her fury rose again.

"He's gay, Rob," she shouted. "Gay. Alex is his partner."

Rob's eyes widened, then he glanced through the open car door. Both Donny and Alex peeked over the seat backs.

Donny smiled lamely.

Alex nodded sheepishly.

"Then you're not getting married?" Rob said.

Erica stared at him for a minute, and although she was not a violent person, she shoved him. He stumbled, catching himself on the door frame of the car before he fell.

"No, I'm not getting married! But that doesn't matter! You

can't toy with my life and then walk away again. You don't get to be the one who says, 'Sorry, I have goals and dreams, babe.' Not again!"

She spun and began walking. She had no idea where she was going. She just needed to leave. To get away from the only man who'd ever made her feel—both love and hate.

She high-stepped through the snow. Her boots, sturdy but more fashionable than functional, slipped several times. But not even that tempered her determination to get away from Rob.

She made it a few feet before strong arms captured her from behind, lifting her bodily.

"Let me go," she screamed, flailing with her elbows and her feet. "Just let me go."

He held her fast, taking her hits, but not loosening his grip. Finally, exhausted, she fell limp in his arms.

"Erica, I'm sorry." He nuzzled her neck, his lips brushing the cool skin of her neck. "I'm so sorry."

She heard him, but she didn't respond. She had no idea what to say. Part of her just wanted to go back, back to the airport, back to before she saw him again. Back to when she could believe she'd gotten over him.

Another part wanted to turn in his arms and kiss the breath out of him. Wanted to have him make love to her right there in the raging snowstorm. She wanted to feel like she had once. Feel the way only Rob could make her feel.

She started to turn, started to ask him to do that. But before she could fully face him, he scooped her up in his arms and plodded through the drifts back to the car. Bracing her against his hard chest, he managed to get the door open and slide her onto the seat. He followed her in, reaching across her to find her coat. Tenderly, he tucked the suede and faux fur over her.

Donny and Alex still peered over the seats like stunned owls.

Rob watched Erica for a moment, his eyes dark and filled with worry.

She started to speak, but the words wouldn't come. Instead, she closed her eyes, her body feeling weary, her outburst having exhausted her.

"Will the car start again?" Rob asked Donny.

Erica heard the vinyl creak as Donny turned back to the steering wheel. He twisted the key in the ignition, and the engine rumbled and growled, but after several attempts refused to turn over.

"It's dead," Donny finally pronounced.

"Shit," Rob muttered. "We'll freeze if we stay here."

Erica shivered. Even though she knew she had to be cold, that her clothing must be damp from the melting snow, she didn't really feel cold. It was the numbness inside her that caused her to shiver again.

"What is that up ahead?" Alex pointed to a light barely visible through the blowing snow.

Rob opened his door and stepped out with one foot to see better. He stuck his head back inside. "It looks like it might be a hotel."

"Could we be that lucky?" Donny said in disbelief.

"Well, it's definitely something. Let's go," Rob stated.

Erica slid across the seat, tugging on her coat and scooping up her purse as she went. Rob held out his hand to help her. She hesitated, then accepted it, placing her icy fingers in his warm ones. He squeezed them, and even after they were outside, he held them fast.

She didn't fight him. It was too late to fight. Even after all the memories and the pain, even after her furious outburst, her attraction still survived.

Chapter Five

Rob gripped Erica's fingers, feeling as though it was his only, his last, connection with her. Since their fight, she'd remained silent as the foursome trudged through the deep snow. She didn't look at him, didn't acknowledge him. So he held her fingers. As long as he had those, she couldn't pull away completely.

The wind whipped, slashing biting snow against their faces. He tried to shield Erica as much as he could, but it was impossible. Like it was impossible to ignore the truth in her angry words. He had been the one to walk away from her. Or rather, to let her walk away.

Bang.

The door. He pretended to keep reading his book, but the words blurred. What had he done?

He tossed aside his book and crossed to the window. Erica was walking down the sidewalk as fast as the snow and her cumbersome boots would allow her.

She wasn't gone yet. He could call her back. Apologize. Try to explain to her that he needed to be a success. He needed to do better than his parents, who struggled every day to make ends meet.

No, she should realize that. She should see that his success was important. That money was important. She could go to her artsy little college, and paint and sculpt, and not worry about the future. He couldn't.

Erica disappeared around the corner, and the street was empty.

He still couldn't stop looking out the frost-covered glass, couldn't stop staring at her boot prints notching the snow. But he finally did look away, and returned to the couch. He picked up his book and determinedly began to read. He was right. Success was the most important thing. Far more important than silly love.

Silly love.

He glanced at Erica, her shoulders hunched forward against the cold. Ironic that once again, she was trekking through the snow, hating him.

Hate. She should hate him, but God, he hoped she didn't. He didn't want that. But he was afraid of what he did want.

"It *is* a hotel," Alex cried out, pointing ahead. A white building with two levels and an orange neon vacancy sign rose out of the snow, welcoming them.

Rob squeezed Erica's cold fingers again. "Looks like we're going to make it."

She peeked up at him. Snow clung to her long amber lashes. Underneath, her hazel eyes were dark and hurt, but she smiled. "Yep."

He fought the urge to pull her into his arms. To kiss her. She was offering a truce. That was the Erica he knew—and loved. He'd take it and make sure he never hurt her again.

"I have good news, and I have bad news," Rob said, approaching Erica where she sat clutching a Styrofoam coffee cup in her reddened hands.

"Good first," she said, taking another sip of the coffee, then grimacing at the taste.

Damn, she looked cute, her small nose crinkled, her cheeks rosy, and her hair tangled.

Focus. "They have rooms."

"And?"

"They only have two."

"Oh."

From that one word, Rob couldn't tell how she felt about the prospect of sharing a room. He didn't imagine she was too thrilled.

"But each room has two beds, so I can bunk up with Donny and Alex for the night." Not his first choice, to say the very least.

Erica smiled, amusement dancing in her eyes. "For a guy who travels in a business suit, you're pretty open-minded."

"What's that supposed to mean?" He frowned, trying to look offended. "Are you saying I look uptight?"

She shook her head, but she still grinned. "I didn't say that."

"You do think I'm uptight."

"No, I don't."

"What's wrong with traveling in a suit?"

"Not a thing," Erica assured him, but there was a hint of a smile still on her lips.

"This is an expensive suit."

"I'm sure it is."

Rob studied her for a moment. She still smiled at him, her eyes never going to his clothes. His Kenneth Cole, limited edition. Because it didn't matter to her. He could be wearing bargain bin castoffs, and she wouldn't care. Money didn't impress her. It never had.

"You can room with me."

At first, because he was caught in his own thoughts, he believed he misheard her. But when he realized he hadn't, his heart skittered around in circles like an excited dog.

"Thank you," he said sincerely. He had a few more hours to be with her.

"Well, I don't think you'd get a lot of rest with them." She gestured to Donny and Alex with a jerk of her head.

The couple stood on the other side of the lobby, bickering in hushed tones.

"You are with me because I look like Sting, aren't you?"

Alex rolled his eyes. "You don't look like Sting."

Donny huffed, that comment not making him happy either. "If I had to pick out anyone you look like, it would be Niles from *Frasier.*"

Donny gasped, then headed toward the stairs.

"Niles is cute," Alex insisted, following him.

"You think everyone is cute." Both men disappeared up to the second level.

"I don't think your Sting comment soothed things over as well as you'd hoped it would," Rob said, very happy that it hadn't. Not because he wanted Donny and Alex to spend their Christmas Eve fighting, but because he wanted to spend his with Erica.

"Well, now that Alex said it, he does look a bit like that guy from *Frasier.*" She chuckled.

"So you're okay about us sharing a room?"

Her smile faded, but she nodded without hesitation. "There are two beds?"

"Yes."

She rose, and a violent shiver shook her. "Fine. Besides, all I can think about is getting out of these wet clothes and into a warm bed.

Rob's body reacted immediately. Erica naked, in the bed right next to his. Shit, he was going to die of a heart attack.

Erica could feel Rob behind her, following her up the stairs to their room. Their room. A room where they both would spend the night.

With each step, another memory of making love with Rob flashed through her mind. The perfection of their embraces. The satisfaction and contentment she'd never been able to duplicate since. She did want that again, with him, even if for one last time.

Erica waited at the door of their room. Rob slid the key card into the slot, then pulled it back out rapidly. In again, and out. The light on the door handle turned green, and the lock clicked.

As far as erotic symbolism went, that definitely wasn't the best, but it didn't take much to get her hot and bothered at the moment.

But still, she skirted far around him as she entered the generic room with its standard two double beds, chair and table in the corner, and armoire. She went toward the bed closest to the door and tossed her purse down. Then she wandered over to examine the print on the wall, the usual unexciting artwork that hotels usually contained. The commonness of her surroundings only made her more aware of the one thing in the room that was so beyond ordinary.

"Not exactly a Toulouse-Lautrec, is it?"

She swung around, surprised he still remembered one of her favorite artists.

He leaned against the wall, his arms crossed over his chest, looking intensely masculine and . . . delicious.

"No," she murmured, unable to stop admiring him. The broadness of his shoulders, the leanness of his hips.

"Are you still painting?"

She nodded, wishing she had her paints right now. She would paint him. The way the single lamp in the room created shadows across his face, showing the cut of his jawline, the straightness of his nose, and emphasized the compelling darkness of his eyes.

She swallowed. "Yes, as much as I can. I'm showing in a few galleries now. And I'm very busy at the museum."

"Museum?"

"I work at the Art Institute of Chicago."

His eyes widened in surprise, and she immediately assumed that he hadn't expected her to use her art history degree to get a "real" job. After all, she did just slap paint on a canvas.

So she was confused when he said, "You live in Chicago?"

"Yes. I have for almost five years."

He laughed. "That's amazing. I just moved to Chicago about four months ago. I work at an investment firm near Grant Park."

Now it was her turn to be surprised. "Wow, we're practically neighbors."

He grinned, but she couldn't quite return the gesture. She knew tonight was going to be torture—but she thought short-lived torture. Now, how was she going to live in the same city, knowing he was so nearby?

His smiled faded, the dimple sinking back into hiding. "You've got to be freezing. Why don't you take a hot shower?"

"Right. Right. That's a good idea." She started back toward where he stood, his shoulder still resting on the wall. The bathroom door waited just on the other side of his tall, hard body.

She hesitated, then twisted sideways to squeeze past him, afraid if she rubbed against him, she wouldn't be able to stop. But even as careful as she was being, his big body took up too much of the hallway, and her shoulder grazed his arm.

"Sorr—" She didn't get the chance to finish her apology, as she found herself pulled against his chest, his hands splayed across her back.

She squeaked, startled at his abrupt movement and her immediate roaring need.

"Erica, I didn't intend to turn your life upside down." His voice sounded gruff; the rough resonance rasped over her skin, adding excruciatingly to her hunger. "I . . ."

His Adam's apple bobbed as he swallowed, his eyes dark, nearly black. "I saw you, and you were so beautiful, more beautiful now than I remembered. And I couldn't think of anything other than touching you. I shouldn't have kissed you, but I couldn't stop myself."

She stared back at him, her whole body crying out for him to do it again. She wanted the hands that he held motionless on her back to move, to slip under her wet sweater to caress the chilled skin underneath, heating her inside and out. Then she wanted those same hands to flick open her damp jeans to stroke the flesh between her thighs, which she knew was equally damp, but not from melted snow.

She trembled, pure need bursting through her like shivery shards of electric energy.

"You're frozen," he said, misinterpreting the tremor. He released her. "Go get that hot shower."

She nodded absently and stumbled into the small bathroom. She glanced back at him. Rob watched her, his eyes smoldering, his lips set in a grim line.

He nodded at her and pushed off the wall, wandering into the room, his broad back to her.

She closed the door gently. The click of the latch echoed off the tile walls and grated in her ears. A loud reality that she was on one side and Rob was on the other.

Leaning on the sink counter, she breathed in deeply, but the rush of oxygen only fed the heat in her veins. God, she wanted him.

Finally, she did manage to calm herself enough to leave the support of the counter and turn on the water. Steam filled the room as she stripped off her clothes, each article clinging to her as if it knew she shouldn't even be thinking about sleeping with Rob. But she was. She was considering that idea very seriously.

She gasped as she stepped under the warm water, the droplets streaming over her sensitive skin, beading on her swollen nipples.

"Rob," she murmured, the sound ragged, desperate.

"Yes?"

She jumped, then clutched the shower curtain to peek out at him. He stood in the doorway, a blue blanket gripped in his hand.

He held it up. "I was just sneaking in to leave this for you. I figured your clothes would be too wet to put back on."

"Oh." *Ask him to join you. Order him to.*

"I'll leave it right here." He pointed to the counter, then placed the blanket there, his gaze never leaving her.

"Thanks," she mumbled.

"Okay. I'll let you enjoy your shower." His dark eyes burned as they glanced at the spot where she grasped the shower curtain, then snapped back up to her face.

"Okay," he repeated. Then he nodded and backed out of the steam-filled room.

Stop him! Say something!

The door clicked shut, again jarring and discordant.

She dropped the curtain back into place, turned the nozzle, letting the water pelt her.

"You coward," she muttered to herself.

Chapter Six

Rob paced the small room, listening to the muffled splash of the water from the other side of the wall. He could visualize Erica standing nude under the cascade, rubbing soap over her silky, wet skin. The way the bubbles would slide down over her rounded breasts. Then slip lower, down across the slight curve of her belly, lower still into the curls below.

"Shit," he growled, and ran a frustrated hand over his face. Control. Focus.

His cock pulsed in his pants, mocking his chant, telling him there was no way in hell he'd be able to focus on anything but Erica and his arousal.

Irritated with his wayward body, he shrugged off his suit coat, then unbuttoned his shirt. Once he was stripped down to his cotton boxers, he sat on the bed. He glanced down at his crotch. His cock bulged against the thin fabric, threatening to escape the slit along the front.

He threw back the covers on the bed and slipped under. The sheet and comforter were an insubstantial armor to put between himself and Erica, but it would have to do.

She'd made it clear in their fight that she'd forgotten him. That she'd moved on, and she wanted to keep it that way. He wouldn't do anything to upset her again. She deserved that. And he should go back to the life he'd so single-mindedly built. His new job, his penthouse apartment, his . . . His career was enough.

He reached for the radio alarm clock on the nightstand between the two beds. He flicked the dial on and fiddled with the stations until he found Christmas music.

Surely thoughts of a fat man dressed in red, and reindeer with glowing noses, and talking snowmen—not to mention the birth of Christ—would be enough to take the edge off his carnal thoughts.

As he flopped back onto the pillow, the sound of "Hark! The Herald Angels Sing" filled the room. The memory of Erica singing in the car popped into his mind.

Fortunately, the song ended quickly, only to go into one of the many versions of "This Christmas," in which the singer declares that he is going to know her better—this Christmas.

He groaned, tempted to cover his ears with the pillow. Even Christmas music seemed determined to drive his libido and imagination into overdrive.

As he leaned over to flip the radio off, the shower stopped.

He sat up and stared toward the bathroom. Now, the real torture was going to start.

Several minutes later, the door creaked open. Erica stepped out, shrouded from her neck to the tops of her narrow feet in fuzzy blue blanket.

But he knew what she had on under that thick material. Absolutely nothing. Again, he almost groaned.

Erica stayed by the bathroom, her hand still on the door as if she were debating whether to dart back in and lock the door behind her.

Rob didn't doubt for one minute that he was watching her like he was ready to pounce. He settled back against the pillow, trying to show her he would behave. Well, some parts of him would behave. Another part prodded the covers—pushing for the pounce.

"You look—comfortable," she said, her voice sounding a little unsteady as she shuffled into the room.

Not really, he thought, casting a look down at his crotch, making sure the comforter wasn't pitched like a tent. When he looked back at Erica, she was struggling with the covers on her bed, trying to spread them back while keeping her makeshift muumuu in place. He caught a glimpse of a smooth, curved shoulder and one of her long, shapely leg from her ankle up to her silky thigh, before she finally managed to crawl under the comforter.

She fluffed her pillow, punching the defenseless thing with great vigor. Suddenly she stopped and turned her gaze to him.

"I—I have a suggestion. And if you think it's inappropriate, you can certainly tell me. But—here it is." She took a deep breath, bracing those lovely shoulders under the fuzzy blue. "You—you said that back at the airport, you couldn't help but touch me. Well, to be honest, I've wanted to touch you, too." Her eyes dropped to his bare chest, and she bit her lower lip. He imagined nipping her lip in just the same fashion. Nibbling their fullness. Tasting their ripe softness. But he forced his eyes to meet hers as she continued.

"Rob, I want it very much."

She stared at him, her eyes wide as if she couldn't believe she'd actually told him of her desire. He couldn't quite believe it either. Had he fallen asleep while she was in the shower, and this was just a dream? Had he died and gone to heaven?

"I shouldn't have said that," she said quickly, not looking at him, instead plucking at her blanket. "It's just that this night has been so—emotional. And seeing you has brought back so many memories. I—I don't want things to be awkward. And I don't want you to think that I—"

As Erica rambled on, Rob threw back the covers and rose, striding the short distance to her bed.

She lifted her head, her mouth snapping shut when she saw him, towering over her, wearing nothing but some now very ill-fitting boxers and a smile.

"I'm not thinking anything," he said, "other than that I

want you, and if you want me, too—well, we should do something about that."

He reached for the covers, tossing them back. Then he tugged at the blanket that enveloped her. The edges peeled away like she was his very own Christmas gift. Carefully, he spread the blanket open until she lay bare before him, all shower-fresh skin and breathtaking curves.

"Rob," she whispered as he gazed at her.

"You are so beautiful." He couldn't remember anyone looking as beautiful as this woman. The gentle swell of her breasts topped with nipples the color of sugarplums. The flare of her hips. The curve of her stomach, indented by a small belly button. The dark golden curls at the juncture of her thighs. Hell, even the tiny dimples in her knees. She was flawless.

Then his eyes rose to her face, and it was the expression in her eyes that truly stole his ability to breathe. Their golden green depths were bright with hunger—hunger for him.

He crawled onto the mattress and pressed a kiss to her dimpled knee. Then he worked his way up to her soft belly, sampling her golden skin as he went. He lingered at her sweet breasts, licking those sugary nipples, toying with their delicious hardness.

Erica whimpered, her body squirming under his, her soft skin a silken friction against his. Her hands kneaded the muscles of his shoulders and back. Her legs tangled with his, sliding up and down their length.

His cock, still confined in his boxers, throbbed in response to the repeated strokes of skin against skin.

He ignored it, ignored his need. He was more desperate to hear Erica's moans of satisfaction. To rediscover all the places on her luscious body that made her scream.

But first, he had to taste her mouth again. To kiss the only woman who could make him vibrate with just the pressure of her mouth and the flick of her tongue.

He captured her lips, tasting her heat. She responded with a pleased moan and sank her fingers into his hair, clutching him, pulling him closer. They tasted each other, the need building in them both, their embrace becoming more needy, more fierce. Her hips rocked against him, her legs bending to cradle his hips, to invite him in.

He pulled away, trying to slow the pace, to make this last.

"Let's see what I remember," he said, then kissed her neck. At a point near her earlobe, he licked her. The tip of his tongue teasing the small spot.

She rewarded him with a gasp and a shiver.

He smiled against her neck, then slid down her body.

"And wasn't here?" He nipped the soft, fragile skin at the side of her stomach, just above her hipbone.

She cried out, her hands knotting into his hair, her hips lifting off the bed.

"Rob, you're killing me!"

"Really?" He nibbled her again. She jumped again, gasping.

He grinned, then slid lower. He stopped between her thighs, resting his chin lightly on the springy curls there.

"And as I recall, I used to do something down here that really made you scream."

She stared down the length of her body to him, her eyes heavy-lidded with passion, her lips parted, rosy and damp.

"You are evil, do you know that?" There was anticipation rather than reproach in her breathy voice.

He beamed, then shifted to nudge her legs wider apart. He pressed his mouth to the curls and the moist heat hidden just beyond them. His tongue delved, slipping deeper, lapping over the hot, silky flesh, finding the tiny seed of her clitoris.

She gasped as he stroked it, using the tip of his tongue to flick over her again and again. He spread her even wider, then his lips joined his tongue, suckling her.

Her hips writhed against him. Her fingers dug into his shoulders. Her legs locked around his torso. She groaned, the sound so deep within her, he swore he could feel the vibration against his tongue.

He groaned, too, her response agonizingly arousing. It was a heady experience, that he could make her feel this way. That he could bring this gorgeous woman to the brink of her sanity.

He drew on her clitoris again, then he grazed the swollen nub, just a fleeting scrape, with the edge of his teeth. And just like that, she screamed and bucked under him, her orgasm shuddering through her in repeated waves. He continued to taste her until her shudders diminished.

He skimmed back up her body.

"Hmm, I'm not sure. Was that the right spot?"

She cuffed his arm and then laughed, the sound still shaky from her release. "Yes, you conceited oaf, you. That was definitely the right spot."

He grinned and tenderly caressed her wild curls from her cheeks. God, had he ever enjoyed anyone or anything more than this woman?

"But before you get too sure of yourself," she said with a devilish grin of her own. "You did forget one spot. One very, very important spot."

"I did?"

She nodded, and she pushed at his shoulders so he would rise a little, and she snaked her hand down between their bodies. She pushed at the waistband of his boxers.

"But I think you'll need to lose these to get there."

He rolled off her so she could work the clothing down his hips.

When the boxers were cast away, he started to move back on top of her.

"Oh, no," she said. "You got to look at me, so I get to look at you."

She pushed him back on the mattress, and her eyes and her hands began to explore his body. Laying her full palms on his burning skin, she brushed down over his chest. Over his stomach, fanning out to shape the hard muscle of his thighs.

"I seem to recall you had a few favorite spots, too," she

murmured, her fingertips grazing the thick curls around his arousal.

"When you touch me, everywhere is a favorite spot," he assured her raggedly.

She laughed, then pressed open-mouthed kisses over his chest, teasing his nipples, before traveling lower. His stomach tightened, need contracting his muscles as taut as a bow, as she dipped her tongue into his navel, then licked a hot path down toward his erection.

She raised her head then, but her hands circled him, holding his cock in a firm, wonderfully torturous grip. Her mouth lowered, her lips pressing to the tip in a heart-stopping kiss. Then he watched as one of her hands released him, only to be replaced by the slow glide of her mouth over him.

"Oh, God. Erica!" he breathed, his head falling back on the pillow as her hot, wet mouth moved up and down him. Her tongue licking him like he was her own personal candy cane.

With each steamy stroke, she urged him closer to the edge. Toward a chasm of glorious release. But he didn't want that. Not this time. Not for the first, and maybe the last, time that he would ever make love to her again.

Quickly, he reached forward and captured her, lifting her bodily so she was fully on top of him, face-to-face.

Shock made her eyes impossibly big. "Did I do something wrong?"

He laughed at that. If she only had a clue. "No, you did it too right."

He rolled and pinned her under him.

"I have to be inside you," he muttered roughly. "I have to feel you tight and hot around me."

Her eyes still wide, she nodded. "Yes."

He positioned himself to enter her, the head of his penis nuzzled by the curls of her sex, when somehow, a moment of reality seeped into his passion-frenzied mind.

"Contraceptives?"

She blinked up at him as if he was a lunatic. "What?"

"Do you have any condoms?"

She immediately shook her head. "No."

"Me neither. Are you on the pill?"

She gave him a pained look, then shook her head again.

He groaned, dropping his forehead to hers. This was absolute torture.

Then he raised his head. "Donny and Alex. Maybe they have some condoms."

"You would go ask them?"

"To make love with you? I'd start knocking on doors one by one all the way down the hallway until I found some."

Her eyes filled with amused dismay. "Go ask Donny and Alex first."

He leaped off the bed, tugged on his cold, wet trousers, and rushed out of the room.

It took him only a few moments to locate Donny and Alex's room and to pound on their door.

After a few moments more, the lock clicked and the door opened. A sleepy Donny stood there, annoyance on his face until he recognized who it was.

"Hi," Rob greeted. "You wouldn't happen to have a couple of condoms, would you?"

Donny stared at him, then grinned. "Well, well, someone is having a Merry Christmas."

"Yes," he agreed wholeheartedly. The best Christmas he'd had in years.

"Wait a minute." Donny let the door swing shut.

Rob waited, tapping his bare foot on the hallway carpet.

After what seemed like an eternity, the door opened again. "You're in luck." He held up a strip of three condoms.

Rob immediately grabbed them. "Thanks. You're a lifesaver."

Donny sighed. "Well, at least someone is having a nice Christmas. Have fun."

Rob practically sprinted back to his room. He planned to have more than fun.

When he entered the room, Erica still waited on the bed. Her bare skin glowed in the lamplight, her hair a golden halo against the pillow.

She levered herself up on her elbow as he walked toward the bed. "That was quick."

"Not quick enough," he said, unfastening his trousers, letting them fall to the floor.

"Did you get one?"

"No," he said. "I got three."

She grinned as he held them up. "I knew I liked those guys."

"They are definitely growing on me, too," he agreed. Then he crawled up her body, done thinking about his new gay pals. Done thinking about anything but Erica.

His lips found hers, pressing her back against the pillows, showing her with his tongue how he longed to enter her body.

She groaned, her arms coming around his neck, then roaming down his back to his buttocks.

Despite the slight delay, his body was still ready. And every touch made him feel like he would combust if he didn't get inside her—soon.

As if she'd read his mind, she spread her legs, cradling him. "Rob, please. I need you now."

She ripped open one of the condom wrappers, and they rolled the latex down his erection, her fingers holding it, his hands guiding her.

Positioning himself over her again, he entered her with a slow, steady glide of his hips.

"Rob," she gasped, arching her back. "Oh, my God!"

Then they began to move, their motions synchronized. Each instinctively knowing what the other needed. Rob thrust over and over, her body clasping him in a precise fit. His hardness filling her completely.

As if they had been made for each other. Only each other.

"Rob," she moaned, her breath coming in pants. "Now! Now!"

She spasmed around him. Contracting muscles, searing heat.

His body answered her, his orgasm ripping through him, violent and overwhelming. And nothing short of heaven.

Erica curled against Rob, her hand stroking up and down his belly, the fine hair bisecting his stomach soft against her fingertips, the muscles underneath hard. He felt wonderful.

She felt wonderful. More satisfied, more content than she had since—the last time she'd made love with him.

As if he were reading her mind, he suddenly asked, "Have you dated much—I mean over the years?"

She rested her chin on his chest to look at him. He looked sinfully tousled, his dark hair curling over his forehead, his eyes dark and intent. She forced herself to stop admiring him and to focus on his question.

"A bit. I had two relationships that were pretty steady. But nothing that ever got too serious." She'd never let them. She'd always held herself back. Until this moment, she'd have said her hesitation to commit was because she was being choosy, making sure everything was perfect. Now, she realized, it was because she just couldn't give her heart. Rob had it—even when she believed he was forgotten.

"What about you? Any close calls?"

He smiled at her wording. "No. I was too busy with my work to get serious. Just casual dating."

"And casual sex?" The question was out of her mouth before she thought better of it. "You don't have to answer that."

He lifted his head, his expression serious. "No. That's a valid question. I haven't been a monk over the years, but I tended to date women who knew where I stood, and who were fine with that arrangement."

Erica nodded, then turned her face away from his, pressing her cheek to his chest. She wished she'd never asked. She didn't want to think about Rob with other women. And she didn't like that she had just joined the ranks of those ladies. A woman who knew the score—who knew that she could never have his heart the way his career and his success did.

204 / *Kathy Love*

His hands caught her under the arms, and she found herself pulled up fully onto his chest, her face aligned with his.

"I need to kiss you," he stated, lifting his head off the pillow so he could capture her mouth. He moved his hands from her arms to the sides of her head, pulling her harder to him, deepening the kiss. His mouth devouring hers. A possessive kiss, a demanding kiss.

When he finally released her, her heart was racing, her blood pounding. And all the places he'd just finished lavishing great attention on throbbed for more of his undivided attention.

"I could spend the rest of my life right here with you," he murmured, stealing another kiss.

His words aroused her to the point of pain. How she wished he truly meant those words. But she nestled her head under his chin and allowed herself to bask in his words all the same. "Me, too."

The radio broadcaster announced that Santa had been sighted over the area, and that all the local boys and girls would be getting the presents on their Christmas lists.

Erica felt like she'd almost gotten hers. She'd gotten Rob, not for forever, like she wanted, but she wasn't going to dwell on that now. She still had the rest of the night to enjoy her gift.

"It's our song," Rob said, drawing her back from her thoughts.

She listened. "There's No Place Like Home for the Holidays" by Perry Como. She laughed, picking up her head to grin at him. "We had to be the only teenagers in the eighties who lost our virginity to Perry Como."

He grinned, too, his dimple deep and so adorable. "Even now, this song makes me horny." To demonstrate, he rubbed his pelvis against her. His very erect penis nudged the juncture of her thighs.

She moaned, wriggling down just a bit to better position herself against him.

"I need to make love to you again," he murmured against

her ear, the vibration of his voice exciting every nerve ending in her body. "I need to be inside you."

She whimpered, but didn't waste any time and reached for another condom. She straddled him, her legs on either side of his narrow hips. Rising up, she rolled the latex down his girth, then positioned him so the head of his penis spread her labia.

She hovered there, giving him just a hint of the wet heat that soon would surround him, and in turn, teasing herself with a sample of the heavy, hard thickness that would soon fill her. Perfect and right.

"Erica," he murmured, watching her perched above him. His eyes roamed over her face, her breasts, and her belly, down to where they made contact but didn't quite join. "God, you are gorgeous." He smoothed his hands up the fronts of her thighs.

His words made her heart swell, her vagina constrict. She lowered herself a fraction of an inch. The head entered her, stretching her.

He groaned, jerking his hips slightly to slide deeper.

"What do you think you're doing?" she asked with feigned sternness, although the effect was not what she hoped, as her breathing was uneven with want.

"Nothing," he said contritely, dropping his hips back against the mattress.

"Good boy. Santa will be pleased that you're such a good boy."

"Oh, Santa is definitely pleased with me." His hands massaged the tops of her thighs. "Very pleased."

She smiled and slipped down a little more. "Good."

He closed his eyes, a ragged, needy moan escaping his parted lips.

Another fraction of an inch, but still she didn't accept his full length. Then a bit more.

Rob growled, his eyes dark and ravenous. She grinned down at him, feeling powerful that she could drive him so mad.

Then the hands on her thighs left, one sliding up to her breast, the other slipping between her thighs. He found her pebbled clitoris, pressing a fingertip again the nub. Need shot through her.

Then his other hand began to pluck at her distended nipple, in repeated gentle, rolling squeezes. Her need rocketed.

"Two can play at this game," he warned, his eyes dark with hunger.

He twirled and tweaked and swirled and stroked until her breath came in loud gasps. Her need soared, building quickly, intensely. She couldn't stop herself, couldn't tease any longer. She needed him in her, hard and deep.

She impaled herself on his rigid length, screaming at the devastatingly incredible feel of him buried within her. Rocking up and down, she squeezed him, stroked him, like he had her.

It was Rob's turn to shout out, his hands gripping her hips, directing her in a rapid, relentless motion.

Their movements became more frenzied, more desperate, until it was simply too much, too intense. She splintered, shards of ecstasy ripping through her. She didn't know if she screamed; she didn't know if she called Rob's name. She was aware only of Rob and the fierce orgasm shaking her.

When she finally regained her senses, she was lying on Rob's sweaty chest, her limbs boneless, her body exhausted.

Their fast breathing harmonized, then gradually slowed, until it was even and low and barely audible under the soft Christmas music.

She felt Rob kiss the top of her head, the gesture sweet. She smiled and kissed his chest in response. Then she fell into a sound sleep.

Sometime during the night, Rob had rolled them onto their sides, facing each other. She woke to find him watching her. Without saying a word, he reached for the final condom.

Then he pulled her leg to hook over his hip, and he angled his body so he could slowly slide into her.

This coupling wasn't frantic, but unhurried and tender. A leisurely adoration of each other's bodies. A slow, steady build toward release. No less thrilling, but somehow more awe-inspiring.

As their orgasms engulfed them in long, rolling waves, they maintained eye contact, seeing the satisfaction on each other's faces. And the love.

At least Erica knew the emotion was clear on her face.

Chapter Seven

The next morning, Rob and Erica didn't get much chance to talk. Donny called their room early to say he'd contacted the car rental company and had arranged for a new car.

A tow truck pulled the old car out of the snowbank and swung by the hotel so they could retrieve their luggage.

Once all the logistics were worked out, they all piled into the new rental, which was a tad nicer than the old one. Christmas Day had arrived sunny and brisk, and the driving was much smoother.

Rob and Erica once again rode in the small backseat. But this time, she curled against him, dozing.

Several times, he noticed Donny and Alex glancing back at them, curious about the state of their relationship.

He wished he knew. Even though they lived in the same city and they could continue to see each other, Erica had made no suggestion in that direction. She hadn't even hinted at continuing their relationship. And he couldn't bring himself to propose the idea. He didn't want her to feel pressured. She had said she'd moved on. He had said horrible things to her that Christmas Eve all those years ago. Maybe they were things she couldn't really forgive. And maybe last night was about closure.

So when Donny stopped the car in front of her folks' house, Rob simply went to the trunk and pulled her luggage out. He waited while Erica thanked Donny and Alex.

"I hope your sister forgives you for being late for her wedding," she said.

Donny shrugged. "Well, it is her third one."

"You know what they say: Third time's the charm."

"Lord, I hope," Donny said dramatically.

"Bye." Erica waved.

Rob walked her to her front door like he had a hundred times before. "Have a Merry Christmas."

"You, too." Her smile seemed bittersweet, but he just couldn't tell if it was because she didn't really want to say good-bye or because this good-bye was for good.

"I'm glad I got to see you again." His words were so inadequate, and they didn't even begin to describe how he felt about last night. But he added nothing else.

"Me, too." She nodded. "Good-bye, Rob."

"Good-bye."

She entered her house, the door banging closed behind her, just as it had once before.

He stood there for just a moment, then returned to the car.

"Are you okay?" Donny asked. Apparently, Rob's misery was clear on his face.

He nodded. "Yeah. Thanks."

"Just remember, anything worth having is worth fighting for," Alex told him, then he reached out to caress Donny's shoulder.

Rob nodded again. But he didn't know if he should really listen to two men who spent their Christmas Eve fighting over who they did and didn't look like.

When Rob arrived at his parents' house, he was greeted at the door by his folks, Mo, Neil, and the baby. He was quickly enveloped in chatter and laughter.

Later, they sat in his parents' living room, on the furniture they'd had since he and Mo were in grade school, and they exchanged gifts.

Dad oohed and ahhed over a tie that Mom got him—even though she gave him a tie every Christmas. Mo and Neil tried to get Stewie interested in a toy they'd gotten him, but the baby was much happier gumming away on the crumpled wrapping paper.

Rob's mother unwrapped the gift he had bought her—an expensive ruby-and-diamond pendant.

"Robby," she said when she saw it. "This is lovely." She hooked the necklace around her neck, then announced she needed to check the turkey.

When she walked past him, she leaned down and hugged him. "I love my gift," she said softly. "But don't you know that having you home is the best gift of all? The only gift I needed." She kissed his cheek. She disappeared into the turkey-scented kitchen.

Rob looked around him, no longer seeing the shabby furniture and faded wallpaper. Instead, he noticed only the people. His dad, who talked in a silly voice to Stewie. Mo and Neil, who gazed at each other, love so clear in their eyes. His mother, who sang "We Wish You a Merry Christmas" in the kitchen.

And suddenly, the truth hit him. Erica had been absolutely right all those years ago. Success isn't measured by money or promotions. Success is measured by the people who love you.

Ambition is fine, but it doesn't keep a person warm at night. And it isn't important without someone to share it with. And he knew with whom he wanted to share his success and his life and his love.

He stood. "I have to go."

His mother came back into the room. Everyone, even Stewie, stared at him.

"I have to go tell Erica Fetzer that I love her."

If his family thought his sudden announcement was odd, they didn't say so.

* * *

The doorbell rang.

Erica sat on her parents' couch watching *It's a Wonderful Life* and feeling very bad for herself, but she yelled that she'd answer the door.

"Rob," she murmured, shocked to see him there on her parents' front porch. His hair was windblown, his cheeks reddened, and he breathed heavy, as if he'd run to get there.

"Hi."

"Hi." She peered at him, puzzled. Why was he here? Her heart leaped with hope, but she ignored it. He wasn't here to proclaim his love. If he loved her, he could have told her last night, or earlier today in the car.

"Did you have a nice Christmas?" she asked politely, not sure what else to say, and he didn't act as though he planned to speak.

"The best," he said.

"And your family wasn't too disappointed that you weren't home on Christmas Eve?"

"I was home for Christmas Eve," he stated.

She frowned at him, starting to think maybe he'd somehow gone mad between last night and now. Or, at the very least, had drunk a bit too much eggnog.

"I was home because I was with you."

He had gone mad. But his certain insanity still didn't stop her heart from pirouetting in her chest.

"Rob—"

He held up a hand. "Erica, I want you to know that you were right. The Christmas Eve when we broke up, you told me that I'd changed. That all I cared about was success. That was true, but I now know that success is nothing if you're alone."

She nodded, waiting for him to continue.

"I'm sorry, Erica. I'm sorry for hurting you. I'm sorry for saying those awful things about your college and your studies and your art. I'm sorry that I was so blind and thoughtless and selfish."

He stared at her for a moment as if he expected her to say more.

What could she say? "I appreciate your apology."

"Erica." He stepped closer, capturing her warm hands in his cold ones, stroking his thumbs back and forth across the backs. Even that small touch prickled awareness over her skin. "I don't want you to move on. I don't want you to forget me. I want you to share my successes. I want to share yours. I want to know all your dreams. I want to tell you mine. But most of all, I want us to spend the rest of our lives together."

She stared at him for a moment. This is what she'd dreamed of, yet now that her dream had happened, she didn't quite dare to believe it.

He stared back, and she could see the sincerity and the nervousness in his coffee-colored eyes.

He was serious. He wanted them to be a couple. Her heart clattered painfully against her ribs. She couldn't pull in a breath.

"Erica," his voice sounded anxious, uncertain. "You're killing me here. Please tell me I can have another chance. I love you, and I can't lose you again."

Before he could even finish, she flung her arms around him.

"Yes," she said against his mouth. "Yes."

Then they were kissing.

"I love you, Erica. So, so much."

"And I love you. I always have."

"And you forgive me for being the world's biggest idiot? For all the years we lost?"

"Oh, I plan to make you pay," she warned.

"Oh, yeah?"

"Mm-hmm. Every night."

He grinned, his eyes smoldering, that dimple she loved deepening. "Yes, I definitely do need to pay—with interest. I know these things—I'm a banker."

She laughed and kissed him again, tasting the love on his lips.

Finally, he lifted his head. "Now, take me inside. I want your parents to meet the man you're going to marry."

She linked her fingers with his, tugging him into the house, and the door gently closed behind them both.

SEDUCING SCROOGE

Katherine Garbera

Chapter One

Jackson Peterson saw the immediate response to his e-mail by Krista Miller and smiled to himself. Krista was his go-to girl. The only one on the entire finance staff seemingly not bitten by the holiday fever that had swept the building. He clicked on her name, telling himself it was the fact that she was a hotshot accountant and not that she had a killer pair of legs that excited him whenever he saw her name.

He froze in his chair as he read the e-mail message. *I'm out of the office until January 2. Please direct all inquiries to Marsha Graham at mgraham@northernsports.com.*

Not believing what he was reading, Jackson picked up the phone and dialed her extension. Her cheerful voice answered on the first ring. "You've reached the office of Krista Miller. I'm out of the office until January second. Please contact Marsha Graham at extension 7158. Thanks."

This was why he hated the holidays. This was why everyone in the office called him Scrooge. He'd counted on the information that Krista was pulling for him. He needed it to finish his report before he left for the evening. And now he was going to have to do the work himself.

He knew better than to depend on anyone. At Christmas time people got caught up in the holidays and forgot commitments. He was just surprised that Krista was one of them. She'd been very dependable up to this point.

The knock on the door frame startled him. He glanced up to see a bottle of some sort of wine and two long-stemmed champagne glasses under the mistletoe someone had hung on his door just to needle him.

"Scrooge McDuck, you in here?"

"Krista, I just called your office. I thought you'd left."

"Did that piss you off?" she asked, sashaying into his office like she owned it and sitting on the edge of his desk.

"Hell, yeah."

"How do you feel now?" she asked, setting the two pieces of stemware on his desk and pouring the sparkling liquid into them.

"Like I wish you'd stop pouring . . . what are you pouring?"

"Champagne. Continue with what you were saying."

"I wish you'd stop wasting time and tell me why we are drinking and not going over the numbers in the report you were supposed to have on my desk,"—he glanced at the Swiss Army watch on his wrist—"two minutes ago."

She handed him a glass and hopped off his desk. She took a quick sip of hers then smiled at him with pure devilry in her eyes. "I think you better drink the sparkling wine while I explain. In fact, you might wish for something stronger but since this is the office and we're technically still at work, I thought I'd better stick to what was okayed by Human Resources for the holiday celebrations."

"I don't celebrate the holidays," he said, knowing she knew this. He'd thought Krista a kindred spirit. A fellow workaholic who understood that a hard day's work was what really mattered, not a calendar full of social obligations during the workday.

"Believe me, I know. But I've come up with a diabolical plot to force you out of your Chief Financial Officer/Scrooge persona for this one night."

He finally took one of the long-stemmed glasses from her

and took a sip. There was something sexy about the way she said *diabolical*. And the glimmer in her eyes echoed the one inside him. He'd wanted her since she'd walked into his office six months ago and aside from one accidental kiss on the elevator late at night three weeks ago, he'd managed to forget about that side of her . . . until this moment.

But he was from the never-let-them-see-you-sweat school. "Go on, I can't wait to hear the rest of this."

"Well, you're being blackmailed, Jack. I'm not going to supply you the numbers you need to finish that report unless you come to dinner with me."

"Why are you blackmailing me?" he asked, not sure what he hoped her answer would be.

"Because I want to get Scrooge and make him understand there's more to life than work. I studied the story and thought about following it to the tee."

"What story?"

"*A Christmas Carol* by Dickens. You do know why the staff calls you Scrooge, right?"

"Krista, I'm considered a patient man by most but you are tempting me to lose my temper."

"Hot damn!"

"Okay, smarty, what made you decide not to follow the story?"

"You live in a gated community and have a really good security system. For me to visit you three times I think I'd have to take a little trip to the police department. And I really don't want to spend Christmas Eve in lock-up. Not exactly conducive to what I have in mind."

"What do you have in mind? And why can't you just give me my report? If you did that, I'd be able to actually get out of here and go enjoy this life you don't seem to think I have."

"No, you won't. That information's not due to Roger until after the first of the year. That means you'll immediately jump into doing the pro forma on the new chain of West Coast retail stores that we have scheduled for January."

He hated that she knew him so well. When had his work habits changed from dedicated and driven to predictable? Most of his staff never looked at him. Never saw him as anything other than a hard boss who rewarded them financially with bonuses twice a year. Why did she?

Krista knew the instant she had Jackson. She saw it in his face as he saved whatever spreadsheet he was working on and leaned back in that big leather chair of his, tunneling his fingers through his thick black hair.

She almost groaned. He always did that with his hands when he was thinking. Inevitably his hair was the slightest bit ruffled and she always wanted to smooth it back into place. She balled her hands into fists and then realized that it was a telling gesture and she didn't want him to guess she was the least bit nervous.

She'd taken a big risk tonight, all based on one kiss that she wasn't sure really happened.

"So, Scrooge, what do you say?" she asked, afraid to let too much time pass. She'd planned this evening perfectly, knowing that her window of opportunity was a narrow one. Honestly, she wasn't sure her nerves were up to a lengthy show of bravado.

"Stop sassing me or I'll have to get tough with you. Exactly what are your terms, blackmailer?"

She paced away from his desk to resist the temptation of him. "You and I leave this place and go to an undisclosed location for an intimate dinner for two during which we don't discuss work. Then we return to the office, I give you your report and we both go home."

She waggled her eyebrows at him when she said *undisclosed*. Everything about her attitude right now was sexy, seductive. Meant to make him lose that legendary cool of his. And she knew it was working because she saw just the smallest hint of a smile in his eyes.

"We both go home alone?"

She arched one eyebrow at him. "That totally depends on you, Mr. Scrooge."

"If you wanted to go out with me, why not just ask?" he asked. "Northern Sports has a very open fraternization policy."

To be honest, she normally wasn't the type to ask a guy out. She'd always been an expert at dropping subtle hints that men had never failed to pick up on and then ask her out. But she'd given up waiting for Jackson when it had become apparent he wasn't going to make the first move.

"Stop stalling. Make your decision. A two hour dinner break or seven hours worth of doing the research and pulling the figures together on your own."

"If I do this, you're going to have to meet some stipulations."

"What kind? I don't want to negotiate with you. I prefer to keep things simple."

"Blackmailers always do. But as the blackmailee—"

"Is blackmailee even a word?"

"Who knows? I'm a math geek, not a wordsmith."

"No way did anyone ever call you a geek," she said.

"You think?"

"Am I wrong?"

"Nah, I'm a jock. Numbers just come easy to me. Back to what I was saying . . . I know that I have to set limits or you'll be back again."

He had no idea how much she hoped she'd be able to seduce him away from work not just this once. But she knew if this didn't work she'd have no choice but to leave Northern Sports and find another job. She didn't think she'd be able to face him every day if this didn't work.

"I don't see this happening again."

"I do. So here are my terms. I want to see the report now so that I can verify you've done the work. I will then enter the numbers into my report and save the worksheet. We will both leave together and go to dinner at the undisclosed location. And then we'll go home."

"What about printing and distributing the report?"

"That can wait until after Christmas."

He surprised her and she could tell he liked it. His personality was too dominant to let her have control of anything for too long. She stared at him. "How do I know you'll keep your word?"

"Have I ever broken a promise?" he asked.

"You've never really made me one." But she did know that his word was his bond. More than one recalcitrant client had been brought around once Jackson entered the boardroom. There was something solid and dependable about him.

He pushed away from his desk and came around it, stopping when only an inch of space separated them. The heat of his body wrapped around her. Nervously she licked her lips and waited.

Why was she waiting? This was her plan. Her seduction. She wasn't letting Jackson Peters take it over now.

She slid half an inch closer. So close that she could smell his totally sexy aftershave and feel each exhalation of his breath against her neck. This was so not fair. He was seducing her without even trying.

"I want something else from you, Krista."

"What?" she asked, trying to pretend the raspy quality of her voice was planned.

"Remember that kiss in the elevator?"

As if she could forget it. They'd both been working late and Jackson had come to her office to make sure she'd left the building when he did so she wouldn't be alone. Then when they'd gotten on the elevator, the lights had flashed out and the car had stopped with a jerk. She'd lurched into him and he'd caught her.

She'd been surprised at how muscular he was under his white dress shirt and tie. She'd tipped her head back and in the strange green-glow of the security light she saw an answering desire in his eyes. He'd lowered his head and kissed her.

She'd closed her eyes for a split second and as soon as she did, he lifted his mouth from hers and set her aside. He'd called security and went back to being all business.

And she'd followed his lead. But forgotten that brief kiss. That brief promise of something exciting and more profound than running quarterly numbers on skis and tents. No way.

"What kiss?"

He laughed, the sound of it catching her off guard. He never laughed. He joked with her sometimes because she refused to leave his office without getting some kind of reaction from him. More than once she'd made him smile, but this was the first laugh.

"I thought I warned you about sassing me."

"You keep assuming that you're charge."

He lifted one hand to the back of her neck. Held her with a light touch, his finger rubbing up and down her neck. "Aren't I?"

She stood on tiptoe, leaned into him, bracing her hands on his shoulders and brought her face close to his. Brushed her lips over his once before pulling back so that she could see him.

"No, you're not."

Then she lowered her head and kissed him.

Chapter Two

Krista's kiss wasn't tentative at all, but then neither was the woman. That energy was part of what made her so exciting to be around. Jackson couldn't think any more. Only feel. She didn't shove her tongue down his throat but tunneled her fingers through his hair and held his head as she just kissed him.

She kept her eyes open, something few women he'd ever kissed did. She tipped her head to the side, sliding her tongue along the seam of his lips. He opened his mouth and tangled his tongue with hers.

She moaned and canted her hips closer to his. But her hands stayed on his head. Jackson pulled her closer, his blood flowed heavier in his veins. Her breasts brushed his chest.

She tilted her head to the side. He angled closer to her, anchoring her to him. Stroking his hands down the column of her neck, he couldn't believe how soft her skin was. She opened her mouth to his thrusting tongue as he pulled her closer to him, felt the soft mounds of her breasts brushing his chest.

She ran her foot up the backside of his calf, sucked his lower lip between her teeth and her eyes drifted closed.

She tasted sweet and felt so right in his arms. This was why he'd resisted her. He didn't give a damn about anything except Krista when she was in his arms.

The kiss deepened until he had to pull away or give into the urge to lift her on his desk, spread her legs and take her now.

"Wow," she said, pushing against his chest and edging back.

He let her ease away from him. He realized that if he didn't get his ass back in his desk chair the chances of him finishing anything work-related tonight were extremely slim.

He'd come over to her to prove something but couldn't remember a damn thing. Couldn't think of anything except him and Krista naked and having hot sex.

Her lips were wet and swollen from his kisses. There was something damned seductive about seeing Krista aroused from his kisses.

Her skin was flushed, her pupils dilated, and she fingered her own mouth for a second before she realized he was watching her. Then she dropped her hand and tipped her head to the side.

"Was that supposed to prove something?" she asked. Her voice was huskier than it had been before. And he didn't for a second believe she wasn't aroused.

"Only that we both want each other." Like he needed that kiss to prove it.

"Did you doubt it, after that kiss in the elevator?"

"What kiss?" he asked, teasing her. Keeping Krista at arm's length was impossible and even though he knew there was no place in his life for her, he wanted to enjoy her.

"How can I trust you to go to dinner with me?" she asked, crossing her arms under her breasts. Her nipples pushed against the thin layer of her silk blouse.

He wished he'd cupped her fullness, caressed her. That kiss was too short. He needed more.

Why had he pulled back?

He saw his framed MBA degree hanging on the wall and remembered the promises he'd made to his parents. Work. Focus. Breathe.

But every breath he took filled his lungs with her scent. Soft, sweet and so damned womanly.

"Jackson?"

He pushed his hands through his hair. She'd asked for his guarantee that he'd honor his end of the blackmail deal.

"I give you my word that if you surrender the report, I'll go to dinner with you."

She nodded and pulled her USB flash drive from her pocket, holding it up to him.

He reached for it but she pulled it back out of his reach. "What's the deal?"

"You won't discuss business when we go to dinner," she said.

"You can't keep adding stipulations."

"Sure I can. I have something you want and need."

"Krista, damn it, honey, you have more than one thing I want and need."

For the first time he saw a flash of something other than sass and determination in her eyes. He couldn't identify it. "Really? What would that be?"

"I'll tell you later. Now, give me my info so I can finish my work."

She tossed the flash drive to him and he caught it one-handed and went back around his desk. Seating himself, he concentrated on getting the information he needed but it was hard.

She seated herself in one of his guest chairs, crossing her long legs. She wore a pair of spiky black heels. In his mind he stripped her clothing from her body and saw her standing in his office. He'd take her bra also so he could see her hardened nipples ready for his mouth. Her panties would be black lace.

"Do I have a run in my hose?" she asked, jarring him.

"What?"

"You're staring at my legs."

Good thing she couldn't read his mind. He needed to get her out of his office or he wasn't going to be able to make heads or tails of her information. "You have great legs."

"Thanks. I hoped you'd notice."

"Is that why your skirts have gotten shorter lately?"

"Have they?"

He glanced at his computer screen. Verified the information that he needed was there. "You know they have. In fact, I've been thinking of getting HR involved."

"In what?"

He integrated her numbers into his master sheet and then watched the automated formulas calculate.

"In your flaunting of the dress code."

"I haven't broken any rules, I'm dressed professionally."

"You might be, but every man who sees you in that short skirt and those high heels isn't thinking of business."

"Every man? Even Scrooge?"

"I'm still human, Krista," he said. The information was in the computer and he saved the new file.

Krista left Jackson to close up his office and retreated to hers to touch up her lipstick and regroup. Her palms were sweating. She was more than a little nervous but now that she and Jackson were leaving together she felt . . . *oh, God, don't let this backfire.*

His words echoed in her mind and gave her a moment's pause. He was human. He'd made the choices he'd made for a reason. What made her think she had the right to force him out of his comfort zone?

Then she remembered the way he'd kissed her earlier. She wasn't pushing too hard at him. He wanted her. But was there more than lust?

She grabbed her purse and her coat and turned, stumbling into Jackson. "Gotcha."

"I didn't see you," she said, inanely.

"Really, I thought you liked the feel of my arms around you."

"You're such a big strong man," she said, batting her eyes at him.

"Does that sassy mouth ever not get you in trouble?"

"I can handle it."

"I'll bet. So where are we going for dinner?"

He tugged her jacket from her arms and held it up for her. She slipped her arms into the sleeves and he settled his hands on her shoulders, pulling her back against him for a moment.

"Are you sure about this, Jackson?" she asked. Even though she wanted him and believed he wanted her. Even though she was sure that they'd both be happier because of her actions this night. Even though she knew that he was as lonely as she was, she still wanted to have some reassurance from him.

"I thought I didn't have a choice," he said, tugging her hair from under the collar of her coat.

"You don't, but you rattled me."

"How? I need to make a note of what worked so I can use it again."

"Oh, ha. When you reminded me you were human," she said as they walked down the hallway to the elevator.

"Am I really that bad?"

"No, but you are a bit of a bear sometimes. Why is work so important?"

"Why isn't it to everyone else in the office?"

She shrugged. Honestly, she had no issues with Jackson's workaholic tendencies. She spent a good deal of her time at work as well. It was one of the things that had made her notice him.

"Holidays are just a special time of year. I think everyone just feels more relaxed."

"Too relaxed. They are still being paid to work."

"Hey, I'm not trying to start an argument."

The elevator car arrived and they both got on. Jackson pressed the lobby button. "You hit one of my hot buttons."

"I'd rather hit a different one. But you evaded my question."

"Which one?"

"Work—why is it so important to you?"

He shrugged his shoulders. "It just is."

He wasn't going to tell her what she wanted to know but she had other ways of getting the information from him. She'd come back to it later.

When they exited the building a light snow fell and she stopped. "A Christmas snow. I love this. My mom always said that snow on Christmas Eve means that the wishes of your heart will be waiting the next morning."

Jackson said nothing. Stood there waiting in his time-is-money mode. She wasn't budging. "The blackmail starts now, Jackson. You gave me your word you'd cooperate."

"I'm here, aren't I?"

"Yes and no. Tip your face up to the snow and tell me what you feel."

She watched him and saw the moment when he decided to pacify her. He tipped his head back and she slid her hand into his. Laced their fingers together and stood close to him.

In a small voice she told him of the magic of Christmas. Told him the story her mom always shared and wove her spell of peace and desire around him.

After a few minutes he turned to her and she saw something in his eyes she'd never seen before. She couldn't identify this new emotion but she knew it was a strong one.

"Where is your family from, Krista? Why aren't you with them this year?"

"My parents' wedding anniversary is tonight and it's their twenty-fifth, so Dad flew her to Florence."

"So you're alone this year?"

"No, I'm with you."

"Things must be desperate if I'm the only one you could come up with."

"I'm with the person I want to be with."

"Why?"

"Because I know you're not the Scrooge you pretend to be."

"Don't kid yourself, honey. What you see is what you get with me."

230 / *Katherine Garbera*

"I like what I see," she said. She pulled a black scarf from her pocket.

"What's that for?"

"I'm going to blindfold you. I don't want you to have too many details about your blackmailer for the cops."

"Are you still my blackmailer?"

"Oh, yes." She fastened the scarf over his eyes and then took his hand and led him across the snow-covered parking lot to her car.

Chapter Three

Jackson didn't like being blindfolded. The out-of-control feeling was almost overpowering. He stopped walking, forcing Krista to do the same. "What?"

"I'm not really into this role."

"What role?" she asked.

"The submissive one. What do you say we change this entire set-up around?"

"Um, let me think about it. No, thanks."

"Krista—"

"Trust me," she said.

"Why should I?" he asked.

"Because deep inside you know I'm worthy of your trust. Come on. I promise this will be fun and that you won't regret it."

"If you don't deliver, I'm going to come looking for payment on that vow."

"Fair enough. Can we go now?"

He started walking, letting her guide him with her small hand in his. He liked the feel of her hand in his. When she'd slipped her fingers through his and made him look at the falling snow he'd felt almost connected to her. Jeez, one kiss on Christmas Eve and he was getting sappy.

"One day I'm going to get you back for this," he said.

"Really? Will you be blindfolding me and doing something kinky? I'll be waiting. Okay, here's my car."

"You like kinky?"

"Maybe."

He heard her opening the car door, and then she helped him into her car. He hit his head, cursing. "Why am I blindfolded now?"

"Stop whining. You barely bumped your head."

"I don't whine—that's something women and children do. And my head hurts."

"What do you want me to do about it? Pack it in snow?"

"Honey, that's cold. What about kissing it better?" he asked.

He didn't think she'd do it. He knew he was asking and hated himself for it the moment the words left his mouth.

After an awkward few seconds he felt the gentle touch of her fingers against his skin. And then the warmth of her breath before her cold lips brushed over his forehead.

"I'm so sorry you hit your head."

She closed the door before he could respond. A few minutes later she was in the car and they were driving. Her radio of course was tuned to the all-Christmas-tunes station. "Can we please listen to something else?"

"Nah. This is part of your desensitivity training to stop being such a Scrooge."

"This isn't helping," he said. A few minutes later when he heard "Frosty the Snowman" come on, he groaned. "I actually think you're giving me new reasons to not like this time of year."

"Don't like Frosty?"

"Give me one thing that Frosty has to do with Christmas?"

"Snow and Santa. I gave you two because I'm so nice."

"Yeah, tell that to someone who doesn't know you."

"You don't think I'm nice."

"We both know you lean more toward naughty than nice."

"Really?" she asked.

He'd never noticed the cadence in her voice before. But deprived of sight, he realized that she had the faint rhythm of the South in it. He liked to hear her talk. Liked to tease her and see what she came up with next. Liked that he could never predict what she'd do next.

"Really."

She squeezed his shoulder. "Thanks, Jackson. I swear you're the first person to call me naughty."

"You say the strangest things."

"Not really. If you'd spent your entire life having everyone think you were boring—"

"Who has ever called you boring?"

"Well, no one. But being called naughty . . . I like it!"

He fought the urge to laugh.

"So what's your favorite song of the season . . . 'You're a Mean One, Mr. Grinch?' "

"No. I don't think I have a favorite."

He felt the car slow and heard her turn on her blinker. Maybe he should have paid better attention to the route they were taking.

"What about when you were a kid? Every kid loves Rudolph."

"I guess," he said, not really wanted to remember his childhood. "Where are you taking me?"

"Dinner. So not Rudolph?"

"Nope."

"The Chipmunks song?" she suggested. "When I was a kid I thought he wanted a hoo-la-hoo, not a hula hoop. Isn't that funny? My brother, Dan, used to make fun of me."

"No, not that song. How many siblings do you have?"

"Just Dan the Mean. Although now he's not so bad. He's an ad exec in New York. He lets me stay at his swanky apartment whenever I visit and sends his car for me at the airport. Who'd have guessed he'd turn out so good?"

Her family sounded close. He analyzed that fact, filing it away for another time.

"What about—"

"Nothing commercial. My parents didn't believe in TV. or things like Santa or the Easter Bunny. They believed in hard work."

She was quiet and he regretted saying anything.

"What about fun?"

"Work is fun."

"You seriously needed me, didn't you?"

He said nothing. He wasn't admitting another thing to Krista. But not saying it out loud didn't change the fact that he did need her.

"We're here."

Krista parked her car on the corner near the restaurant where they had reservations. She leaned over to untie Jackson's blindfold. She put her hands on the sides of his face, framing it. With the blindfold on he looked different. His square jaw and firm lips were brought into contrast. She never really studied his mouth before because his eyes always fascinated her. And she didn't really want to get caught ogling him at work.

She swiped her tongue over her own lips, wetting them before leaning forward and pressing them against his. Whereas before she'd had the control to want to savor his taste, to learn each nuance about his mouth, this time she didn't. The first touch made her ravenous and she couldn't keep it slow and easy.

Jackson's hands came up to her waist and lifted her over the gearshift into his lap. His hands were under her coat, caressing his way up her ribs.

"This is much better."

"What is?"

"You in my arms," he said, against the skin of her neck. His hands roamed over her body like he owned it. And she thought maybe that wouldn't be a bad thing.

"You like to be in charge, don't you?" she asked, settling in his lap. It was nice. She couldn't remember the last time a man had held her like this. Jackson wrapped his arms around her and she liked the feeling of security that came from it.

"Don't say that like it's a bad thing. So do you," he said in that wry tone of his that had first made her realize there was more to Jackson Peters than work.

"Yeah, I know. That's one reason why I made these plans."

"What was another reason?" he asked.

She wasn't sure she wanted to reveal too much to him but she wanted him to tell her his secrets and so she hedged. "I didn't think you'd ever make the first move."

"You're right, I wouldn't have."

"Why not?" she asked. She knew from the past that it was easier to reveal things in the dark. The blindfold had served two purposes, really. Now that were away from work she had a finite amount of time to convince Jackson there was something worth pursuing between them.

He brought his hands up to her face. Stroking his forefinger over her cheekbone and down the curve of her ear. Touching her so . . . reverently. "You were a distraction that I didn't have time for."

"Were? Does that mean you changed your mind?"

"I kind of had very little choice."

She laughed. "When I see something I want I go for it."

He said nothing for a minute and then pulled her head toward his with that touch on her neck. She rested her forehead against his and he said quietly. "I'm glad."

Her heart ached. Jackson needed the kind of caring she wanted to shower on him. He was too alone and everyone in the office didn't see that behind the Scroogelike attitude was a man who was just highly focused and driven.

She cupped his face and rubbed her lips along the line of his jaw. The faint shadow of his beard abraded her lips. She liked the texture.

His arms around her were strong and sure. There was no hesitancy in him. Though she'd blindfolded him, he was in control.

And she found she liked it. She liked a man who gave as good as he got and Jackson certainly did. She shifted in his embrace as he scraped his teeth down the side of her neck.

Then soothed the sensual sting with his tongue. He cupped the weight of her breast in one hand, rubbing his thumb around her nipple. Not touching, just circling so damned close that she thought she'd go crazy.

She shifted her shoulders, trying to move his touch where she desperately needed it but he ignored her hint. Instead he suckled at the base of her neck. She moaned deep in her throat and clenched her legs together.

She didn't want to make love to Jackson in the front seat of her car so she pulled back. But she ached for him. Her breasts felt full and sensitized. The base of her neck where he'd suckled tingled. Lust washed over her in waves. Should they skip dinner and go back to her place?

She pulled off his blindfold and climbed awkwardly back into the driver's seat. She wanted more than a night with Jackson.

He didn't glance out the window to see where they were, just stared at her in the muted light provided by a street lamp three cars up. She felt raw and vulnerable. Out of control.

Regroup, she thought. But she couldn't when he watched her like that.

"Um . . . I thought we'd stroll by Fields and check out the Christmas windows before dinner."

He shifted in the seat and she tried not to notice that he had an erection. "This is your show."

She nodded. "I think you'll appreciate the theme this year."

"Let me guess. *A Christmas Carol*?"

"Aren't you glad it's not Frosty?"

He gave her a very sweet smile. "Yes, I am."

He opened his door and came around to meet her on the sidewalk. The snow had stopped but the wind was still very chilly. She buttoned her camel-colored wool coat to the neck.

She slipped her arm through Jackson's and led him across the street where the windows were. The sidewalk was busy with families and couples. People hurrying to make a few last-minute purchases.

"Did you get your shopping done early?" she asked.

"I guess."

She raised one eyebrow at him.

"I don't exchange gifts."

She stopped on the sidewalk and stared at him. But it made a certain kind of sense with what he'd said earlier. His family focused on working hard for things.

"Are you shocked?"

"Nah."

"Just another piece of evidence that I really am Scrooge?"

"No, Jackson, just another reminder that you really need to be shown the magic of Christmas."

Chapter Four

Jackson was relieved when they were seated in the restaurant. The piped-in Christmas music was soothing and soft. Festive without being intrusive. Around them families and couples were seated and for once Jackson felt a pang for what might have been.

There was a large tree in the center of the room and as luck would have it they were seated with a perfect view of it.

"Isn't this nice? I've never eaten here before but Shannon in R&D recommended it."

"You told her what you were doing?" he asked, not sure he liked the fact that anyone else knew about this.

"Do you really think I would?"

She sounded hurt. He shrugged. "I guess not."

"Well, thanks for that." The waiter approached and Krista ordered a Bellini and he ordered a scotch neat.

"My mom's Italian so we always have seafood on Christmas Eve. I tried to find a place where we could get some traditional dishes but then I thought you might not like fish."

"I like fish."

"Good. So do I," she said with a smile. "You don't have many traditions, do you?"

Not around holidays. His family was spread across the

country. "No, I don't, I'm always looking forward to something new."

"Like what?" she asked, taking a sip of peach flavored drink.

"Projects and such," he said, distracted by the way she licked her lips.

"Just work? Aren't you afraid of turning dull?"

He played hard no matter what anyone thought. "No. I take two weeks off in January and go on a trip."

"Where?"

"Wherever I feel like. Usually some place warm."

"That sounds nice. My parents have a condo in Florida and we all try to meet there in August."

"That also sounds nice. Where is it?"

"In Fort Pierce on the Atlantic Ocean side."

He was getting an image of Krista as a woman who surrounded herself with family and friends. But he already knew that from watching her at work.

"What about you, do you go alone?" she asked.

She leaned forward as she spoke, giving him a glimpse of her cleavage. His palm tingled remembering the weight and feel of her. "Usually one of my brothers joins me."

"You have brothers?" She sounded almost indignant.

"Am I not supposed to?"

"Why didn't you say anything when I mentioned Dan?"

He shrugged. The last thing he wanted to talk about on a date with a beautiful woman was his brothers. "I have two brothers. Patrick, the youngest brother, always plans the trip for me."

"So you're close?"

"I guess. Why are we discussing my brothers?"

"Because I want to. Your trips with them sound like a tradition."

"You're not going to let that go, are you?" he asked, unsure what point she was trying to make. His life wasn't the Norman Rockwell classic Americana. That didn't mean it sucked.

"I'm kind of tenacious about things and I'm trying to figure out what makes Jackson Peters tick."

"You're kind of a pain," he said, fighting a smile.

"That's not very nice."

"So?"

"What kind of response is that?"

"The only kind for a woman like you."

The waiter arrived. Krista smiled and flirted with the waiter, asking for his suggestions and then ordering. He felt a stirring in his gut that felt like jealousy. He wanted to keep her to himself.

"Jackson?"

"Hmm?"

"Do you want an appetizer?"

"Sure," he said, not paying attention to the details of the meal. Krista had brought him here for more than just one night. And he wanted that. In his mind he started playing the variables of making something like this work.

He'd never dated anyone at the office. But he knew that they couldn't continue to work together and date at night. He didn't need another complication at work but Krista was worth it.

He placed his order and the waiter left.

"Is everything okay?" she asked.

"Yes, I was just trying to figure you out."

"Want to know what makes me tick?" she asked. "Be careful, that can have you labeled a pain."

"I think being labeled Scrooge kind of says that."

"Does it bother you?"

"Men don't get bothered by stuff like that."

"I don't believe that."

"Sweetheart, I don't get upset, I get pissed. And I'm not bothered by something, I'm ticked off."

"Oh, I get it. Semantics. Do you believe in love?" she asked. Taken aback, he could only stare at her. He had never thought about love. He'd had some affection for his brothers but figured that had to do with the familial bond. Beyond that he knew he'd experienced lust and some friendship. But love? Who knew what that was?

"Not any more than I do Santa Claus."

She closed her eyes and sank back in her chair. Jackson wished he could have given her a different answer but lying went against the grain. Better that Krista know exactly the type of man he was before she built a fantasy around him he couldn't live up to.

Krista had changed the subject and they'd finished their dinner. But in the back of her mind lingered the fact that she'd taken a huge risk tonight. She shrugged as she remembered her mom saying nothing ventured, nothing gained.

She slipped her arm through Jackson's as they walked away from the restaurant and toward her car. The crowds were lighter now and she paused in front of one of the windows. Ebenezer Scrooge was standing on the edge of his bed, arms outstretched and a look of total loneliness and pain was etched on the sculpted figurine.

She glanced up at Jackson. He stared at the figure and she wondered what was going on in his head. He revealed so few emotions around her. Around anyone, really, but she wanted him to be different with her.

"Thanks for dinner," he said after a few minutes.

"You're welcome," she said.

He'd gone for his wallet at the table but she'd firmly insisted on paying. This was her set-up, not his. Next time, please God, let there be a next time, he could pay.

"As far as blackmail goes, this has to be one of the better deals."

"You don't wish you were still in the office working on that new pro forma?"

"Well . . ."

Taking a step away from him, she punched his arm. "Hey, I'm more exciting than running numbers."

He grabbed her around the waist and tugged her into his arms. "If you say so."

A family of four stopped next to them, but Krista wasn't ready to move on. However, when the kids started dancing around them in circles she tugged on Jackson's arm and moved them down a few windows.

She saw that it was Christmas Present. This was what she had based her seduction of Jackson around. By showing him a great time tonight she hoped to lay the groundwork for the future.

"How does this Christmas stack up against the ones in the past?"

He pushed his hands though his hair and studied her for a long moment. She tried not to fiddle but when he watched her like that she had to. Patting her hair, licking her lips, wishing she'd remembered to touch up her lipstick before leaving the restaurant.

"This night's been okay."

She forgot all about her lipstick. "Just okay? That's cold. I blackmailed you into leaving your office. Blindfolded you to add to the intrigue of the night and then treated you to a very good meal."

He closed the small gap between them. Wrapping one arm around her waist, and tucking her firmly against his side under his shoulder. "You left out kissing my socks off."

She tipped her head back and realized he was watching their reflection in the glass. She followed his gaze and saw the two of them. They looked good together. His height made it seem like he was protecting her. Cherishing her . . . she told herself it was just a reflection but her heart beat a little faster.

"And still all I get is an okay?" she asked, her voice dipping huskily at the end.

He shrugged his big shoulders and then brought his face to hers. "I'm not going to become Mr. Holiday Spirit overnight."

"I don't want that. I just want—" she broke off. She wasn't going to be insecure. That was the deal she'd made with herself. If she was seducing him then there was no place for doubts.

"What do you want?" he asked, cupping her face and tilting her head back.

She rested her head against his shoulder. The scent of his aftershave filled each breath she took. His eyes were crystal clear and for the first time all the plans she'd made faded away. This wasn't about plans or seduction. This was about two lonely souls who'd found each other.

No matter what Jackson said aloud she knew he felt it too. Taking a deep breath she said, "You."

He watched her through half-lidded eyes. Making her hyperaware of him and at the same time of her body. She felt his gaze moving over her. She shifted in his arms, sliding around to stand pressed breast to chest with him.

"Good."

She bit her lip to keep from laughing. He was too confident, too sure of himself, and with plenty of cause. He lowered his head and she held her breath.

Brushing his lips over her cheek, he held her close but with a tenderness no man had shown toward her before.

"Is that all you can say?"

"I thought it covered everything."

His long fingers caressed her neck. Slow sweeps of his fingers up and down until she shivered in his arms. She needed more from him. She grabbed his shoulders, tipped her head and opened her mouth over his.

He sighed her name as she thrust her tongue into his mouth. Sliding his arms down her back he pulled her close never breaking their kiss.

His tongue moved on hers with ease, tempting her further, tasting her deeper and making her long for him. Her skin felt too tight. Her breasts were heavy, craving his touch. Between her legs she was moistening for him, ready for him.

She lifted her head to look up at him. His skin was flushed, his lips wet from her kisses. She flexed her fingers against his shoulders.

God, he really was solid muscle.

"This is going to be complicated," he said.

"How?" she asked. Her car was down the street and her condo was only a few blocks over.

"Work."

She'd thought about it. Already had a plan in place but she didn't want him to know it. "You're a resourceful man. I'm sure you'll figure something out."

"I think we both will."

That sounded good to her.

Chapter Five

Krista's house had never seemed so small as it did with both her and Jackson in the foyer. She looked at the deacon's bench she'd purchased on an antiquing trip with her mom and felt a flood of nervousness. She wanted this man and everything felt so intense.

"I like this neighborhood. Doesn't Stuart live a few streets over?"

Stuart was their big boss. He and Jackson were both on the steering committee together. "Yes, he does. If you'd attended his Christmas party last weekend you'd know that."

"I wasn't the only one to skip it."

"Just pointing out the obvious."

"Why?"

"I think I'm nervous that you're finally here."

"Finally? Does that mean you'd planned on seducing me at Stuart's party?"

She flushed a little. The idea had actually come to her at Stuart's party when she'd watched several of her coworkers hooking up and leaving together. "I think I better take the Fifth."

He laughed. "Show me your place."

"It's nothing special."

"Yes, it is. It's your home. I live in a one bedroom condo so I'm not going to be comparing your place with much."

She turned on the lights and moved into her small living room. Jackson stopped in the archway and studied the room. She had a decorated tree inset a little off center in the front window that looked out on the street. The tree had been heavy and she hadn't been able to position it as she would have liked.

"Nice, but I really want to see the bedroom."

"You're kind of pushy."

"With your type that's the only way to be."

"My type?"

"The blackmailing seductress," he said.

"Then you have to know there's no way you're going to be in charge."

"I'll take the Fifth," he said.

She took his wrist and led him down the short hallway to her bedroom. She flipped the light switch and pivoted on her heel, leaning up to kiss him.

"Take your shirt off," she said. She'd been longing to see his chest all night. But her fantasies had really started last summer when he'd gotten caught in a late afternoon storm. She'd come into his office to drop off a report. Water had matted his hair and made his dress shirt cling to his muscles.

He reached between them, the backs of his fingers brushing her breasts as he unbuttoned his shirt. She shook from the brief contact and bit her lip to keep from asking for more.

He unbuttoned her blouse when he was finished with his shirt. Running his finger down the center of her body. Over her sternum and between her ribs. Lingering on her belly button and then stopping at the waistband of her skirt.

He slowly traced the same path upward again. This time his fingers feathered under the demi-cups of her ice-blue bra. Barely touching her nipples. Both beaded and a shaft of desire pierced Krista. Shaking her.

She scraped her nails over his chest. Traced the muscled ridges of his stomach and dipped her hand lower. Teasingly scraping one fingernail along the edge of his belt.

His breath rasped out and his stomach clenched. She watched his erection grow against his zipper. She slid her fingers down his length. He widened his stance, allowing her fingers to slip between his legs.

She needed more. She wanted more. Her heart beat so swiftly and loudly she was sure he could hear it. She hooked her fingers around his belt buckle and led him to the bed. Once there, she pushed him down first and he sprawled on his back. He moaned and the sound rumbled up from his chest. He leaned back, bracing himself on his elbows.

And let her explore.

His muscle jumped under her touch. She circled his nipple but didn't touch it. Scraped her nail down the center line of his body. Following the fine dusting of hair that narrowed and disappeared into the waistband of his pants.

His stomach was rock hard and rippled when he sat up. He reached around her back and unhooked her bra and then pushed the cups up out of his way. He pulled her closer until the tips of her breasts brushed his chest.

"Krista," he said her name like a prayer. Holding her against him.

His hard-on nudged her center and she shifted on him, trying to find a better touch but it was impossible with the layers of cloth between them. Her skirt was hiked up but it wasn't enough.

He kissed his way down her neck and bit lightly at her nape. She shuddered, clutching at his shoulders, grinding her body harder against him.

He loosened the fastening of her skirt and slipped his hands under the cloth. His big hands slipped into her panties, cupping her butt and urging her to ride him faster. Guiding her motions against him. He bent his head and his tongue stroked her nipple, and then he suckled her.

Everything in her body clenched. She clutched at Jackson's shoulders, rubbing harder and faster against his erection as her climax washed over her. She collapsed against his chest.

He held her close. Krista hugged him to her and closed her eyes.

Jackson had never seen anything more beautiful than the woman in his arms. She was so responsive to his touch and he wanted more.

She was the best Christmas present he'd ever had but he wouldn't say those words out loud. He'd wanted her but until this moment, he had not realized how fiercely.

She pushed his shirt off his shoulders, and he tugged it off, tossing it away. She shrugged out of her blouse and bra. She was exquisitely built, soft, feminine. Her breasts were full and her skin flushed from her recent orgasm.

He ran his hands slowly over her torso, almost afraid to believe that she was really here.

Her nipples were tight little buds beckoning his mouth. He'd barely explored her before and he needed to now. He needed to find out how she reacted to his every touch.

"I'm so ready for you," she said. Her voice was pitched low and a slight blush covered her cheeks and neck.

There was something very fragile inside this ultra-competent and professional woman. He pulled her more fully into his arms. Cradling her to his chest with one arm. She closed her eyes and buried her face in his neck. Each exhalation went through him. God, he wanted her.

He was so hard and hot for her that he might come in his pants. But he was going to wait. Then he felt the minute touches of her tongue against his neck. Her hand sliding down his chest and opening this belt, unfastening the button at his waistband and then lowering his zipper.

Hot damn.

Her hand slid inside his pants and his boxers. Smoothly her touch moved up and down his length. He tightened his hands on her back. He glanced down his body and saw her small hand burrowed into his pants. Saw her working him with such tender care and he had to grit his teeth not to end it all right then. But he wanted to be inside her the next time one of them climaxed.

Glancing down he saw her smiling up at him. She knew exactly what she was doing to him and was enjoying every second of it. Little minx.

"That's it, honey," he said, his voice raspy.

She pushed off the bed and slowly eased out of her clothing. His breath caught in his throat. She was exactly as he dreamed she'd be. Nipped in waist, long slender legs and full breasts. She put her hands in her hair and fluffed it out around her face.

"Like what you see?" she asked.

"Hell, yes. Turn around."

She did, slowly. Stopping when her back was to him and glancing over her shoulder. She had a sweet ass and he longed to caress her again. He reached out and touched her. She stood still and let him.

"Bend over," he said.

She leaned forward, bracing her hands on a dresser that was against the wall. He slipped his fingers between her legs. Felt her wetness against him and felt his own body harden even more. He needed to be inside her.

He pulled his hand from her body. "Come to me."

She did, crawling on top of him. He nudged her over on her back. Leaning down and capturing her mouth with his as he shoved his pants farther down his legs. She opened her legs and he settled between her thighs.

The humid warmth of her center scorched his already aroused flesh. He thrust against her without thought. Damn, she felt good.

He wanted to enter her totally naked without a condom, at least this first time. But that was a huge risk and one he knew better than to take.

He pushed away from her for a minute, fumbled with his

pants, taking them all the way off along with his boxers, then found the condom he had put in the pocket earlier today.

He glanced over at her and saw she was watching him. The fire in her eyes made his entire body tight with anticipation. He put the condom on one-handed and turned back to her.

"Hurry."

"Not a chance. I'm going to savor you."

"Betcha can't," she said.

"You really want—"

"I really want you, Jackson. Come to me now."

She opened her arms and her legs, inviting him into her body and he went. He lowered himself over her and rubbed against her. Shifted until he'd caressed every part of her.

She reached between his legs and fondled his sac, cupping him in her hands. He shuddered. "Not now. Or I won't last."

She smiled up at him. "Really?"

He wanted to hug her close at the look of wonder on her face. "Hell, yes."

He needed to be inside her now. He shifted and lifted her thighs, wrapping her legs around his waist. Her hands fluttered between them and their eyes met.

He held her hips steady and entered her slowly. Thrust deeply until he was fully seated. Her eyes widened with each inch he gave her. She clutched at his hips as he started thrusting. Holding him to her, eyes half closed and her head tipped back.

He leaned down and caught one of her nipples in his teeth, scraping very gently. She started to tighten around him. Her hips moving faster, demanding more but he kept the pace slow, steady. Wanting her to come again before he did.

He suckled her nipple and rotated his hips to catch her pleasure point with each thrust, and he felt her hands in his hair clenching as she threw her head back and her climax ripped through her.

He started to thrust faster. He leaned back on his haunches and tipped her hips up to give him deeper access to her body.

Her body was still clenching around his when he felt that tightening at the base of his spine seconds before his body erupted into hers. He pounded into her two, three more times, then collapsed against her. Careful to keep his weight from crushing her. He rolled to his side, taking her with him.

He kept his head at her breast and smoothed his hands down her back. Knowing his instinct had been right and this woman was the one meant for him.

Chapter Six

Jackson knew his entire world had changed in the last few minutes. He couldn't think or analyze and that worried him. He could always do an analysis. Always—but lying in Krista's bed, her naked body pressed to his, he couldn't.

She sighed. "That was nice, Jackson. You know how to keep your blackmailer happy."

"I do my best," he said.

"I'll say. So have I reformed you?"

"Was that your intent?"

"Yes."

"No," he said. He knew he wasn't reformed. He was still going to demand that everyone on his staff earn every dollar that went into their paycheck.

"Oh," she said, slipping from the bed and taking her robe from the closet. "I . . ."

"I'm still going to be a demanding boss, but that doesn't mean that I'm going to be working round the clock any more, sweetheart."

"What will you do to occupy yourself?"

"Hopefully spend some time with you."

She gave him a brilliant smile. "That's been my plan."

He closed the gap between them, caging her face between both of his palms. Tipping her head back he stared down into her wide brown eyes. He felt something he couldn't describe when he looked at Krista. His gut clenched and his groin tightened but his heart also beat a little faster and there was this feeling deep in his soul that if he lost her . . . things would never be right again.

Her mouth was made for long, drugging kisses and he took his time tasting her. Getting his fill of this woman who'd come so unexpectedly into his life

"I'm not going anywhere," he said when he lifted his head.

She bit her lip and pushed away from him. "Don't stay because I blackmailed you."

"That's not why I'm staying."

"I'm not so sure."

"Well, hell, woman I am. And I'm the boss."

"Not ton—"

He cut her words off with his mouth. Bringing his lips to hers and making her stop talking. He'd never met a woman so damned frustrating as this one. He damned well knew that he wasn't going anywhere and neither was she.

Jackson's kiss overwhelmed Krista. He thrust his tongue deep in her mouth. When she tried to angle her head to reciprocate, he held her still.

This was his embrace and she felt the fierce need in him to contradict what she'd just said. She'd lashed out at him to save herself. To remind herself that men didn't fall in love with her this easily.

And now she was finding the proof she was searching for that Jackson was different from every other man she'd ever met.

Her nipples tightened and her breasts felt too full as he pulled her fully into his embrace. He canted his hips toward hers. The ridge of his erection bumped against her. She moaned deep in her throat and clung to him.

His biceps flexed as he shifted her in his arms, pressing her back against the dresser while he ran his hands down her back.

His mouth moved down the column of her neck, nibbling and biting softly. He lingered at the base of her neck where she knew her pulse beat frantically. Then he sucked on her skin. Everything in her body clenched. Not enough to push her over the edge, just enough to make her hungry—frantic for more of him.

She scored his shoulders with her fingernails. His skin was hot to the touch and she wrapped her arms around his body, pulling him closer to her.

He pushed her robe off her shoulders. He pulled back, staring down at her. Then he traced one finger around the her nipple.

She shook with need. Couldn't wait for him.

She reached between their bodies, caressed the hard length of his erection, then reached lower, cupping his sac in her hand. His breath hissed out.

His mouth fastened on her left nipple, suckling her. She undulated against him, her hips lifting toward him.

He lifted her leg up around his hip. Then he shifted his body. She felt him hot, hard, and ready at her entrance. But he made no move to take her. She looked up at him. "You're mine."

She couldn't respond to that.

"I . . ."

"Watch me take you, Krista, and know that this is real. Not blackmail or holiday crap. But real fire and passion."

He thrust inside her then. Lifting her up, holding her with his big hands on her butt as he repeatedly drove into her. He went deeper than he had earlier. She felt too full, stretched and surrounded by him.

He bit her neck carefully and sucked against her skin and everything tightened inside her until she felt her climax spread through her body. Her skin was pulsing, her body tightening around his plunging cock. A minute later he came.

Crying her name and holding her tightly to his chest.

She rested her head on his shoulder and held him. Wrapped

completely around his body, she realized the truth of what he'd said. They belonged to each other.

He staggered back to the bed and lowered them both onto it, adjusting their bodies so that she was cradled on his lap with his arms around her.

"You do us a disservice when you say something like I'm with you because you blackmailed me."

"It's true, though."

"The only truth is that I've wanted you for a damned long time."

"Then why did I have to make the first move?"

"I'm not that kind of guy, Krista. But now that you have my attention I'm not letting go."

She didn't know how to respond to him. She'd made a fool of herself once for love and the last thing she wanted is to be proven wrong again. Especially now.

He cupped her face so gently, rubbing his forefinger along her jaw. "I'm not good with words. I can't say it the way you'd want to hear it but I want you."

"That's sex."

"Yes, sex. I want you in every way I can think of until neither of us has any energy left. But I also want your smile and your laughter over the dinner table every night."

"I can't cook."

"I can."

"Why am I not surprised?"

She felt dazed by all he'd said. By his kisses, his actions and his sweet seduction. How had he gone from Scrooge to an odd kind of Santa Claus giving her the one thing she really wanted for Christmas?

"And you're mine."

"Yes. We'll take this slow if we have to but I'm not going anywhere."

"I'm not going to let you. Not now that I've found you."

"Hey, I want credit for this. I found you. I lured you into my lair and seduced you."

"Whatever you say," she said.

"I like the sound of that. Why don't you shift around here so I can make love to you again?"

"What are you going to do for me?" she asked.

"Everything. I'm going to keep you happy for the rest of our lives."

February 14

Krista saw an immediate response to her e-mail to Jackson. She knew he was still at the office. It was almost six and they had plans for the night but she knew he wouldn't want to leave until the last report was finished.

She opened the e-mail. *I'm out of the office until February 22. Please direct all inquiries to Marsha Graham at mgraham @northernsports.com.*

Where was he?

A rap on the door frame made her look up. She saw a bottle of Korbel and two long-stemmed glasses. One of the glasses had a black velvet ribbon tied at its base.

"Come in."

"Still working, sweetheart?"

"I'm waiting on some numbers from you."

"I've got them but it'll cost you."

"Really?"

"Yes," he said, sauntering into her office and hooking one hip on the edge of her desk. He popped the cork on the champagne while she saved her document.

"What's the price?"

"It's very steep."

"I'm listening."

He handed her the glass with the black ribbon on it and as she took it she realized there was a ring attached to it.

Her hand shook and a drop of bubbly spilled on it. Jackson took the glass from her, licked the back of her hand and smiled down at her. He loosened the ribbon holding the ring and dropped to one knee in front of her.

"Marry me, Krista. Promise me all the Christmases of the future as well as a life filled with love, laughter and hard work."

"Yes," she said, pulling him to his feet and wrapping herself around him. "Oh, definitely yes!"

THE GOOD GIRL'S GUIDE TO A VERY BAD CHRISTMAS

Kylie Adams

Acknowledgments

For the sassy, sophisticated ladies of Minks Only . . .

Lea Barton—Artist, fashionista, ferociously fearless. She's a Brooklyn girl by way of a small Mississippi town. But listen up. Because she *always* has something to say.

Jennifer Hall—A locomotive in lipstick and high heels. Caution: When this girl wants something, give it up or get out of the way. Because she *will* prevail.

Janet Scott—If ever you needed living proof that fifty *is* the new forty, then look no further than this tall, blonde, gorgeous, fabulously fit, pistol-packing sharpshooter.

Rita Wray—She knocks down goals like ninepins and does it with the kind of cool, super confidence that makes everyone in the room want to *be* her when they grow up.

Men vote with their feet. If his shoes are pointed toward you, so is the thing in his trousers.
—Diane Farr

FROM: tinababy@aol.com

TO: peri@earthlink.net

SUBJECT: DON'T BOOK THE BAND!

Peri,
There's really no delicate way to put this, so I'm just going to come out with it. Your fiancé, Mike Mason, is a scumbag. And I've got proof. It's not pretty. In fact, it's pretty ugly. But you have to see it. As much as it may hurt. Unless you want to be like most girls. You know, the ones who continue booking the band, ordering the flowers, and scheduling the fittings no matter what, because the prospect of having an idiot husband seems better than having no husband at all. But I *know* you're not that girl. Last night I got an e-mail from my ex, David. He's the guy I dated for a few months before I met Kent. You might recall that I broke up with him over his addiction to Internet porn. Anyway, David came across Mike on one of the sleazy sites he frequents and remembered him from that time the four of us went to the Dave Matthews Band concert. I attach the link below only *for your own good*. Call me if you need to talk.
Tina

http://bankersgonewild.com/talesfromthestrip/mike.video

Chapter One

"Peri, I'm sorry about your engagement. I know that's gotta suck," Louie said. He tied his black smock and stepped out of the way.

"Thanks. And it does. But life goes on." Peri punched the clock with her time card. *Shit.* She was just late enough for Owen to dock her a quarter-hour's pay.

"Sometimes the best medicine when you find out your guy's been cheating is to go out there and nail somebody yourself," Louie went on. "And I'm here for you if that's what you need. I'll be that guy."

Peri looked at him.

Louie stared back earnestly, as if he'd just offered a place to crash for relatives in town for a funeral.

Peri grinned. The boy was speaking from the depths of his twenty-two-year-old, party animal heart. "I appreciate that so much. It's very thoughtful. But I think I'm going to pass."

"Am I on crack, or was there supposed to be a fucking shift change ten minutes ago?" Owen bellowed to no one in particular from some place unseen.

Peri and Louie darted out of the office to take their positions behind the counter as baristas at Rush Hour, an anti-Starbucks coffeehouse on Thompson Street in New York's trendy SoHo.

"Sorry I'm late," Peri said, moving fast to relieve Sabrina, who'd just come off the graveyard midnight-to-eight gauntlet.

"Please take over before I throw something in that bitch's face," Sabrina half-begged, half-threatened in a low whisper. "She acts like I've never made a cappuccino before."

Peri glanced up to see one of Rush Hour's like-clockwork regulars—a high-strung assistant fashion editor for *Vogue*. The impression always lingered that if her Guatemalan Huehuetenango cappuccino wasn't prepared just so, then furniture would go flying.

"I've got this," Peri assured Sabrina with an amused laugh. "Go. Leave this place. Sleep." She finished up and sent the fashionista with the Obsessive Coffee Disorder on her way. And then *he* approached the counter.

Chase McCloud.

Almost instantly, Peri's heart began beating as fast as a little bird's. It seemed impossible. But each time she saw him in person, he appeared to be even more handsome. Like today, in his distressed brown leather bomber jacket, vintage Lynyrd Skynyrd rocker tee, destroyed-wash denim jeans, and motorcycle boots, Chase McCloud was dressed to torture women. And for that matter, certain men, too. The black cashmere skull cap that covered his forehead and ears only added to his appeal, because it accentuated his piercing blue eyes.

Chase smiled at Peri. "Caramel Frappuccino," he said.

Peri smiled right back. "You're breaking my heart." And he was. And he did. Every time she saw him. In person. Or on television.

Chase shrugged, grinning, showing perfect teeth, displaying even more perfect dimples. "Okay, okay. I'll take the usual."

It was their little joke. After all, Rush Hour was *the* choice for coffee hardliners. Skinny latte drinkers were encouraged to queue up at one of the corporate chains where the java slaves wouldn't know a well-brewed coffee from a cup of week-old Sanka.

Peri moved like lightning to prep Chase's ritual request—a Nicaraguan ristretto. Definitely a morning hit for the serious-minded, as it was like an espresso but with *half* the amount of water.

"Any luck on the acting front?" Chase asked.

"I got a part in a play," Peri answered modestly, casting her eyes downward. "Off, off, *off* Broadway." She laughed a little.

He nodded and laughed along with her. "I've been in some of those. But that's okay. Work is work."

Oh, God, was he hot. For a millisecond, Peri indulged in the exquisite art of just drinking him in. "When it lasts. In the middle of our first cast reading, we found out that the financing fell through. So . . . ."

Chase glanced around for a moment, searching for the right words. "Oh . . . well, I've been in some of those, too, actually." Now he laughed a little.

And this time Peri joined in.

"Have you ever auditioned for *Physical Evidence*?" Chase asked.

Peri shook her head. *Physical Evidence* was only one of the hottest shows on television, running a close second to *C.S.I.* in the ratings race, thanks to the viewing public's insatiable desire for gory forensic crime dramas. Chase had a supporting role in the series. He played Bingo Grant, a cooler-than-cool junior investigator with a penchant for mouthing off to superiors. As far as Peri was concerned, he never got enough screen time.

"The show needs at least fifteen guest actors for each episode. Pick up a copy of *Back Stage* and give it a shot." Chase leaned forward confidentially, giving her the full benefit of his aftershave.

Peri recognized it as Dior Higher. Hints of pear, basil, and frosted citrus were strong in her nostrils as she hung on every syllable tripping off his spectacular lips.

"A single-day walk-on pays about seven hundred bucks. A speaking part could take a week to shoot. That pays a little over two grand."

Peri's eyes widened. "I had no idea."

Chase gave her a severe nod. "Before I lucked out with this *Physical Evidence* gig, I *survived* on the *Law & Order* franchise." He chuckled. "Once I was a lawyer on the original *Law & Order*, a prison inmate on *Special Victims Unit*, and the boyfriend of a murder victim on *Criminal Intent*. All in the same week. But I paid my rent that month. And I had more for dinner than Ramen noodles, too."

Peri could feel her central nervous system adjusting to the current reality. This marked the longest conversation she'd ever had with Chase McCloud. Why did he have to be nice, funny, helpful, empathetic, encouraging, and self-deprecating? Now her fan-girl crush was morphing into something much more.

In a nervous gesture, she played with her brunette hair, moving it behind her ear. "I auditioned for a TV show once, and the casting director told me I was 'bland and way too half-hour.' God, I was so embarrassed. Since then, I've pretty much been sticking to theater."

Chase paid for his caffeine fix and dropped a ten-dollar bill into the tip jar. "That's *one* guy. You can't listen to him. I had a woman tell me once that I'd be lucky to get cast as a fraternity extra in a National Lampoon movie. I kept at it and got lucky." He winked. "You will, too."

The man in line behind Chase cleared his throat impatiently.

Chase patted the counter with a gloved hand. "Take it easy." He started out, and she wondered if he was aware of her eyes burning into his back, because he stopped at the door, spun quickly, and hollered out, "Get *Back Stage* today! I want to see you on my set!" He paused a beat, smiling at her, realizing that he was causing a minicommotion. "What's your last name, Peri?"

"Knight," she called out.

"Peri Knight," Chase repeated thoughtfully. "Now that's a name for television!" And then he was gone.

Peri could feel the blush staining her cheeks.

"A double espresso with hot milk on the side would be nice," the next customer barked. "Any time you feel like it, honey. I was only supposed to be at work five minutes ago."

"Coming right up," Peri chirped, practically floating and feeling no irritation whatsoever. *Nobody* could get under her skin today.

Nobody except her mother, of course.

"Tina's a troublemaker," Suzanne Knight was saying. "I've never liked that girl. She wants to spoil things for you. Just so she can have Mike for herself."

"Mom, that's the dumbest thing I've ever heard you say," Peri argued, struggling to fish cash out of her coin purse without taking off her gloves.

The newsstand guy, gloveless and unaffected by the bitter cold, just stood there like a statue in the park until she produced the necessary funds to claim a copy of *Back Stage* as her own.

"Anyway, Peri, you're overreacting to this situation. How can you be one hundred percent sure that it's Mike on that video?"

"Okay, *that's* the dumbest thing you've ever said. The bit about Tina comes in second." Peri stuffed the casting weekly into her tote bag and started down the frozen sidewalk, cellular clamped to ear.

"It could be anybody on that tape. Think of all the things they can do with trick photography."

Peri sighed. "Mom, the distinctive birthmark on Mike's ass is clearly visible. And at one point in the video, you can distinctly hear him yelling, 'Mike Mason rules! Fuckin' A,' while he's having sex with the stripper." One beat. "So there's really no room for conspiracy theories. It's him."

"What am I supposed to tell his mother? Since you broke off the engagement, Caroline Mason has left me two messages. I can't avoid her forever."

"I don't know. Tell her that she raised a pig. See where the conversation goes from there."

"Peri, I can't believe you're willing to throw away an entire future over this . . . *incident*. At the end of the day, it's a meaningless encounter."

"Meaningless to him maybe. Not to me." Peri charged on, even as the bitter winter wind sliced into her, chilling her to the very marrow of her bones. This thrift-shop coat was for shit. But the train station was just a few blocks away. She could make it. And driving her mother insane would be just the entertainment to keep her mind focused on something besides the cold.

"The Masons are a strong family, Peri. Mike is a fifth-generation banker at Manhattan National. His future is secure. You'll live in a fine apartment. You'll summer in the Hamptons. Your kids will have access to the best schools. You could build a great life with him."

"It's not the life I want," Peri said. "In all honesty, this breakup hasn't been that devastating. I'm relieved. God, I'm even *grateful* . . . that Mike gave me this out. I've known for a long time that he wasn't the right guy for me. But I accepted his proposal, and part of me just didn't want to admit that I was wrong to do that. So I stuck with it, and I interpreted things to support the idea that I loved him. But I don't. And I don't think I ever did. He just doesn't thrill me."

"He just doesn't thrill you," Suzanne Knight echoed, her voice weary with impatience. "Sometimes you have to grow up, Peri. There's more to life than *thrills*. Look at your situation. You make an hourly wage behind a coffee counter, so you can pursue this acting thing, and you couldn't *buy* a cup of coffee from all the money you've earned from your so-called craft. You don't have any health insurance. You had to take in a crazy roommate to stay in that horrible apartment, and you *still* need me and your father to subsidize the rent every month. That kind of vagabond lifestyle is only cute when you're twenty. After that, it's pathetic and irresponsible."

Peri's blood began to boil a little. It always came down to money. If her parents handed it out, then they thought that it put them in the captain's chair to control her life.

"There's a meeting I want you to attend tonight," Suzanne announced.

Peri was instantly suspicious. Right away she thought it might be some kind of intervention involving the Masons. "What kind of meeting?"

"The American Promise Makers."

Peri groaned. "You can't be serious."

"Oh, I'm very serious. It's just an introductory seminar, but I already paid the two-hundred-dollar registration fee, and you *are* going. It's being held in the auditorium of a Brooklyn high school. Check your e-mail when you get home for the details."

"Mom, I'm not schlepping out to *Brooklyn* in this weather to listen to some wack job tell me that feminists are evil and that *The Surrendered Wife* should be required reading."

"See, you're already judging the information before you've had a chance to hear it."

"I know about this group," Peri persisted. "It's just a bunch of crazy women who want to pretend that it's the fifties again. Tell them to send me a pamphlet. I'm not going."

"Yes, you are," Suzanne said sharply.

"No, I'm *not*," Peri shot back, her tone equally sharp. Thank God. There, right across the street, was the subway. "Listen,

I'm about to go into a train station, so I'm probably going to lose you . . ."

"Wait just a minute."

"I have to—"

"Patricia Perriman Knight! You don't have to do anything but listen to your mother!"

The use of her full name combined with the primal scream stopped Peri in her tracks.

"For years, your father and I have indulged you with this dream of becoming an *actress*. We've paid for training and head shots and God knows what else. All I'm asking you to do is attend one Promise Makers meeting with an open mind. Is that so much to ask?"

Yes, it was.

"The reason why women are unhappy and unfulfilled in marriage today is a simple one: They try to do too much." Paige McCoy stopped talking, looked out at the sea of attentive listeners in the auditorium of Brooklyn's Cobble Hill School of American Studies, and smiled in quiet acknowledgment of the hundred or so female heads bobbing up and down in unified agreement.

But Peri's head did *not* move.

Paige McCoy walked to the lip of the stage, her smug, listen-to-me-because-I-know-the-secret voice carried by one of those wireless, headset microphones, the kind Britney Spears uses even when she lip-synchs in concert. But Paige McCoy was no Britney. In her pink-and-black boucle jacket, black wool crepe ruffle-hem skirt, and wedge-heeled Mary Janes by Taryn Rose, she was oh-so Charlotte from *Sex and the City*.

In fact, as Peri swept an assessing gaze over the crowd, she discovered that the auditorium was chockablock full of Charlotte types—attractive, fashionable, yet with a conservative touch, and palpably yearning for the *Modern Bride* fantasy of marriage and family to come true.

And here sat Peri Knight, the definitive odd-girl-out in her youth-hostel-chic ensemble of ethnic headwrap, thrift-shop coat, baggy cargo pants, and lace-up shearling boots, fresh from a self-imposed engagement bust-up and unable to wipe the mystified expression off her face as Paige McCoy blathered on.

"Don't listen to the feminists, ladies. They tell us that the key to happiness is equality. But I've been there, sisters. Once upon a time, I crashed through the glass ceiling. I earned the kind of income that made my husband's salary look like lunch money. I had a say in *everything* that went on in our household, from how we approached finances to when or if we would make love. And you know what? I'd never felt more miserable. Seek relationship *equality*, sisters, and you will only get emotional *inequity*."

Peri knew that her mouth had dropped open, that her eyes were wide with shock, that her chest was tight with the fury of silent protest. And yet, as she looked around, it seemed as if every other woman in the room was just smiling in lockstep agreement.

"Sisters, you are here today because you want to make a promise. A promise to yourselves. And most importantly, a promise to your husbands, present or future." Paige McCoy walked back and forth across the stage, making eye contact with the first few rows of disciples, beaming *gotcha* looks to each and every one. "A true Promise Maker surrenders to her husband's leadership in all aspects of marriage. A true Promise Maker knows that her best talents are utilized in avoiding boredom in the bedroom."

"This Stepford bullshit is un-fucking-believable," Peri muttered under her breath.

The objection was loud enough to incur scowls and hisses from the women in her immediate orbit.

"It's like I always say," Paige McCoy went on, "a true

Promise Maker is something of a Wonder Woman. She's Betty Crocker in the kitchen and Jenna Jameson in the bedroom."

A cacophony of chuckles filled the auditorium.

"But a true Promise Maker is not indulgent to fantasy. She's not one of those 'desperate housewives' who covets young, virile men or the mysterious neighbor next door. She doesn't harbor erotic thoughts about celebrities, either. Her husband is her king. And she is there to make him feel like one. *Especially* in the bedroom. Do this, sisters, and you will *never* have to worry about your husband's wandering eye. And if he does stray, then that's your cue to double up your efforts at making his bedroom a more exciting place to play."

By now, Peri was beyond disgusted. She began gathering her things to leave and made no attempt to be quiet about it.

"Sisters, I challenge you to write down five erotic fantasies involving a man other than your king," Paige McCoy said.

A ripple of shock moved through the crowd. Uncertain glances were shared. Some titters, too.

Peri hesitated.

"Go ahead," Paige McCoy encouraged them. "Give voice to these desires. State them for the record."

Peri watched as shameful pens went to work on shameful legal pads. Suddenly intrigued by the assignment, she joined in and began to write.

1. Have sex with Chase McCloud.
2. Have sex with Chase McCloud while he's wearing his Bingo Grant costume.
3. Have sex with Chase McCloud after waking up with Chase McCloud and eating a breakfast that Chase McCloud prepared.

4. Have sex with Chase McCloud again.
5. Repeat items 1–4 with Chase McCloud.

"And now, sisters," Paige McCoy instructed, "I implore you to renounce these thoughts as psychic garbage and symbolically rip them to shreds!"

The sound of paper being torn echoed through the auditorium.

But Peri Knight merely slipped her private page into her tote bag and walked out. Somewhere between the frigid walk on Baltic Street and the takedown of a cab to whisk her to the train station, she decided what to do with her secret fantasy list. Peri was going to post it on the door of her refrigerator.

The thought of how horrified Paige McCoy would be about that conjured up a secret joy in Peri that triggered a spell of uncontrollable laughter.

How's *that* for a promise, bitch?

BACK STAGE

Open Casting: Film & Television

Project Type:	Television
Full Project Name:	PHYSICAL EVIDENCE
Union:	SAG
Rate:	Scale
Location:	New York
Shoot Date:	Not Set
Casting Studio:	Silver Screen Studios
Audition Date:	December 16, 9:00 A.M.
Production Co:	Fingerprints & Fibers, Inc.
Address:	Chelsea Piers, Pier 62

Seeking

Attractive actress to believably play assistant district attorney between ages mid-20s and early 30s. Sexy, intelligent, confident, take-no-prisoners attitude, fast talker.

Performers of all ethnic and racial
Backgrounds are encouraged to attend.

Chapter Two

"Owen, *please*," Peri begged. "I have to make this audition. Let me go, and I'll forego my Christmas bonus."

"I don't give Christmas bonuses," Owen snapped.

"That's what you always say," Peri countered. "And every year, you slip us a little red envelope with a hundred-dollar bill inside. By the way, we're out of Ethiopian Yirgacheffe."

"It's on order," Owen said automatically.

Peri followed the Rush Hour owner-manager into the storage room, where he proceeded to rip open a box of custom-made china filters.

He glanced up. "You're on the clock, and we've got a line of customers going out to the sidewalk."

Peri pleaded with her big brown eyes. "If I leave right now, I can make it on time."

Owen sighed defeat. "I need to find some slackers with zero ambition. This is killing my schedule. Everyone here wants to be an actor."

"Actually, that's not true," Peri said, ripping off her Rush Hour smock. "Angela wants to be a dancer, Julie wants to be a singer, and Louie's working on a screenplay." She made a dash for the door, then suddenly halted. "You didn't take my offer to give up the Christmas bonus *seriously*, did you? Because I'm broke and was really counting on it."

Owen waved her off without eye contact.

Peri took that as a yes, raced to grab her tote bag and week-end carryall, bundled up, and clocked out. She weaved in and out of cranky customer bodies to reach the exit door.

Once her feet hit the sidewalk, she experienced a thrilling sense of freedom and lurched forward to get a good running start. But merely a few strides into her escape, she crashed into a hard body and went down fast on the cold concrete.

"Peri?"

For a moment, she was dazed. And then she saw Chase McCloud kneeling down in front of her, reaching out both hands to help her up. "Are you okay?"

She nodded, embarrassed, feeling like a clumsy fool and horrified to see the contents of her tote bag littered along the sidewalk. Did the entire population of New York really need to see her past-due notice from Providian Visa and know that this week's train reading was *The Stud* by Jackie Collins?

"Is the coffeehouse on fire or something?" Chase asked with a laugh as he piloted her to the standing position. "You almost mowed me down."

Funny he should ask about fire, as his touch was burning through the thick fabric of her winter wear. Peri smiled apologetically, watching in helpless wonder as Chase solicitously bent down to retrieve her wind-strewn belongings.

He came across the latest issue of *Back Stage*. It was folded back to the film and television casting pages, a single notice circled in red marker. He looked up at her, beaming. "You're going for it. Good for you."

"I know," Peri said excitedly. "I'm auditioning for your show in, like, *twenty* minutes!"

Chase moved fast to collect the rest of her things. "Then you better take off. I'll put in a good word when I get to the set. My first call isn't until noon." He transferred the tote bag and weekender back to her. "Good luck."

"Thanks," Peri said, almost breathlessly.

All of a sudden, Chase let out a piercing whistle and hailed a cab. He shoved some cash at the driver and said, "Take this lady to Chelsea Piers, number sixty-two," before ushering her into the rear cabin and shutting the door. He smacked the hood with his gloved palm, and the taxi took off.

Peri watched the events unfold in some kind of awestruck daze, deliriously hopeful for the future, totally amazed that these random star sightings were developing into a real connection, and completely unaware that her list of top five sexual fantasies had just blown onto Chase McCloud's foot.

Peri did a quick change in the backseat. Off went the thrift-shop coat. On went the caramel herringbone seamed jacket with flutter sleeves. Good-bye Old Navy cargo pants. Hello matching flat-front slacks with wide legs. Luckily, the black turtleneck she routinely wore to Rush Hour could stay. When she fastened the three big buttons of the snug-fitting jacket, the hot-milk stain was completely covered up. Taking a deep breath, she fingered her grandmother's iridescent starburst brooch for good luck.

A terrible fear lanced her brain. Shoes! Frantically, she unzipped the weekend bag. There were the dark-chocolate nappa leather boots. Relief flooded through her bloodstream. For a moment, Peri thought her entire audition had just ended before it began. After all, how could she show up for the role of a no-nonsense legal eagle in a battered pair of Uggs?

The driver stopped at Pier 62.

Peri swung out and made a dash for the entrance, the cold breeze coming off the Hudson fighting her the whole way. But she won that battle. It was the next one that would be impossible to win. Lined up in the gray-carpeted hallway were what looked to be hundreds of women just like her—dressed to prosecute and desperate for a speaking part on a hit television series.

She slumped against the wall at the end of the queue, feeling her hope of success fade as quickly as her labored breathing from the sprint.

The statuesque blonde beside Peri gave her a glance that translated into "What are *you* doing here?"

As Peri studied the competition, she began asking herself the same question. It was wall-to-wall beautiful women, longer legs, bigger breasts, better clothes. And unlike Peri, they weren't afraid to do the low-cut blouse, the tight skirt, anything to ratchet up the sensuality.

A fresh-faced girl who looked young enough to be a college intern emerged from an office and started down the line, passing out a single script page as she said, "You're reading for the part of Elise Mills. Please have your head shots and resumés ready. We'll get to you as soon as we can. Thank you for coming."

Peri cooled her heels for almost two hours before her turn arrived. She stepped into the room to find two women and one man seated behind a table, looking weary and unimpressed.

"I'm Peri Knight," she muttered, punctuating the announcement with a nervous laugh. "Here's my head shot and resumé." With great awkwardness, she placed the pages on the edge of the table and returned to the center of the room.

One of the women scanned her resumé. The expression on her face told the world she'd just tasted something bad. "No television experience?"

"No," Peri answered apologetically. "I've had several callbacks for commercials, though. So . . . almost." Her nervous laugh returned for an encore.

"We're casting for Elise Mills today," the other woman launched in robotically. "She's assistant D.A., very confident, very sexy, a take-no-prisoners attitude."

Peri nodded to the beat of each character trait, even as she realized that none of them had ever been used to describe her. She took a deep breath. Okay. So this is why they called it acting.

The man spoke up for the first time. "And just as an aside—this bit of background might inspire a different spin on your reading. Elise has a personal history with the Bingo character. They slept together once, and he never called. Now they're forced to work one-on-one to prep his testimony for a lawsuit against the crime lab."

"Does this mean I'll be reading with Chase McCloud?" Peri asked. Her heart took off while she waited for the answer.

"Not today," the first woman answered. "Chase will be reading only with the final three."

"Okay," the other woman cut in. "Ready when you are."

Peri glanced at the page of script, sucked in a terrified breath, and shut her eyes for a moment, working hard to channel the spirit of Heather Locklear from *Melrose Place*. What would Amanda's body language be? How would Amanda say it?

Suddenly inspired, Peri stalked toward the table and delivered her reading directly to the man. "I'm not here to bust your balls, Brett. I'm here to *save your ass*. It's *your* team's shoddy work that put what should be a nuisance case on the fast track to trial. I'm guessing you're not the kind of man who'd take advice from a woman, especially one that didn't breast-feed you. But here goes. Try worrying less about my attitude and more about your resident cowboy's. Christopher Dockett is one of the top plaintiff's attorneys in the country. I wouldn't want to be cross-examined by him about what I ate for breakfast. Meanwhile, Bingo's walking around like this is a small claims matter in Judge Judy's court." She stepped closer to the table and lowered her voice for emphasis. "If this goes the wrong way, Brett, the award could easily go double-digit millions. That'll be a nice footnote for your career."

Peri stopped. Suddenly, she was out of her Elise Mills zone and aware of her surroundings again. She glanced down at the script page. "Um . . . should I read the next part?"

The casting team exchanged a series of odd looks, then

turned back to Peri, seemingly regarding her in a whole new light.

"I like her," the first woman said. "We've had a parade of supersexy types file in here, but I actually *believe* that she's a lawyer."

"She knows she has a brain," the second woman added. "And she doesn't advertise *sexy* to get attention."

"Which in and of itself is sexy," the man put in. "She's pretty in an accessible way."

"Women will like her for that," the first woman agreed.

"So will men," the man pointed out. "The *Sports Illustrated* swimsuit model is what we fantasize about, but at the end of the day, we're terrified of her."

"Great job," the second woman praised. "Can you come back tomorrow for a reading with Chase?"

"This is *amazing*!" Tina squealed. "Oh, my God! You're going to get this part. I can just feel it."

Peri blocked out the thought. She didn't want to jinx it by jumping that far ahead. "Look, right now I'm just thrilled to have a callback." She breathed a sigh of relief into her cellular.

"But you have an *in* with Chase McCloud," Tina said, her voice up several octaves. "He said that he was going to put a word in, right?" She let out an annoyed sigh. "Hold on. Don't buy anything from her. All her clothes smell like cigarettes. Shoo her away before she stinks up the shop. Okay, I'm back."

Peri smiled. Tina Rich managed Something Borrowed, one of the city's most popular vintage-clothing and consignment boutiques. She became a fast friend after Peri made it a ritual to duck into the store at least once a week to dig through the racks for new finds.

"I can't believe this," Tina went on breathlessly. "You're going to be on *Physical Evidence*. You have to tell me when, so I can set my TiVo."

"Tina, stop," Peri protested lamely. Deep down, she enjoyed her friend's optimism. Maybe saying it out loud would make it come true. "It's only a callback, and I don't have *any* television experience. It really is a long shot."

"No, it's not," Tina said sharply. "They already know about your lack of TV experience. And trust me, these people didn't call you back just to make you feel good. You're a fresh face, and that's what they're responding to. People are plucked from nowhere to star in shows all the time. Like that girl from *Lost*. She beat out big names for that part."

"I just don't want to—"

Beep.

Peri glanced at the screen to identify the incoming call. She didn't recognize the number. "Tina, this could be the casting office. I'll call you back." She disengaged Tina and clicked on the mystery caller. "Hello?"

"I believe congratulations are in order." It was Chase McCloud.

Peri shut her eyes and jumped up and down. Chase McCloud was calling her cell phone!

"It's Chase," he said. "I scammed your number from casting. I hope you don't mind."

"No, of course not. I didn't get a chance to thank you for the cab. That was sweet."

"I'm just glad things worked out. Rumor has it that you really wowed them today."

Peri laughed modestly. "I don't know. I just feel lucky to have a callback."

"How about dinner tonight?" Chase asked. "And afterward, we can run lines together. That way, you'll kick ass again at tomorrow's reading."

"That sounds great."

"One of my favorite spots is Mas in the West Village. How about meeting there at ten?"

"Perfect," Peri chirped. But right away her brain went to work deconstructing the invitation. Was this just a friendly actor reaching out to a struggling nobody? Or was this a date?

PHYSICAL EVIDENCE

Season 3: Episode 57

"Blood on the Cross"

SHOOTING DRAFT

7 INT. SATURN 3—UPSCALE BAR/NIGHTCLUB—EVENING

A trendy, professional after-work gathering spot. The scene is crowded with lawyer types. Elise Mills is sitting at the bar, fingering the stem of a near-empty martini glass.

Bingo Grant walks in and generates a ripple of awareness from the women bored with suit-and-tie guys who only want to discuss their master plan to become partner at a firm.

Bingo
(sliding onto the empty seat next to Elise)
No fair. You're way ahead of me already.
(gestures to the bartender)
Draft beer, bud.

Elise
(still offering no eye contact)
I had to do something for the twenty minutes I've been waiting.

Bingo
(sarcastically)
Sorry. I couldn't decide what to wear. I must've changed clothes five or six times.

(glancing around at the other patrons)
You know, part of me wants to start a bar fight right
now. Some of these guys in here deserve a black eye and
busted lip just on principle alone.

Elise
(rolling her eyes)
Ooh—a man with open hostility for lawyers. You're nothing if not original.
(signals to the bartender for another martini)

Bingo
I'm surprised you wanted to meet here.

Elise
Here being what? The scene of the crime?

Bingo
Was it a crime? I thought we just had a night of meaningless sex.

Elise
You should ask around. Sex with you is considered a
criminal act.

Bingo
I guess anything that makes you feel that good has to be
illegal.

8 INT. BINGO'S APARTMENT—LATER

As if following moonlight, camera pans living room floor,
tracking scattered clothes—a man's and a woman's—along
a path to the bedroom, where two lovers are locked in a
feverish embrace.

Elise
(in a low, passionate, breathless growl)
You bastard. I'm supposed to be preparing you to take the stand.

Bingo
Don't worry. You won't leave here until I get a thorough cross-examination.
(silences her with a kiss)

Chapter Three

Somewhere between the second glass of wine and the poached lobster, Peri began to feel the tingle of the alcohol and the energy of animated flirtation.

Chase McCloud knew how to charm.

Mas was a quaint restaurant nestled on Downing Street in the West Village, a secret hideaway teeming with intimacy and French-countryside flavor. The wait staff was slavishly attentive, the menu deliciously eclectic.

After accepting Chase's dinner invitation, Peri had made a mad dash to Tina's Something Borrowed boutique, where she found an exquisite camel-colored cowl-neck poncho in Italian wool and a gorgeous, squeal-worthy pair of Spanish leather knee boots in her size. She put them together with her favorite pair of Seven jeans, her best black silk blouse, and vintage chandelier earrings. With her dark hair sexy-messy in that morning-after-a-great-night way and her makeup flawless, Peri felt like she had no change left from a million.

Which was a good way to feel when sitting across from Chase McCloud. There was handsome, there was beautiful, and then there was superhumanly gorgeous. He definitely stood behind door number three.

"So," Chase began, settling back between courses and taking a slow sip of wine. "What did you think of the new pages?"

"Shocked, to put it mildly."

Chase smiled. "The part's been upgraded to lead guest star. That means it'll pay more than five grand."

Peri's mind swirled with the news. "I still can't believe I'm up for it."

He raised his glass in salute. "You're not only up for it. You're the one to beat."

Peri refused to believe it. She filed this under flattery. Nothing more.

"I'm serious," Chase said, picking up on her doubtfulness. "And I might have you to thank for a better story arc."

"What do you mean?"

"The show's been criticized for too many stand-alone episodes that focus just on the investigations. Viewers are interested in the characters, too. Finally, the producers and writers are starting to come around. It's been implied that Bingo's a player, but do you realize that they've never even shown him on so much as a dinner date? Seems like all I do on the show is dust for fingerprints and mouth off to the bosses. Don't get me wrong, though. I realize that it's a great gig. But after a few years of the same scenes over and over again, it's easy to forget how grateful you should be." He shrugged. "But now, because of you, I've got something else to do."

"Because of *me*?" Peri asked.

"This was originally a glorified bit part—one brief scene with the Brett character and another one with Bingo on the witness stand. You showed them something this morning. They started talking, it went back to the writers, and now I'm involved in a major subplot with backstory. You're good luck. I should take you to Vegas."

Peri smiled demurely and busied herself with finishing her wine.

"Is this too late for you? I didn't finish my last scene until nine. Otherwise, I—"

"It's fine," Peri cut in. "I'm a bit of a night owl anyway."

Chase grinned. "Good. After dinner, I thought we'd go back to my place and run lines."

Peri felt the blood rush as she gestured to the script pages on the banquette next to her. "*These* lines?"

"Yeah, *those* lines," Chase teased. "Something wrong?"

"No, it's just . . ."

"I brought home some pieces from wardrobe," he announced. "That way, I'll be in my Bingo Grant gear, and it'll feel more like a real audition."

The sigh of relief that came next was ready-made with a hint of internal disappointment. "For a second there, I thought you meant we'd rehearse the second scene."

"You mean the love scene?" Chase asked.

Peri nodded.

"Oh, we should at least run through it." One beat. "Are you comfortable with that?"

Peri hesitated, not quite sure how to answer. The truth: She was so comfortable with it that she wanted to improvise what wasn't on the page. And her version could definitely take things to a too-hot-for-prime-time level.

"Trust me," Chase assured her. "It's better that we break the ice before the real audition. We can get past the initial awkwardness and establish a real chemistry. Our characters have already been intimate, so we don't want it to look like we're kissing for the first time."

The main entrées arrived, Peri could hardly concentrate on her lamb dish. It was delicious, but she basically took a few bites and pushed the rest around her plate to disguise her lack of appetite.

She asked Chase about his background, even though she knew it by heart, having consumed every bit of information published about him and occasionally Googling him for Internet mentions.

He grew up in Dallas, attended the University of Texas, played college rugby, majored in business, tried out for a campus production of *Cat on a Hot Tin Roof*, got the lead, then dropped out of school altogether, moved to New York a month later, and started to get jobs right away. Yes, he was *that guy* for whom it seemed everything in life came easily—career, friends, sports . . . women.

Peri had seen the paparazzi photos. Chase at the People's Choice Awards with an unknown blonde. Chase at the Screen Actor's Guild Awards with a vaguely familiar brunette actress. Chase at the opening of the new Helmut Lang store with a *Maxim* model.

And now, here he sat with her, the struggling actress and part-time barista. Peri was hardly the pinup type. The question begged to be asked: Why was he with her?

Chase smiled at her while digging into a sinful mixture of peppermint ice cream and flourless dark chocolate cake.

Peri grinned back. "What?"

"I'm trying to picture you in this part. It's definitely not typecasting. You're so cute and sweet. It'll be fun to see you channel your inner vixen."

Peri swooped her spoon in for a small bite of cake. "I can be bad," she said silkily.

"Oh, yeah?" The look he gave her was hotter than lava.

"Don't put Baby in a corner," Peri said, referencing that notoriously awful line from *Dirty Dancing*.

Chase laughed.

Peri drank deeply from what was now her fourth glass of wine. The slight buzz made her feel alternately bold and reluctant. But one impression lingered. How many dinners like this had Chase orchestrated? The desperate actress. The audition. The love-scene rehearsal. It was either a real dream-come-true or the worst casting couch cliché being played out at her expense. Peri felt herself withdraw.

Instantly, Chase picked up on it. "Is something wrong?"

"No, of course not," Peri lied . . . badly. And she called herself an actress? "It's just . . . I can't help but wonder how often you do this."

"Order dessert?" Chase joked. "Hardly ever."

Peri smiled at his evasive answer, then narrowed her gaze playfully, letting him know that there was no getting around a straight answer.

He raised his right hand in the peace sign. "Scout's honor: I've never scammed an actress's number from the casting office before. Yours is the first."

Peri believed him. So she wasn't the flavor of the week. This was a good sign.

"These days, I'm more used to women giving me *their* numbers." He pointed at her accusingly. "But *you* never did. Forgive me if I'm clumsy, but my muscles in the fine art of female pursuit have atrophied a bit."

Peri roled her eyes skyward at his sweet attempt at self-deprecation. "Well, I'm sure it's kind of like riding a bike."

"I'm not a serial dater," Chase announced. "I went through my man-whore phase during the first season of *Physical Evidence*." He shook his head at the thought, almost shuddering. "You wouldn't have wanted to know me then."

"That bad?"

"Pretty bad. But I got it out of my system. The second season I tried to date seriously, but nothing made it past the three-month mark, and even then, I was struggling to make it that far."

"This is your third season. So what's it going to be—marriage or celibacy?"

Chase arched his brow. "According to one of my co-stars, there's no difference." He sipped slowly on his wine. "I never want to settle, you know? To stay with someone or, God forbid, *marry* someone just because it's good enough. I see so many people around me do that. It's like the *idea* of a relationship is enough for them. But that kind of happinesss fades fast."

Peri raised her glass. "Truer words have never been spoken."

"So you can relate?"

"Oh, yes."

"Sounds recent," Chase said gently.

"It is. By a matter of days."

"Rough time of year to go through a breakup."

"Not when it's for the best. I'm not moping around wondering how I'll make it through the holidays. I actually have a chance this year at having a Merry Christmas. I don't think there's anything more lonely than being with the wrong person." Peri gazed at Chase sunnily. "In fact, this just might be one of my favorite Christmases ever."

"Really?"

"Even if I don't get the part. I know that—"

Chase interjected. "You can't think that way. The part is yours. You have to own it. Don't be that doubting actor with the overactive voice in your head that constantly tells you what's *not* going to happen."

Peri let out a guilty sigh. "I do that to myself all the time." She halted. Oh, God, did she sound like a teetering neurotic? Granted, she had her I'm-not-worthy moments, but deep down, she wasn't that girl. "When it comes to acting, I've never had much of a cheerleading squad. My parents think it's a silly dream, and my fi- . . . *ex*-fiancé never took it seriously either."

"That's easy to reverse," Chase said with philosophical directness. "Just find a conscious place where you tell yourself what *can* happen."

For show, Peri shut her eyes and pretended to try. *I can bounce back from a bad relationship with an amazing guy like Chase McCloud.*

"I want to hear you say it," Chase whispered.

Peri opened her eyes. "I can . . ."

"Can I tell you a secret?" Chase whispered, saving her from the words that died in her throat as she got lost in the infinite pools that were his eyes.

Peri nodded blankly.

"I really am a Caramel Frappuccino guy."

She smiled at him. "What are you talking about?"

He laughed a little. "It's true. I hate that Nicaraguan stuff. It's like drinking tar."

Now Peri was laughing. "Well, why do you order it then?"

Chase shrugged in that charming way that guys who've done something stupid do. "Because. The first time I walked through the door of Rush Hour, I took one look at you behind the counter and went, 'Wow, I'm in trouble.'" And I knew this was a serious coffee joint, and I didn't want to half-ass it and create a bad first impression, so I went for the tough stuff."

Peri shook her head, still laughing at him. "That is so adorable. And it was so unnecessary. I was already a fan. God, you could've ordered a chocolate milk, and I still would've thought you were Cary Grant."

"See, it's those damn seduction muscles again. They're not properly conditioned."

"Well, maybe you need to work out more," Peri said.

"You want a pickup line? I've got a great pickup line."

Peri smiled. "You pretty much had me at Caramel Frappuccino, but lay it on me."

"Some love doctors in Japan came up with it. Apparently, it has just the right number of linguistic triggers to make a girl go crazy. Are you ready?"

Peri nodded.

"Rainen no hono hi mo Issho ni waratteeiyoh."

"What does it mean?"

Chase took both of her hands in his now, his smile warm, broad, welcoming, and full of infinite possibility. The sight of him was practically a Christmas miracle. "This time next year, let's be laughing together."

"It doesn't take long for you to get back in shape, does it? I'd go anywhere with you right now."

"Let's get out of here." Chase said.

He opened the steel door to his SoHo apartment on Mercer Street, and Peri stepped inside a spacial wonderland. It was a swamping twenty-three-hundred square feet with thirteen-foot ceilings; exposed pipes, beams, and brick; dark walnut floors; and a gleaming Viking kitchen with a bar that stretched on forever.

"This is incredible," Peri said, marveling at the sophisticated, understated decor.

Chase began flicking on lights, then dimming them for mood creation.

An enormous Maine coon cat sloped in from what appeared to be the bedroom, gave Peri and Chase a bored look, then sloped back.

"That's Bingo the Second," Chase explained. "He's kind enough to let me live here, too."

Peri laughed. "I would love to have a cat, but my roommate's allergic." She thought of Anna Stallings and her allergies, phobias, strange work hours, and obsessive amounts of time spent in Internet chat rooms. "Among other things."

"I know that voice," Chase said, moving over to a sleek butler table to open a bottle of pinot noir. "That's the crazy roommate voice."

"*Oh, don't get me started*," Peri said, doing her best Fran Drescher.

Chase laughed. "Believe me, I've been there."

"How long have you been here?"

"Just a few months. I kept thinking *Physical Evidence* was going to be canceled. Finally, once we started the third season, I decided to ditch the studio walk-up and the smelly roommate."

Peri accepted her glass of wine and drank deeply. "It took you until the third season?"

Chase shrugged. "I should probably practice what I preach about that little voice, huh? But I'd been a part of so many pilots that didn't get picked and series that got the ax after just a few episodes. I was a little gun-shy about a mortgage."

"Well, it's a beautiful place."

"Thanks. I can't take much credit, though. My sister's an

interior designer in Dallas. She flew in to help out her baby brother."

A silence descended. It was uneasy . . . but in a good way. The tension wire between them tightened.

Chase gestured to the bar. "Why don't you have a seat? I'll get changed into my Bingo gear, and we can run through the first scene."

Peri sought out the script pages for a quick review, slipped onto one of the bar stools, and mentally prepped for the reading, calling forth the same attitude she had brought to the character earlier that day.

Chase stepped back into the room.

But Peri merely zeroed in on her wineglass, as the scene called for.

"No fair. You're way ahead of me already," he said.

"I had to do something for the twenty minutes I've been waiting." Peri turned to Chase, and the sight of him in full Bingo Grant gear—the police vest, the C.S.I. patch, the laminated photo ID badge—startled her.

For one long, surreal moment, everything stood still. From the very first broadcast of *Physical Evidence*, Peri had been hooked, never missing an episode. There was just something about Chase McCloud. Maybe it was his charisma and sex appeal, which seemed to run on a divine grade of superhuman fuel.

"I don't think you're supposed to be looking at me like that," Chase said quietly. "At this point in the scene, your character can't stand me."

"Who do you think I am—Meryl Streep?"

Chase smiled the smile of a man who *knew* he wasn't waking up alone the next morning. "Is it warm enough for you? I can turn up the furnace. I don't want you to be cold when I take off your clothes."

Peri was momentarily taken aback by the intentional, gentlemanly . . . *rudeness*. It might've been the sexiest thing any man had ever said to her. In fact, his polite yet potently sexual delivery left her a little bit undone.

She had to admit to herself that she was standing at the lip of the landslide of her fantasy—the one that she lived out every week after the final credits of *Physical Evidence* rolled, the one that smoked her mind each time he stood in line for his Nicaraguan ristretto, the one that she'd had the temerity to write down in that high school auditorium while sitting among the Promise Makers.

And now here she was, being gently piloted away from the bar, through the living room, and toward his bedroom. For a moment, Peri wondered how many others had run this gauntlet. But then all outside thoughts receded, and the only thing that existed was the two of them.

Chase lifted off her poncho and placed it carefully on the impressively tidy floor. Then he undid the middle button of her shirt and slid his hand inside to fondle her breast while his mouth moved in to claim hers.

Peri's lips parted in semi-amazement. She felt a thrilling tingle. The way their mouths fit so perfectly together. The charm and elegance of his seduction. It was exotic, erotic intoxication. She was drunk on the reality of finally living out the illicit dream that had stalked her mind like a wolf in the woods for so many months.

Chase drew back and carefully unfastened her wrist buttons before undoing the rest. When it was time to slip off her blouse, the fabric fell silkily to the floor, like a perfectly choreographed love scene from a romantic movie.

He moved to stand behind her, briefly letting his hands travel up the inside of her thighs. His fingertips lingered there, lightly, practically a feather touch, but hot enough to burn through the denim and scorch her imagination.

"You've got the softest skin," Chase murmured, unhooking her black lace bra and sliding it off her shoulders. His hands moved fast to caress her breasts, and he started a trail of soft, wet kisses from her shoulder to her neck to her ear . . . and then back again.

Peri just shut her eyes, basking in the wonderful, terrible notion that something so glorious was happening . . . and that something so glorious would have to end at some point. She felt like she could go on like this forever.

"You're so beautiful," Chase whispered.

Peri moaned her thanks as his tongue found that erogenous spot in the crevice of her ear. She pushed back against him, feeling the physical proof of his arousal hard against her. Oh, God, he knew how to make a woman feel good.

"I'm going to make love to you until we're so exhausted that we fall asleep," Chase promised in a thick whisper. "And then I'm going to make you breakfast, and we're going to do it all over again. I can't remember the last time a woman turned me on like this." He pressed himself into her back. "Can you feel it? That's what you do to me."

Chase eased her onto the bed and made a show out of removing her boots, her socks, her Seven jeans, her panties. And then he just stood there, staring, as if mesmerized by the first nude woman he'd ever seen in the flesh. "Merry Christmas to me," he murmured.

Peri marveled at the effect this had on her. With Mike, she'd always felt so insecure in bed, careful to always suck in her tummy, too afraid to try anything new with him. It was because he knew nothing of courtesy, generosity, or patience. And as a result, she never felt desirable.

But Chase made her feel like the sexiest, most confident woman in the world. And her arousal matched her newfound sensual belief in herself as she lay there watching him undress himself.

The vest, the pullover, the undershirt, the navy khakis, the boots—everything came off effortlessly. He even de-socked himself without breaking the spell. And the moment he was done, he returned to her, starting with her breasts, sucking slowly, licking them like they were the most delicious thing in the world, over and over again.

When he started to travel down, Peri lifted her hands overhead and gripped the sheets, preparing for the volcanic moment to come.

His mouth lingered between her thighs, hovering there, breathing into her, gently exploring her opening with his fingers. "Are you comfortable?" Chase asked. "Do you need a pillow under your back?"

"I'm fine," Peri breathed, arching her pelvis forward.

"Because I plan on being here for a long time." After that announcement, he moved in for the kill.

And Peri died instantly. Her mouth was open as the breath shuddered in her throat. Everything blistered and burned as he probed her with his fingers, relished her with his moans of pleasure, feasted on her with his tongue. From her slick depths to the tiny tip of her pleasure source, he *owned* her.

Peri pushed forward, as if welcoming him with her whole body, as the exquisite quickenings started in her stomach, and the slow melt started from the rest of her. She pulled at the sheets with such force that her knuckles were white. And the sexual adrenaline gave her such strength, she heard the distinct sound of a rip.

"Oh, yes, oh, yes, oh, *yes*," Peri moaned as the incredible feeling took her, lifting her up, spinning her through the sky, and casting her gently down, sweating with steam heat, damp with desire, and basking in the beautiful afterglow.

Chase's face was wet. His expression said that he was happy for her, pleased with himself, and ready for more as soon as she recovered.

God, he was such a gentleman. And it made her feel like *not* being a lady. The contradiction got her so hot that every part of her body felt like it was on fire. She wanted him to take her. But she didn't want it slow and refined. She wanted it firm and fast. The intense look in her eyes transmitted the order.

And Chase McCloud followed it like a dutiful soldier, entering her with just the right amount of force to let her know that he knew what she wanted. It took mere minutes. But every second thrummed with chivalry . . . and just a little bit of bite. By the end, he was screaming her name, she was coming a second time, and they were both dizzy, slick with perspiration, and gasping for breath.

Chase disposed of the condom neatly, then nuzzled into her. "Can I get you something to drink?" he asked.

Peri waited for her heaving breaths to subside before answering. "Am I in bed with you, or am I stuck somewhere on the ceiling? I can't tell."

Chase laughed, kissing her shoulder and pulling her closer. "Does that mean the reality isn't a letdown from the fantasy?"

Peri turned to him, a question in her eyes.

Chase grinned. "I have to confess something else. And this is a little sneakier than me being the Caramel Frappuccino guy." He paused a beat.

Peri braced herself.

"After you got in the cab this morning, the wind blew a certain piece of paper onto my foot."

Instantly, Peri knew what it was. That silly erotic fantasy list she had jotted down at the Promise Makers meeting. Oh, God! It was supposed to go on her fridge, and she'd forgotten all about it. Embarrassment swamped her. Playfully, she punched at Chase's broad chest. "You son of a bitch! Why didn't you tell me?"

Chase laughed at her. "Look at you blushing!"

Peri *knew* her face was burning red. Of course, Chase pointing this out only intensified it. "How did you know that was *my* list anyway?"

"I didn't—at first. It belonged either to you or to a bald guy who dropped his briefcase." Chase pretended to be worried. "Should I have taken him to dinner?"

"This isn't fair!" Peri wailed. "You knew more about me than I knew that you knew."

"Uh, I think I followed that."

"You don't understand. I was in this stupid seminar, and they told us to—"

He kissed her to make her shut up. "You don't have to explain anything. It was my fantasy, too. Now it's *ours*. Of course, breakfast will be a challenge. I never have any food here. I'll have to run down to the corner and pick up some bagels and fruit. Does that count?"

Peri nuzzled into him. "Where did you come from?" she marveled. And then, all of a sudden, she halted, disregardng the importance of his answer. "Wait a minute. That's not my line." She closed her eyes for a moment, sucked in a deep breath, and attempted to get into character. "You bastard, she growled. "I'm supposed to be preparing you to take the stand."

"Don't worry. You won't leave here until I get a thorough cross-examination," Chase said, silencing her with a kiss. *That* part of the scene was art imitating life.

And it was brilliant.

FROM: mmason@manhattannational.com

TO: peri@earthlink.net

SUBJECT: We Need to Talk

Dear Peri,
I've tried calling and stopping by, but you never answer your phone and never seem to be at home. Sooner or later we need to talk about us. You have a right to be mad, but I can't believe you'd end things for good over something like this. I was wrong. I was a jerk. I'll give you that. But I was drunk, and it didn't mean anything. In fact, if the tape hadn't come back to haunt me, then I never would've remembered what happened that night. I don't think you understand much about my job here at the bank. It's a lot of high pressure and high stress. Going to strip clubs is just a way for guys like me to unwind and

let off a little steam. Most wives get that and don't care. They'd rather a husband whoop it up with the occasional nameless/interchangeable club dancer than go out for drinks after work with a hot assistant. Maybe you could try spending some time with people in my circle instead of hanging out with those out-of-work actor types all the time. That might help our relationship. Think about it.
Love,
Mike

FROM: peri@earthlink.net

TO: mmason@manhattannational.com

SUBJECT: Re: We Need to Talk

Dear Mike,
There is no relationship, so feel free to pursue both strippers and hot assistants.
Peri

Epilogue

"I'm surprised you wanted to meet here," Bingo said.

"Here being what?" Elise countered. "The scene of the crime?

"*Was* it a crime?" His question mocked her. "I thought we just had a night of meaningless sex."

Elise gave him a look that most people reserved for messes on the side of the road. But deep down, the impression lingered that she just might want to lick it up. "You should ask around. Sex with you is considered a criminal act."

Bingo's smile was all the way cocky. "I guess anything that makes you feel that good has to be illegal."

Chase gave Peri a nod of approval as she broke character and turned to face the casting panel. Only this time, she had no pre-existing doomsday thoughts that one of them might utter the fatalistic phrase, "Don't call us. We'll call you."

The man spoke first. "I think I need a cigarette. The chemistry between the two of you is *hot.*"

"I say cancel the other readings," one of the women chimed in. "It doesn't get any better than this."

"Merry Christmas, Peri," the other woman said happily. "I believe you're needed in wardrobe."

THE NEW YORK POST

"Page Six"

STOCKING STUFFER

Newbie actress **Peri Knight** sure is having a very Merry Christmas. Last week the struggling thespian was fetching coffee at java hot spot Rush Hour. Now she's landed a recurring role on television's sizzling hit PHYSICAL EVIDENCE *and* her hunky co-star, **Chase McCloud**. The two have been spotted canoodling all over the city. The lucky lady is bouncing back fast from a breakup with former fiancé and Manhattan National heir, **Mike Mason**. The hotshot banker recently caused a scene at stripper haven Scores Westside. It seems bouncers had to eject him after his credit card was declined. Friends say Peri refers to her ex as "the bad dream." It's no wonder. This year TV's new rising star has something far better under the tree.

Please turn the page for a sneak peek at
Erin McCarthy's new novel
THE PREGNANCY TEST.
Available now from Brava . . .

She covered her face with her hand. "God, I think I'm blushing. This is just so unbelievable."

"But in such a good way." Damien put his hand on the small of Mandy's back and herded her in the direction of the hotel shop.

Good thing it was a short walk, because now that he had been given the green light by Mandy, he was more than a little eager. He was on fucking fire.

Mandy hung back in the store, hovering over by the imported magazines displayed both in English and Spanish, her cheeks a charming pink. Damien didn't feel any embarrassment whatsoever. He strode over to the counter and asked the clerk, "Where are the condoms?"

Why waste even five minutes looking for them?

The man, in his late twenties, grinned at Damien and pointed behind him. "Individual or a box?"

"Box." No sense in having to repeat this shopping expedition if things went according to plan.

The clerk slapped the box down on the counter, and Damien studied the busty Hispanic woman in a bikini on the front. The carton was bright yellow, the bikini a violent orange, and while the label was in English, the small script was in Spanish.

He hoped like hell these weren't novelty condoms. He wasn't wearing anything with parrots on it.

"Would you like some Mamajuana, too? Good stuff." The man pointed to a bottle of what looked like alcohol, shelved next to the rum.

"What is it?" Not that he had any intention of getting drunk. He wanted to remember every second of this.

"You drink it. We call it Dominican Viagra." The clerk winked. "Helps you last, if you know what I mean. If this doesn't work, they say you should just go and kill yourself."

Did he look like he needed Viagra? What the hell. He was so hard he could moonlight as a woodpecker. Damien shook his head. "I don't need any help, thanks." He handed over the six hundred pesos for the condoms, which he shoved in his pocket, and turned to find Mandy. She was biting her lip, arms over her chest, staring vacantly at a display of T-shirts.

"Have fun!" the clerk yelled with a knowing grin.

And people thought New Yorkers were rude.

Fortunately, he'd forgotten how to blush. But Mandy looked like she'd spent too long in the sun, so he took her hand and hustled her outside to the quiet walkway that lead to the main lobby.

And kissed her eagerly.

"Damien," she protested, trying to pull back. "There are people around."

"No, there aren't. Not a single one." The path was deserted, everyone still down at the buffet, and it was lush with foliage, and thick with humidity in the glow of faux gas lamps.

But she was still darting her eyes around, hands pressed on his chest to hold him at bay. So Damien dropped his mouth to her forehead and gave her a soft kiss. "My room is in the first building on the right."

"Then it's closer than mine. I'm by the adults-only pool." But she didn't move in the direction he had pointed to. She worried her lip, and Damien watched her, waited for her to say what was on her mind. "I just want you to understand that I don't usually . . . I don't sleep around. I thought Ben really cared about me, and well, I've never really fancied one-night stands. But that's all this can be, because I can't get involved with anyone until I've sorted out my own life."

Damien brushed a hair back that had caught on her lip. "This isn't a one-night stand. It's not just about sex. It's about being together, enjoying each other, if only for a few hours." It was about loosening the suffocating chains of loneliness and reaching out for something simple and uncomplicated. "But I'm not looking for a relationship either."

He couldn't believe he was about to admit this, but he wanted her to understand, wanted her to know what this—she—meant to him. "I haven't been with a woman in three years."

"You haven't been in a relationship in three years?"

"Yes, but I also haven't had sex in three years."

Understanding dawned in her eyes. "Oh. Oh, my." She stroked his forearm. "Since Jess?"

He nodded, not willing to say any more. "That's been a conscious choice I've made, and now I'm making the conscious choice to change that. Let me have you tonight, Mandy."

There was no way she was going to say no. He could read the acquiescence in her eyes, the way she leaned toward him, stroked his arms and opened her mouth. Her breasts pressed against him as she tilted her head to the side and gave a small, sweet sigh.

"Oh, I'm not a bloody idiot, Damien. I have every intention of doing this—I just needed to make sure we were clear on what it was, and that you don't think I'm some sort of swinger who sleeps with her boss in the Caribbean on every job she takes."

He raised an eyebrow. "That definitely wasn't on your résumé."

She gave a soft laugh and wet her lips, making him want to

suck on both her lip and her tongue, taking turns. "What if I don't meet your expectations? Three years is a long time to wait. I'd hate to be a disappointment."

That was a joke. He'd be lucky if he got a full five seconds in her before he exploded. "As long as you don't have some sort of objection to oral sex, we'll be fine. I have it in my head that I'd really like to taste you."

Her breathing quickened. "Funny, that. I had a dream you were doing that very thing to me, and I was really quite enjoying it."

Damien's groin tightened. What the hell were they doing standing here then?

"You know, you're usually much more efficient than this. Move it, Mandy. Before I drop your sundress here on the sidewalk." And he reached for her zipper.

Mandy had taken Damien's threat seriously, and a quick two minutes later they were in his room, her beach bag tumbling to the floor as she reached for the buttons on his linen shirt.

She'd seen the way he looked in his swim trunks that afternoon and she wanted to touch that broad chest. She wanted to explore his hard flesh, make him tremble with want. She wanted to draw this all out and enjoy every blasted second of it since she was facing a future of celibacy.

Damien's own hands were busy unzipping the back of her dress. But whereas she was fumbling, overeager, nervous, he was quiet, studied, intent. Goose bumps rose on her flesh as his fingers trailed over her back. His room was at the end of the hall, remote, the sounds of the resort buffered by palm trees and flowering plants. The whirr of the ceiling fan and the uneven tempo of their breathing were the only sounds in the room.

All her doubts, all her concerns, fear about how she should behave and how he might react to her pregnancy, her body the way it was now, had all evaporated when Damien told her he hadn't been with a woman in three years. She'd seen it then, what he had been telling her. That they both needed each other, just here, just now, to touch and taste and push on each other in uncomplicated pleasure.

She wanted that. She wanted him.

Buttons free, she spread his shirt and sighed as the palms of her hands caressed hard, warm muscle. "You have a lovely chest."

His lip quirked up. "What a coincidence. I was thinking the same thing about you."

Mandy glanced down and saw that with the zipper undone, her dress had slipped a bit, only to come to a crashing halt at her cleavage. Nothing could get past her newly blossoming breasts, and her plump flesh was bursting out of the top of her strapless bra.

"This isn't my natural state, you know," she told him, pushing his shirtsleeves down to his wrists. "Every day I wake up to find they're a bit bigger, like I've taken an air pump to them."

Damien's thumb ran over the swell above her bra. "I like the end result."

"Yes, well, easy for you to say." Mandy gripped his wrist as his thumb brushed lower and lower, skirting her nipple. She gave a sound of disappointment. "But at this rate, I fully expect one day to roll over and have them clap."

He laughed, expression relaxed and amused. "I love your sense of humor."

She was about to tell him that back in England, at The Wycombe Abbey School for Girls, she'd been quite the comedic thespian, but she only had time to open her mouth before he ripped her dress down to her waist, and she promptly forgot how to speak.

Or breathe, when his head descended to her chest and his tongue traced above the rim of her overburdened bra. Back and forth it went, as if it was on a leisurely stroll in the park, and Mandy shivered, appreciating fully how much more sensitive her breasts were now. Torn between wanting to just enjoy his teasing tongue and urging him to dispense with her bra and head south to her nipple, Mandy gripped his wrists and squeezed.

Damien lifted his head, and Mandy expected him to shove her dress down, strip himself, and slide right into her standing up.

Or maybe that was just wishful thinking.

But she had expected Damien to be urgent, to take charge, to rush through to the release they were both seeking.

He was taking charge, yes, but he wasn't interested in rushing. Which had its pros and cons.

As she tugged his shirt off and dropped it to the floor, Damien pulled the clip out of her hair. He stroked in it and smiled. "I love your hair. It's just like you. Sort of free, with a mind of its own, but always in control."

Was that the way he saw her? Mandy thought that was just a lovely way to describe her, even if she felt control was the last thing she possessed. Unable to resist touching him, she smoothed out his dark eyebrows, traced his cheeks, brushed along his lips in a caress that was too intimate, but felt so, so right here with Damien. His lips pressed in a kiss over her fingers and she smiled, knowing she felt as raw and vulnerable as he looked.

Here's a look at
THE ROYAL PAIN
from the fabulously funny
MaryJanice Davidson,
coming from Brava in November 2005.

Shel Rivers looked down at the small foot wedged in his doorway, then up at the ridiculously good-looking woman attached to said foot. She didn't look mad or pissed or haughty. Just had a patient look on her face, like, 'you're gonna get this thing off my foot, right?'

Finally, he said, "That's a good way to break something," after a moment that felt longer than it was.

"Not before you get shot," she replied, and shouldered her way past him. A good trick, since he had, at best estimation, four inches and thirty pounds on her.

He got a whiff of lilacs as she brushed by, and he almost reached out to see if her black, shoulder-length hair was as silky as it looked. "Dr. Rivers and I will be right out," she added, and closed the door on the protests of everyone else in the party.

The princess (princess! in his lab!) looked around the small, cluttered room for a moment, her small hands on shapely hips. Then she glanced back at him. He actually forgot to breathe when those crystal blue eyes fixed on his.

"I don't think we've been properly introduced," she said pleasantly.

"And I don't think your security team is going to like this at all."

"I'm Alexandria Baranov—"

"I know."

"I'm talking now, please. And you're Dr. Rivers. You're also rude and annoying, which is fine, but *nobody* slams a door on me."

"Especially when your family built half the aquarium," he snapped, trying not to look at her breasts.

"Irrelevant. I wouldn't tolerate that behavior if *you* were funding *my* work. What a disaster area," she continued, turning in a circle to take in the whole room. "How do you find anything in here?"

"None of your business."

"I think we could find some paperwork to prove that isn't true. What's so important? What are you working on?"

"Is playing twenty questions part of the tour?"

"No, it's part of being relatively pleasant. And why did you dodge the tour? You don't even know me."

Because she was rich. Because he was busy. Because she was a princess and he was a lowly Army brat. Because she was too beautiful. Because she was trouble with a capital T, and he'd had enough of that to last five lifetimes.

She was waving a hand in front of his eyes. "Dr. Rivers? Hellooooo? Is anyone in there? Is it lunchtime already?"

He jerked his head back and gave her a good glare. "I've got more important things to do than play tour guide for a stuck-up VIP."

He was sure she'd get pissed, but instead, those amazing blue eyes crinkled at the corners and she grinned. "I bet you don't," she said, and turned to reach for the door handle.

"Okay, okay," he said, grasping her elbow. She took his wrist and pulled it away, almost absently, and in the bottom of his brain a small red flag popped up. "I'll give you the damned tour. But no annoying questions."

"You're a fine one to talk about annoying," she retorted.

"And no potty breaks."

"I went on the plane."

"And I'm not going to be doing this all day, either."

"You can't," she pointed out. "I'm having lunch with Dr. Tomlin in three hours."

"Another rich fat cat," he muttered.

"Did you just call me fat?"

"Hardly. In fact, when was the last time you had a meal?" She was gorgeous—she more than lived up to her moniker as one of the most beautiful women in the world—but too skinny. The planes in her face made her blue eyes seem enormous. "Or even a milkshake?"

"I don't know, " she said absently. "It's probably on the schedule somewhere."

Another red flag popped, and he was so intrigued he almost forgot about his experiments. "Well, there's a snack bar on the second floor. Maybe we can grab some fries or something. Although, once you have to watch Dr. Tomlin eat, you're gonna lose your appetite. Assuming you ever had one."

"That's all right, Dr. Rivers."

"Shel."

"Shel. You don't have to worry. I'm not even hungry. And I'm Alex, by the way."

He shook her small, cool hand. His wrist was almost twice the width of hers. Definitely needs a few milkshakes, among other things.

"It's nice to meet you, Alex."

"What a lie, Dr. Rivers."

He smiled in spite of himself.

And we know you'll enjoy
Karen Kelley's sizzling new novel,
TEMPERATURE'S RISING
available now from Brava.

A blue Oldsmobile pulled to the curb.

Oh crap! Troy had told her that his brother drove a blue car. She thought he'd said Lincoln, though. Whatever. She scrubbed her hands across her watery eyes, brushed her hair behind her ears and pasted a smile on her face. At least she hadn't entirely blown the sale . . . yet. He turned the engine off, opened his door, and stepped out.

Tall and dark. He fit the description she'd been given. She smiled. Friendly, that's how she wanted to appear. Like they'd known each other for a while, rather than just meeting for the first time. Real Estate 101—Be their best friend.

"John?" She inwardly winced. She'd inhaled so many fumes that her voice was raspy. No time to worry about that now. *Shake it off. You're a professional.* She walked closer, smile widening.

The man hesitated before he walked around the front of his car toward the sidewalk where she stood. Jessica gave him a quick once-over. Then went back for seconds. Troy certainly hadn't mentioned scrumptious, sexy and downright delicious. Not that he would think of his brother like that.

Her gaze blazed a trail past wide shoulders and across a broad chest covered by a maroon Polo shirt before her glance slid downward.

Liquid heat coursed through her veins. There was just something about a man who wore his jeans low on his hips. It was almost as if he were telling the world he didn't really give a damn, and telling women he could fulfill their every desire.

His jeans pulled taut across nicely developed muscles as a booted foot stepped to the sidewalk. Drawing in a ragged breath, she forced her gaze back to his face, and the knowing look in his eyes.

Oops. Caught staring.

She mentally shrugged. As sexy as he was, he should be used to appreciative looks from women.

"How much?" His roughly textured words scraped across her skin, leaving a heated flush in its wake.

Her thighs trembled. "You don't waste any time, do you?"

"We both know what I want."

"Wouldn't you like to see it first?" Did he turn a little red? She mentally shook her head. It was probably just the way the sun had hit his face.

He cleared his throat. "Why not get the trivial details out of the way, then we can . . . concentrate on other things."

His rich, southern drawl wrapped around her, causing a small earthquake inside her body. Three leisurely steps and he stood in front of her. Slowly, his gaze slid over her, lingering, touching, caressing.

At least six feet, four inches of raw male magnetism invaded her space. She inhaled and caught the scent of his musky aftershave. Much nicer than car fumes.

Pull yourself together. Business before pleasure. Yeah right, at this rate she'd give him the damned property and take the payment out in trade. Okay, deep breath. Jeez, what brand of aftershave was that? *Pheromones for Men?* She couldn't think with him this close. Turning away, she walked a short distance down the sidewalk to clear her muddled brain.

Think about the property.

The building was nice. Not too large. Taxes were low. Only

single story, but it would make a great travel agency, which is what Troy said his brother wanted.

White, stone pillars gave the small commercial building a more prestigious appearance. She bit her bottom lip. Some of the ceiling tiles needed to be changed—water damage, but the owner had replaced the roof. A couple of the interior walls had rather large, gaping holes, though. In fact, the inside of the building needed a major overhaul. Personally, she thought the asking price a little steep, but the facts remained: it was in a prime location, the Texas town was growing, and this district had the fastest rate of improvement.

Only one teensy-tiny problem: The eyesore across the street.

Triple X's flashed on the marquee of what used to be an old movie theater. If that wasn't bad enough, three scantily clad ladies had arrived a few minutes ago to stand on the corner. She grimaced. That wasn't good.

At least there were only three this evening. Two blondes, and she wasn't positive, but the third hooker's hair color looked deep purple. The one in question raised her hand and waved.

As unobtrusively as possible, Jessica motioned for them to leave. One cast her a grin and flashed a little leg. Great. She could see her sale gurgling as it choked its way down the drain.

Oh Lord, he was probably staring at them right now. Maybe she could redirect his attention away from the *women of the night*, and focus it on the property once again.

She wheeled around.

His gaze riveted on her chest.

Well, her boobs practically thrown in his face had certainly drawn his attention.

Her hand automatically fluttered toward the next button before she stopped the nervous habit from making her more exposed. She pointedly cleared her throat. He didn't seem in any hurry to raise his head or appear a bit embarrassed at being caught staring.

"Two hundred," she stated, ignoring the little flare of desire that swept through her, and concentrated on the matter at hand. She wanted this sale. And actually, two hundred thousand wasn't a *bad* asking price for the land and building. She bit her bottom lip and waited for his reply.

Damn, he was cute. Why did he have to be such a distraction? Maybe they could get together after the deal was final. She inwardly smiled as naughty thoughts filled her head. She could easily picture them naked in bed, bodies pressed against each other. She sighed, wondering what he thought of her.

Conor Richmond thought the woman in front of him looked a little desperate. He wondered why she worked the streets. He figured her more for a high-priced call girl than a street hooker.

New in town, maybe? Like him?

Except she wanted to start a business. And the way she looked, it wouldn't take her long to have a whole string of *Johns* begging for her favors and willing to shell out more than a couple of hundred dollars. If she cleaned up a little, that is, and bought some decent clothes. Her hose were ripped so bad she'd do better without them, and her skirt looked like she'd dug it out of the Salvation Army trash bin.

What had driven her to this way of life? Drugs? Her eyes were a little red-rimmed. She *could* be a user, although he didn't see any track marks running up her arms.

But underneath the smudge of dirt on her face and the worn clothes, he saw a sensuous woman, and he had a hell of a time keeping his gaze from straying. The amount of cleavage showing beckoned him to bury his face in her lush curves.

The view only got better. Her long, silky legs drew his attention even if her hose were shredded. They were the kind of legs made to wrap around a man. Pulling him deeper and deeper inside her hot body. Yeah, she was made for sex. The kind that got down and dirty.

A carload of boys driving by whistled and honked their horn. She looked momentarily distracted, then tossed a saucy grin in their direction as they laughed and sped down the street.

The smile transformed her face. Meant to pull an unsuspecting male into her web. He wasn't immune to her charms any more than the next poor sucker would be. But he wasn't her next customer, either. Sometimes he hated his job.

"Don't you think two hundred's a little steep?" he asked.

She wet her lips, her gaze returning to his. A temptress. Conor inwardly groaned.

"Not for what you'll get."

The way she said the words, kind of husky, made him wish just for a few hours he could pretend he wasn't a cop. Made him wish he hadn't seen her standing on the sidewalk. And made him wish that for a moment he hadn't thought she looked out of place and vulnerable.

Man, had he misjudged. She was a pro, all right. Her sultry eyes promised sinful delights. His gaze was drawn to her low-cut blouse when her hand moved toward the buttons . . . just as the gesture was meant to do.

His vision clouded as he remembered the way she'd walked down the sidewalk. Hell, how could he forget! Hips swaying seductively, and the way she'd slowly turned back around so he could see what he'd be giving up if she chose to keep going. He'd burned all the way down to his boots. No, she knew exactly what she did to him.

"And what will I get for my money?" he asked, wanting her to spell it out.

Her eyes widened innocently. "Why everything, of course."

Sliding his hand into his pocket, he emerged with a roll of crisp, green bills. Thumbing them, he drew two out and handed them to her. She took the money, looking a little confused, he thought, but decided it was part of her act. He pocketed the rest.

"A down payment?" she asked, staring at the bills.

Figured. She knew she had him by the balls. Why not twist a little harder? Get as much of his cash as she could.

"Is that okay?" He stepped forward. So near her scent washed over him, bathing him with erotic fantasies. She might look like she'd been sleeping in the streets, but she smelled oh-so sweet. She raised her head. Her lips so close. So kissable. He ached to pull her into his arms and see if her mouth was as hot as it looked.

"I . . . suppose."

Too bad.

In one swift motion, he reached behind him, drew the hand-cuffs from the leather case hooked to his belt, and snapped them shut over her wrists.

A damn shame he couldn't have met her in another place. He had a gut feeling they would've been good together.

"Lady, you're under arrest for solicitation."